MAKE HER MINE

SAPPHIRE FALLS NEXT GENERATION

ERIN NICHOLAS

EN FICTION, INC.

ABOUT MAKE HER MINE

I know that I should just tell my ex to F-off when he announces to our entire hometown that he intends to get me back.

But then I'm given the option to make him miserable instead...

Yeah, I definitely go with door number two.
Even though it means fake dating my arch-nemesis.

Jefferson Riley is my best friend's older brother and the bane of my existence.
But he's also my *ex's* biggest adversary.

Being happily in love with Jefferson will be the perfect way to torture the man who was absolutely horrible to me. And Jefferson agrees. In fact, it's his idea.
Besides, it's only for a week.

So, we'll enjoy watching the creep seethe, and then we'll part ways and keep living our lives as enemies. As always.

At least, that's the plan.

Until Jefferson starts cooking for me. And taking his shirt off. And fostering cats. And kissing me. And talking dirty. And proving that he really understands and supports me. The jerk.
When this is over, he's going to leave me with a bunch of mixed-up feelings, isn't he?

Like maybe actually *liking* him.
And maybe wanting even more from my biggest rival.
Something very much...not fake.

CONTENT NOTES

This is a fun, steamy, small-town rom-com! However, your mental health is important, and I want you to be aware that there is a brief discussion of suicidal ideation (by a secondary character, off-page) and a past history where the heroine was drugged at a party by an ex-boyfriend in the story.
Please take care of yourself!
xo Erin

CHAPTER 1

JEFFERSON

"JACKASS ALERT."

My brother looks to the side, and sighs. "You still have beef with Zach Nelson? It's been years."

I nod and lift my beer. "I will *always* have beef with Zach Nelson."

My arch nemesis stops inside the door, grinning like the cocky asshole that he is. A few people call out to him, and he raises a hand like he's Miss Fucking America. Then his gaze lands on my brother.

Now it's my turn to sigh. "Incoming."

Carver grins. "Of course. I'm the man of the hour."

"Yeah, yeah, you finally decided to marry the woman who has put up with you since you were what? Four years old? I don't see why you should get drinks on the house and all these pats on the back. You're only doing what you should have done years ago and what any even halfway intelligent man would do."

He smirks. "Your jealousy is showing."

I chuckle. Honestly, everyone should be jealous of my brother and his fiancée, Kaelyn. They are a perfect couple. The only reason it's taken Carver this long to officially marry the woman who has been his since before they even went to kindergarten is because she's been working on her PhD and didn't want to also plan a wedding.

Somehow, my dorky older brother managed to lock down an amazing, gorgeous, funny, intelligent woman. I think all the men in town like him in spite of that because it gives them hope.

Kaelyn Spencer decided long ago that my brother Carver needed her. I don't think at the ripe old age of three she really understood all the ways that he needed her, but something told her that the sweet nerd was going to need some help getting through life and she appointed herself his guardian angel.

Fortunately, my brother is an actual genius, and even though he is socially awkward and takes after our father in many ways, he did understand that he wanted to keep Kaelyn close.

They've been inseparable their entire lives, started dating as soon as either of them really understood what that was, and have essentially been an old married couple since they were about thirteen.

But finally, my brother put a ring on it. They're getting married next weekend. And not only are they practically royalty in this town, they decided to say their vows in the town's gazebo on the Saturday of our annual town festival.

So now it's a week-long party complete with snow cones and a Ferris wheel and every person either of them has ever met will be in attendance.

"Riley!"

Even jackasses we all went to high school with like Zach Nelson.

Zach claps Carver on the shoulder. "Congratulations!" He raises his voice. "A round for the bar on me in celebration!"

I fucking hate this guy.

This is just like him.

Go off to college and become a huge football star for the beloved state university team, go on to medical school to become a rich orthopedic surgeon, and then stroll back into town to throw his money around and grace us all with his presence.

This has very little to do with celebrating my brother's upcoming nuptials. Carver is only a year older than us and Kaelyn was in our grade, so Zach knows a ton of people who are coming back this week for the festival and wedding. It's basically a high school class reunion with a fancier party at the end. This is the perfect way for a guy like Zach to show off.

He's probably been in town for about ten minutes. That's how long it would take him to want to get everybody looking at him and ooh-ing and ahh-ing over him.

"Glad to see you, Riley," he says. Then he looks at me. "And Riley. How the fuck are you, Jefferson?"

About a thousand times more annoyed than I was two minutes ago. "Zach," I say flatly. "What are you doing here?" He hasn't been back for a festival in about five years.

Not since he started medical school.

"I couldn't miss this wedding. I hear everybody's coming back for it."

Exactly. I give my brother a side-eye. I blame him for this. They didn't even really send invitations out. They just told everyone to be in the town square Saturday at six.

Ninety percent of the town would have been anyway. The town square is the heart of the festival.

Carver just winks at me.

It takes a lot to get Carver worked up. And 'worked up'

really means excited. Never angry. And the things that get Carver excited are Kaelyn, bugs, and soil samples. Probably in that order, though I'm sure he's smart enough not to tell Kaelyn if that's *not* the actual order.

Carver doesn't have much of a temper. He definitely takes after my father. My dad isn't exactly laid-back. It's more that he's always wrapped up in some project and so in his own head that he doesn't realize what's going on around him. Carver is like that. Our youngest brother Graham gets that way too.

But our sister Ginny and I take after our mom a little more. We're protective. And we're a hell of a lot more social than the others. Which means that we definitely understand that people can be assholes. And that pisses us off sometimes.

"So that means you'll be around for a while," I say. Dammit. It's Friday night a week and one day before the wedding. That's a long time before the big event will be over and everyone can leave town.

"Yep. Took all this time off to come back." Zach takes a deep breath. "It's good to be home."

I scoff and take a drink of my beer. Home. Right. Zach left as soon as he could and has rarely been back. Thank God. While he was in college, he was busy with football and medical school, and his residency has a "grueling" schedule—according to what his mother told his aunt who told my...hell, I don't even remember who I heard it from at this point. He just hasn't been back to visit since his parents moved to Omaha.

"Glad you could make it back," Carver says when I don't say anything.

"Yeah," Zach says happily as beers are delivered to our table as well as all the rest in the room. "It's gonna be great. All the old crowd will be here together. It'll be just like old times."

I lift an eyebrow. It will be nothing like old times.

Back in the day Zach and I used to pretend that we got along. I suppose at the moment we did. I was the star quarterback, and he was the best running back our school had ever seen. We were the Dynamic Duo, as the local papers and sportscasters dubbed us. We were unbeatable for three years. There wasn't a ball I could throw that he couldn't catch, and if Zach Nelson had a football in his hands, we were getting six points.

We had three amazing years of football together. Everything was great. On the surface.

Then we both went to play in college.

But for two different Big Ten teams.

And once a year for four years, and twice a year for two years including the conference championship, we faced off.

The news and fans went nuts. *Sapphire Falls* went nuts. The watch parties, the betting pools, and the way the town divided up was nuts.

He was the good guy who played for the home school. He was starting for the Nebraska Cornhuskers by their fourth game his freshman year.

I was the 'traitor' who went to play for Minnesota. I was starting by our fifth game after our starting QB broke his wrist.

Of course, the sports coverage talked about how Zach earned the spot and I lucked into mine.

They talked about how we'd been 'inseparable' in high school.

And they talked about our State Championship series our senior year.

The year Sapphire Falls won without me.

Everyone *here* knows that Zach and I don't get along. But they all think it's about football.

I *wish* football was the reason I hate this guy so much.

"I need to get going," I tell my brother as I stand from my stool and withdraw my wallet.

Zach puts out a hand to stop me. "I've got this."

I toss a few bills on the table. "You're not covering me."

"I'm at least buying the last round."

I meet his gaze directly. "You're not doing anything for me."

He pulls his hand back. "I see."

It's not like this is the first time I've seen Zach since high school. His parents lived here until about four years ago. He came home for holidays and different occasions. But I didn't have to put up with him for any length of time. I avoided him as much as possible. He did come to some games, putting in an appearance as an alumnus. But even when he congratulated me for coaching two Sapphire Falls teams to State Championships, I gave him tight smiles, let the local newspaper snap a photo of the Dynamic Duo on the Sapphire Falls football field together again, and moved off as quickly as possible.

"Hey, I don't suppose you've seen Harlow around?"

I turn back instantly.

Zach is asking my brother. But I immediately ask, "Why?"

"I tried to call her, but I think she's changed her number. She's always been close with your family. Figured Graham was back in town, and they'd be hanging out."

He figured correctly. Harlow Hansen is our little brother Graham's best friend. And Graham is indeed back in town for the wedding. In fact, he's at Harlow's house right now.

But I want to know why the fuck Zach wants to know about Harlow.

I step back toward the table. "Why do you need to talk to Harlow?"

"Really?" he asks with a grin. "I know you're not the smartest one in your family," he tells me. "But guessing even you can figure this out."

Yeah, yeah, I'm the dumbest of my siblings. I'm still smart enough to know something Zach doesn't—there's no fucking way he's getting close to Harlow again.

And he *should* know that.

"You and Harlow were over a long time ago," I remind him.

"Yeah, well, I want to talk to her about that."

"Spit it out," I tell him. "What do you want with Harlow?"

Zach shrugs as if it should be obvious. "I want her back. This is the perfect chance. I'm settled. When my residency is finished, they've promised me a job with the practice. We've both grown up. It's time I tell her I'm sorry for what happened and work to get her back."

I look at Carver, who wisely keeps his mouth shut. Then I look back at Zach. "Not gonna happen."

Not. Fucking. Ever. Even over my dead body. Because Carver and Graham and Ginny will pick up where I leave off. But as long as I'm breathing, this asshole doesn't stand a chance with the woman we all consider a sister.

"Excuse me?" Zach draws himself up taller.

"You seem to have forgotten my *opinion* about you and Harlow back in high school. I can easily remind you," I tell him, taking a step closer to him and balling my fist.

I've hit exactly one person in the face in my life. Zach Nelson.

I've definitely punched my brothers' arms, legs, and even stomachs a couple of times. I even made the mistake of punching my sister in the shoulder once. That was how I first learned about the excruciating pain of getting kicked in the balls. But I've only hit another human in the face on purpose once.

I'll do it again though. Without hesitation. Happily.

Zach narrows his eyes. "This isn't about you, Riley. Back off. Harlow and I are going to see each other while I'm back."

"Guys," Carver says, warningly.

I glance toward the bar. Dammit. Derek Wright, co-owner of the bar and head bartender tonight, is watching us.

He's friends with my parents. It's not that I'm worried about Derek telling my mom on me. It's that even though Derek is a good twenty-some years older than me, he can definitely physically throw me out of this bar—though that would not be a great look for the town's football coach and guidance counselor. He could also ban me from returning for a couple of weeks, which would just be no fun, *and* tell my mom.

That's how it is growing up here. It's hard to get away with much when your friends' parents are the town's teachers, business owners, cops, bartenders, and even the mayor.

I make myself relax. I force a grin, which I hope drives Zach crazy, and say, "Yeah that's not going to happen. She's taken."

I'm not sure why I say those last two words.

But then Zach's eyes narrow and his face gets a little red.

And yeah, *that's* why.

Because that will really piss him off.

"Taken?" he repeats.

"You didn't really think that she was gonna sit around and wait for *you,* did you? She's taken. You have no chance."

"By who?" Zach asks.

I scoff. "Really? I mean, you're no smarter than me," I tell him. I could've been a fucking orthopedic surgeon if I wanted to. "But I don't think you're gonna have to think real hard to figure that out."

I look at my brother. "See you later." Then I turn on my heel and leave the building.

I saunter out to my truck, casually slide behind the wheel, and pull out onto the street easily.

Just in case he's watching.

But the minute I'm to the end of the block and out of sight of the bar, I smash the gas pedal, and swear loudly.

Then groan.

Fuck. Harlow is going to *kill me*.

CHAPTER 2

JEFFERSON

WHEN I PULL up to Harlow's house, I'm relieved to see my sister's car is still here. That means Graham is still here too and I can talk to him and Harlow together. He'll hopefully keep Harlow from murdering me. But I don't think he'll keep her from yelling at me. He never has in the past.

I park my truck at the curb, and walk up the short, paved path to her front porch. I note all of the cars here. Looks like most of the girl gang is present. The rest could have carpooled over, but I know Sasha is at the bar, working with her dad, and I'm guessing that Whitney Bennett and Mia Hansen, Harlow's older sister, are with Kaelyn doing wedding stuff.

Yes, my brother is the only guy at this girls' night. And yes, that's completely typical.

I climb up onto the porch of Harlow's little house. It's a one story, two-bedroom, one-bath bungalow. It's small, but cozy, full of mismatched furniture with an abundance of cushions and pillows and blankets and just...stuff. She's got more bookcases than any one woman really should and while many are filled with books, there are also plants and photos and knickknacks packing the shelves.

Harlow is a collector of *things*. I won't call it junk because it probably all means something to her. If I had to guess, I'd bet most of it's gifts, actually. That's just who she is. People love her and she inspires things like gift-giving. But there's not much room to walk around or gather. Yet, somehow, this is always where people show up to hang out.

I can't count the number of times I picked up one or both of my siblings from this house. Drunk, hung over, or late for something. If they're not showing up for something on time, my mother will send me to go find them, and I always start at Harlow's house without even calling either of them first. Even when she was living with her parents. This has been going on for years.

It's a pleasant night for mid-June in Nebraska so her windows are open as is the front door. Through the screen door, I can hear conversation and laughter from inside.

I'm surprised they're not on the back deck I remember her dad, brother, and several of the other guys building three years ago.

I take a deep breath and then knock on the wood frame.

"Come in!" someone calls. I don't think it's Harlow.

Yeah, they're expecting more people to join them.

I pull the door open and step inside, just as Harlow comes around the corner from the kitchen.

She stops short when she sees me, her smile dying. Then she frowns and continues forward.

She's in short denim shorts, a black tank, and is barefoot, her toenails painted bright blue. The shorts show off the tattoo that decorates the outside of her right thigh. A goldenrod. The state flower of Nebraska.

I can't see it, but I know there's also a deer silhouette

tattooed on her right shoulder blade. It's another symbol for our home state, but there's deeper symbolism to deer and I'm certain Harlow is aware of that.

As she approaches, I note the sparkling blue gem pierced through her nose, the many ear piercings, and the multitude of rings on her fingers.

She's got her full jewelry on even though she's definitely dressed down and has her long dark hair up in a messy bun on top of her head and I find myself wondering if she ever takes it all off. To shower? To sleep?

I do *not* need to be wondering about Harlow Hansen showering or in bed, I remind myself as she comes to stand in front of me.

Tendrils of hair are escaping her bun, framing her face, and brushing against her long neck and I can see the faint lines where her bathing suit crosses her shoulders and wraps around to tie behind her neck.

She's beautiful. There's no doubt about that.

I might even be attracted to her if she didn't hate my guts.

"No fucking way." She plants her hands on her hips.

But she does. So I'm not.

And, I remind myself, I don't like her much either. She's a pain in the ass who always thinks she's right, was a bad influence on my brother, and thinks I'm a bad guy for no fucking good reason at all.

"No way what? I haven't even said anything."

"You can't have them yet."

I roll my eyes, even though it makes sense that she thinks I'm here to pick up Ginny and Graham. Rolling my eyes with Harlow is just an instinct.

"Graham has been home for two days and this is the first time I've had him," she informs me. "He and Ginny are sleeping over."

I shift my weight and tuck my hands into the front pockets of my jeans. I give her a smirk. "Did Mom say that was okay?"

My sister is twenty-six, Graham and Harlow are twenty-four. Obviously, no one gives them direction on where they're sleeping.

Harlow sticks her tongue out. "I know you don't have any friends, but that's your own fault for being an asshole. Leave *my* friends alone."

I frown. "I have friends." She knows that very well. She knows all of them.

"Do you? Or have they just all been stuck with you because this town is so tiny?"

"Says the woman who's having a sleepover tonight with people she's known literally her entire life."

I've got a point and she doesn't even have to say so. "Well, you can't take Ginny and Graham. So get out of here."

"I'm not here to pick them up. I..." Might as well rip the band-aid off. "I need to talk to you, actually."

She's predictably surprised. "About what?"

"Something happened tonight that you should know about."

She straightens, her expression immediately turning concerned. "Is Alex okay?"

Alex Fallon is something Harlow and I have in common besides my siblings. And our hometown.

He just graduated, after coming to live with a foster family here three years ago. Harlow is a social worker and child advocate who has been working with Alex. She has gotten close to him and the affectionate feelings are very mutual. Alex is also one of my star football players. I love the kid.

And part of me loves that she immediately thought of Alex and was concerned.

I blow out a breath. "No, this isn't about Alex. Sorry. I see why you might've jumped to that."

She breathes out in relief. "Geez, Jefferson."

"It's something about you, actually."

"What is?"

"I need to tell both you and Graham."

She narrows her eyes and starts to say something—an argument I'm sure—so I step around her and head toward the kitchen.

I hear her give a little growl behind me and can't help but smile.

Everyone thinks she's so sweet and sunny. I know better.

I step into the kitchen. The group is gathered around the middle island. She only has a tiny wooden table with two chairs near the window because that's all there's room for, so when there's more than two people here, obviously they have to stand and cluster around the counter. They don't seem to mind.

In the center of the island is a fondue pot filled with melted chocolate. There's a plethora of other items spread everywhere —crackers, fruit, marshmallows. I notice there are potato chips and pretzels and know that's what Harlow is using. She's not really into sweets.

I frown as I realize I know that. I mean, I probably know what most of these people like for snacks. I've known them all forever. But...no, I don't. I know Graham is going to go for the fruit, and Ginny will be all about dunking cookies into the chocolate, but I don't know what Sloan or Margot prefer.

"Jefferson is here," Harlow says flatly, right behind me.

"Hi," Ginny says, surprised to see me.

"We're staying here tonight," Graham informs me.

I roll my eyes again. "You're twenty-four. I'm not here to pick you up."

"Then why are you here?"

Everyone in town knows that Harlow Hansen and I do not get along. *No one* would expect me to be invited to a get-together at her house or for me to just show up as a friendly drop-in. *Least of all* my siblings.

"I need to talk to you and Harlow about something."

Harlow reaches for a thick wavy potato chip. "Something that just couldn't wait until he *wasn't* crashing the party and ruining the fun."

Yeah, well, I definitely didn't think about what *she* was doing tonight before I opened my mouth in front of Zach.

She leans over, barely dunks the chip into the chocolate, then leans her elbows on the island. "So, what is it?"

"How about we do this in private?" I ask.

They all just stare at me.

I forgot for a moment that this group never does anything without the rest of them knowing.

"No way," Harlow says biting into the chip. She crunches for a moment. "If you wanna talk to me about something, I want to do it in front of witnesses."

"And near weapons?" I ask, my gaze dropping to the tiny fondue forks.

She gives me a grin. "Maybe."

Her gaze moves to my left and I follow it to the butcher block full of knives. When I look back at her, she simply dunks another chip into the chocolate.

I sigh. "Fine. Zach is in town for the wedding. Plans to be here for the whole week. I ran into him down at the Come Again."

There's frowning, grumbling, and Ginny says, "Well, we expected him."

I don't look at anyone but Harlow, though.

She's studying the chip in her fingers.

Everyone gathered in kitchen hates Zach. And we all hate

him because of how he treated Harlow. I am the only one who has additional beef with him.

"Thanks for the warning, I guess," Harlow says after a few seconds.

"Yeah, well, there's more. You need to pretend to be dating Graham this week."

Everyone goes still and quiet. Everyone looks at Harlow. Including Graham.

Her gaze bounces up to mine. "What are you talking about?"

Suddenly the back door to the kitchen bangs open. "You guys, guess what!" Sasha Wright asks as she steps into the house. She stops when she sees me. She visibly deflates. "Oh. Did you tell them?"

"That Zach is back? Yes," Harlow says.

"And that he now thinks you have a boyfriend and that everyone at the bar is very curious about who it is?" Sasha asks. "I am *very* curious about who it is and why Jefferson knows and I don't."

Harlow looks from her to me. "Boyfriend? Why does Zach think that?" She looks back to Sasha. "Did you tell him I don't?"

Sasha shakes her head. "Of course not. I wasn't going to argue."

"But you know I don't have a boyfriend," Harlow says, straightening.

Sasha gestures toward me. "But Jefferson said it. I thought maybe Graham knew and told him or something."

Harlow turns slowly to face me. "*You* said I have a boyfriend?"

Here we go. "Yes."

"*Why?*"

I cross my arms and meet her gaze directly. "Because he

said he was here to get you back. And that's a terrible idea. I thought you having a boyfriend would make him back off."

Harlow is staring at me. "*What?*"

I nod. "He said he's ready to settle down. He's finishing his residency, and has a job lined up. So now he's come home to win you back." I frown. "And I hate the idea that he thinks you've been waiting for him."

Harlow tosses down the potato chip that she still hasn't eaten, and crosses her arms, mimicking my stance. "You mean you wanted to make him mad."

I shrug. "Yes."

It's no secret to our friends and family that I hate Zach. Of course, they all think it has to do with his and my history with football. None of them really know the part that Harlow plays in it. And that's fine. They don't need to. *She* doesn't need to.

Her eyes narrow. "Who does he think this boyfriend is?" Then she looks at Graham, understanding dawning on her face. "Wait, you told him Graham and I are dating?"

"No. But that makes the most sense."

"When Zach asked who it was, Jefferson said that he was pretty sure Zach could figure it out," Sasha says with a grin. "Or something like that. Which has the whole bar talking. Because *everyone* is now trying to figure it out. And..." She turns her attention to me. "Zach is suspicious because no one in town seems to know about this boyfriend."

Harlow growls again. "Great! So you just left it as some random dude. He'll never believe that. Especially when the whole rest of the town doesn't know!"

"They'll all believe it if it's Graham," I say confidently. "You can say that you didn't want to make a big deal of it before you were sure it was serious, but now it is."

Everyone goes quiet for a moment. Then they all start laughing at once.

I frown. "What?"

Ginny shakes her head. "That will never work."

"Of course it will. Harlow and Graham have been friends forever. Now he's dressing better and is more social. He's very successful in his job. They've grown up. He's been away for awhile so it will be easy to believe they missed each other and then realized they had deeper feelings and fell in love."

In fact, I've been continually surprised that they haven't. I was convinced for most of their high school years that they were secretly crazy about each other and that they were just keeping it on the down low. Or that Graham was in love with her and it wasn't reciprocated, which pissed me off and caused me to be...okay, a little mean to her if I'm totally honest.

Harlow gives Graham an affectionate grin. Then she looks at me. "No."

"It makes sense," I insist.

"They've been friends all their lives," Sloane says, speaking up for the first time. "If it was going to be more than friendship, it would've happened by now."

"They were just kids before. Maybe they needed to grow up a little," I offer.

Now it's Margot's turn. "Anyone who has been around Harlow and Graham knows that they're only friends. There's no chemistry. And this entire town has been around them before."

I'm gritting my teeth now. "Look, Zach isn't the brightest bulb in the drawer. We tell him that Harlow and Graham are in love. They spend their time together this week so that Zach can't get close. He leaves town and it's all over. This doesn't have to be difficult."

"They'll never be able to pull it off," Sasha says. "They're going to run into Zach a lot even if he's only here for a week.

They're not going to be able to be convincing as a couple in love."

Margot nods. "I guarantee they can't kiss with any heat. And if they try, they'll probably get the giggles."

Harlow actually giggles at that. Again, she's looking at Graham. He's grinning at her too.

"And Graham is interested in someone," Harlow says. "I don't want *her* believing that he's involved with *me*."

"Harlow," Graham says, his voice low with warning.

She gives him a wink.

Wait, my brother is interested in someone? Who? Why hasn't he told me? Has he told Ginny? Will he tell me if I ask?

Probably not. If he's got Harlow, he doesn't need anyone else. It's always been that way.

Harlow looks at me. "So this is a terrible plan. Big shock. You're bad at matchmaking too."

"Well, excuse the hell out of me for trying to help you with Zach," I say with a frown.

"First of all, I don't need help with Zach."

"You've always needed help with Zach. He's the one person who could talk you into terrible decisions."

Her eyes widen and her cheeks get pink. "Fuck off, Jefferson."

I take a breath. Okay, that was low.

"I'm sorry. I shouldn't have said that. I just..." Then I decide to be fully honest. "I really hate that guy. And he seemed so happy to be home and everyone at the bar seemed happy to see him and...I wanted to see him sad."

I shrug. I never said I was a saint.

Harlow studies me for a moment. Then she smiles. "Did the idea of me with someone else make him seem sad?"

I lift one brow, but say, "Yes. And a little surprised. I think he thinks you still have feelings for him."

She shakes her head. "I hate him."

"He's very easy to hate."

"*Very* easy," she agrees.

Our smiles grow.

"I can understand the urge in the moment to make him sad. Or knock him down a peg. Or whatever," she says.

"I'd love to knock him down," I mutter. And I don't mean emotionally. Or with my words.

"I'd love to see that," she says.

We smile at each other again.

So we have four things in common—loving my siblings, loving our hometown, loving Alex Fallon, and hating Zach Nelson.

"You know," Sloan muses. "People would believe if *you* two were dating."

Harlow and I both turn to look at her.

Then I look around.

Everyone else in the room is nodding.

I turn to Harlow.

She stares at me.

Then we both start laughing.

CHAPTER 3

JEFFERSON

SLOAN SHRUGS. "I'M SERIOUS."

"We hate each other," Harlow tells them. "The whole town knows that. We fight all the time. "

"You treat each other differently than you treat anyone else," Sloan agrees. "You are both so nice to everyone else, but you're rude as hell to each other. You bicker. You argue. But I guarantee, if I told five people in this town that you two were dating, four and a half of them would not be surprised at all."

"How do you get half?" I can't help but ask.

"They would be surprised at first, but when they thought about it, they would realize it made sense," Sloan says with a smile. "The other four would just believe it right from the beginning."

"You're crazy," Harlow tells her.

"There's a fine line between love and hate," Graham pipes up.

"Most importantly," Sasha says. "It would bug Zach *so much* if it was Jefferson."

That much is true. I think Zach would hate to think that

Harlow is taken and not waiting for him no matter what. But if the guy she was dating was his arch nemesis, that would definitely hurt more.

"That's not a terrible…" I start.

"No way," Harlow says. "You don't think Graham and I could pull it off because we have no chemistry. How the hell would Jefferson and I pull it off? We'd be out in public and start screaming at each other and everyone would know it was fake."

"We never scream at each other," I protest. "We needle each other. We definitely bicker. We love to poke at each other. But we don't scream and throw things."

She lifts a brow.

"Okay, we *almost* never throw things."

There was that one time she threw a shoe at me. But I easily ducked that. And there was the time she threw a water gun at me. But that was because it was empty, and I had cornered her during the water fight. And I guess I did then throw a water balloon at her. And soaked that see-through white cropped tee she was wearing and exposed the white and red striped bikini top she had underneath…

"There's definitely passion between you," Margot says with a grin.

Harlow is shaking her head adamantly. "No. That's a terrible idea. Besides I don't need to have a boyfriend to fend Zach off. I will just tell him I am not interested. Which I am *not.*"

"Fine," I say, throwing up my hands. "I'm going to look like an idiot in front of the guy I hate so fucking much I'd rather chew glass than admit I lied to him. But it's my fault. He drives me nuts. He started mouthing off and I just spoke up without thinking."

Harlow studies my face for a moment, then says, "I get it.

He makes me crazy too. How about I'll tell him that I was seeing someone and you just didn't know we had broken up."

That's actually very decent of her. "Thanks," I say.

"You'll have to say it was someone from out of town or something," Sasha points out. "No one in town knew about it. Your parents didn't know."

Harlow rolls her eyes. "It's okay if not everyone in this town knows every detail about my life."

But we all just snort at that. It would be okay, but not at all realistic.

Her dad is the town cop. Her mom is a partner in the busiest bakery in three counties. Everyone knows Harlow and they all keep track of her.

But there's no one in this room for whom that isn't true. Myself included. My mom is her mom's partner in that bakery and my dad and his business partner, Lauren, are two of the biggest employers in town. Really in the entire area.

"Okay, well, I'm going to head out," I say, jingling my keys. "Y'all have fun. Call me if you need a ride home," I tell my siblings.

They just grin.

I let myself out and am down the front porch steps when I hear Harlow call my name.

I turn back.

She's standing on the top step, arms crossed.

"Zach really said that he was here to get me back? In those words?"

"Yes. And he didn't seem to think that it would be much of a challenge."

I don't think even Harlow knows everything I know about her history with Zach. But he was a manipulative, cheating, lying scumbag when they were together.

"Well, for what it's worth, it *will* be a challenge. One he won't win."

"I know you don't need help with him," I tell her honestly. "I believe that you don't want him back. I just really liked the idea of him *not* getting his way *and* him being as miserable as possible in the process."

She gives a soft laugh. "I completely understand that sentiment."

"Is he allergic to anything? Something we could sneak into his food?"

She grins. "No. Unfortunately." She pauses. "But there're always laxatives or something."

I snort. "Well, I guess if I can't break his heart, chaining him to the toilet isn't a terrible option B."

She laughs. "I'll keep thinking." Then she gives me a sly look. "I know I seem very sweet, but I can be really mean when I want to be."

"No way," I deadpan.

"Yep."

"Gotta say, I'm glad to be on your team rather than on the opposing side in this case."

She crosses her arms. "Yeah, well, don't get used to it."

I roll my eyes. "Wouldn't dream of it." I start to turn away but then...for some reason...I say, "Of course, when we are on the same team, some pretty great things happen."

She narrows her eyes.

Yep, she knows exactly what I'm referring to.

"You do not want to go there, do you?" she asks. "Really? We were kind of getting along. For us. Can't we just work on torturing Zach?"

I shrug. "I'm just saying we were a hell of a team when it came to Alex."

She frowns.

But *why* did I say that? I could have just *not* said that.

She's right that we were kind of getting along. We were agreeing to hate Zach together at least. And she'd thrown me a lifeline by agreeing to tell Zach that I just didn't know she and her boyfriend had recently broken up rather than outing me as a liar.

Why do I always want to poke her? Because this topic does poke her and I know it. It riles her up. Makes her mad at me.

"Jefferson," she says, her voice low. "I do not forgive you for Alex. Drop it."

"There isn't anything to forgive," I say. "That all turned out great. *We* were great. Ask anyone. His parents. His teachers. His coaches. His counselors. *Him*."

She's gritting her teeth and glaring at me now.

But that's why I poke her about this. Because I want to hear *her* admit that we were both a part of Alex's success. I want her to acknowledge it.

Alex is a bright, big-hearted, happy kid with a future full of possibilities. Now. But he hasn't always been. He certainly wasn't when we met him. He'd been a fifteen-year-old, angry, grief-stricken, scared kid who'd showed up at a foster home in our town after his mom had been killed by her boyfriend in their home.

We've had to track him down after he's run away from home.

We've given him rides to and from his therapy appointments.

We've sat up with him when he's had suicidal thoughts.

We sat by his hospital bed together when he tried it with pills once.

It's been almost two years since all of that happened.

Now he has friends. He smiles. He lets Harlow hug him. He texts me every other day.

It was a long road getting there, especially that first year, but he made it. *We* made it.

And five weeks ago, Alex left for Colorado. He's moved into his room on campus, started his summer class, and is getting ready for football camp in preparation for the fall.

He's got a very bright future ahead.

And Harlow is pissed at me, because I'm the one who got the scout here to look at him, encouraged Alex to consider Colorado, and then drove him to campus.

She blames me for him being so far away from her. Just like she blames me for Graham leaving Sapphire Falls. And Ginny leaving. And her brother Austin leaving.

"Well, you do like sending people away from Sapphire Falls," she says. "Feel free to turn that energy on *Zach.*"

I sigh. I do not *like* sending people away from Sapphire Falls. It's just that sometimes that's what's best for them.

"I will," I say, deciding not to press this bigger topic any further right now.

"But you might not enjoy *this* as much," she says, "I mean, *I* don't like Zach. I don't want him to stay here. And you seem to especially like getting rid of people I care about."

"You know that's not—"

"'Bye, Jefferson," she says, turning on her heel and heading for the door. "*You* can definitely leave. My house. My front yard. My *life.*" She pulls the screen door open, but pauses to look back at me. "Of all the people you've convinced that Sapphire Falls has nothing to offer, why haven't *you* ever taken that advice and gotten the hell out of here?"

But it's not like she's really wanting or waiting for an answer. She steps inside, letting the screen door slap shut. Then, for good measure, she slams the inside door as well.

She probably also turns the lock.

Yeah, the two of us should totally pretend date. That's a great idea.

CHAPTER 4

HARLOW

JEFFERSON RILEY IS *the* most aggravating person I know.

This has been true for a *very* long time.

And last night was not the first night that I've had a hard time falling asleep because I'm replaying something he did or said.

He's such an ass. He always thinks he's right. And he's great at everything. And everyone likes him.

But he's so fucking...optimistic. It's like he thinks the world is actually a happy place and everything always works out for everyone if they just *believe* hard enough and work hard enough and have a positive mental attitude.

God, that's annoying.

How the man doesn't understand that there are people all around him who are dealing with a lot of hard shit and that just *thinking* and *hoping* isn't the way to solve problems makes me nuts.

I pull in a deep breath.

Okay, that's not entirely fair. I know that he knows there are people who have it tough.

He's smart. I know this. But he sure doesn't act like it sometimes.

Like with this whole thing about Zach.

He thinks Zach wants me back. So what? What business is that of his? And he doesn't need to protect me from Zach. I want *nothing* to do with Dr. Nelson. Ever. I've been over him for almost a decade. And I'm thoroughly offended that Jefferson Fucking Riley doesn't believe that.

But he wants to make Zach sad.

Yeah, well, I get that. But he didn't need to pull me into his little revenge plot or whatever this is.

Jefferson and Zach have always had such a weird relationship. They were *magic* together on the football field. Even as someone who completely resents the sport and my small town's obsession with it, I knew that. I didn't hate it as much back when Jefferson and Zach were the town's golden boys. Hell, for almost a year I was in love with one of them—*not* Jefferson. *Never* Jefferson—and I showed up to every damned game just like everyone else.

Over the course of three seasons, one Friday night at a time, on various fields all over the middle of Nebraska, the Sapphire Falls Miners won one game after another until they'd given our town one near-perfect, and two perfectly perfect seasons and two State Championships.

And it was mostly due to the Dynamic Duo of quarterback Jefferson Riley and wide receiver Zachary Nelson.

Jefferson and Zach's sophomore through senior years were the best football seasons Sapphire Falls has ever had.

To hear people talk about it, even now ten years later, you'd think they'd cured cancer or landed on Jupiter.

I'm so caught up in my internal rant that I don't see him until his hands wrap around my upper arms and he brings me to a stop with a chuckle.

"Hey, there. I was looking for you."

And while I don't want to see either of the Wonder Twins, *this* one is the one I most don't want to see.

"Oh, hi, Zach."

"I understand you have the week off," Zach says, still hanging onto my arms.

I step back, shrugging out of his grasp. I start to ask how he knows that, but then realize it doesn't matter. This is Sapphire Falls. He could've asked pretty much anyone he knows who knows me. Which is everyone.

"I do. Festival week. Plus the big wedding next weekend."

He grins. "Perfect time to come back. Lots of great memories of the festival."

I am not taking his bait. Of course, there are lots of good memories of the festival. For every single person in this town. Every festival. I am not going to let him think that the festival before his senior year when he first, finally paid attention to me was somehow special to me.

"Yeah. I can't wait to see everyone. It's going to be fun."

He nods, his expression softening. "I have high hopes."

"Well, I'd better go. I'm on my way to the bakery." I know my mom and Adrianne are elbows deep, if not shoulders deep, in baking for the wedding and the festival, but they'll still definitely have muffins and scones ready for breakfast.

I love my job, of course, but being only on call this week is a break I've been looking forward to. It's a beautiful summer morning and the walk from my house over to the bakery for breakfast and coffee is perfect.

I love sitting in my mom's bakery and chatting with her and Adrianne. Who happens to be Jefferson's mom. I forgive her for that, since she's also Graham, Carver, and Ginny's mom. Three out of four ain't bad.

"Can we talk for just a minute?" Zach asked. "I was looking

for you. I could buy you breakfast." He gestures to his left, my right.

We're standing on the sidewalk along Main Street, right in front of Dottie's Diner. Which not only means it's the second best place for breakfast, but also means there are several people sitting inside, looking out the huge window, watching the two of us talking on the sidewalk.

I don't think the majority of the town knows what went on between Zach and me. Our "romance" was short and secretive, thanks to him, and ten years ago. I very much doubt that anyone inside is looking at us and thinking, 'oh, look at the exes'.

However, they might be looking at us and thinking, 'oh Harlow and Golden-Boy-Turned-Doctor-Zach are talking, isn't that interesting'.

My mom will know about this before I get to the bakery.

I just turned twenty-five for fuck's sake, but everyone's acting as if my single status is a huge concern. And interest.

It's absolutely not. I love my life, and if and when I find a guy to settle down with, it will be at the right time, the right guy, and they'll all love him.

But it will not be fucking Zach Nelson.

"I don't really think there's anything for us to talk about, Zach," I tell him honestly.

"That's because you don't know what I have to say," Zach says earnestly. "I need to apologize. And just tell you about myself. I've changed."

I don't care.

I realize looking at him now that all the reasons I had a crush on him were legit.

I was young. Things like good looks and being great at football and being beloved by our entire town, were perfectly fine reasons for a fourteen-turning-fifteen year-old girl to develop heart-eyes for him.

Fourteen- and fifteen-year-old girls are a little gullible, and easily won over by things like flirtatious charm and good looks, which I have to admit Zach still have.

Plus, give me a break, our town is small. There weren't a lot of choices.

But looking at him now, I really don't care. He could have won a Pulitzer Prize for science. He could have saved four thousand rescue dogs. He could be running for President. Of anything, really. I wouldn't care.

"Zach, I really am—"

"Please."

I sigh. He's going to keep doing this. He's here for a week. Apparently he thinks I'm one of the reasons he's here. I should probably just get this over with. Yes, I really want one of my mom's orange scones. But I can have one of those almost anytime. The sooner I get this conversation with Zach over, the more peaceful my week is going to be.

"Okay, fine," I say, gesturing at Dottie's.

"I was thinking maybe we could get some food to go and find somewhere a little more private."

Yeah, that is not going to happen. I am not talking to Zach by myself. I need other people around. Not for my safety, but to keep me from screaming at him. Or stabbing him with my fork.

"I think it would be better in public." I turn and open the door to Dottie's without waiting for him.

I hear him sigh but he follows me inside. Like he had a choice.

"Hey, Harlow. Hi Zach," Deanna, Dottie's daughter, who is now running the restaurant, greets us. She's obviously surprised to see Zach but pleased.

I keep from rolling my eyes. He still has everyone fooled about what a great guy he is.

He's really fortunate that I never told my dad some of the shit he pulled.

My heart rate kicks up a little thinking about that. There were a couple of times I almost told my dad. But I kept it to myself for a number of reasons. Not because I thought my dad wouldn't believe me. Probably because I knew my dad *would*.

And besides being a protective father, he's also the town cop. He would've gotten involved on a personal and professional level. Zach would've been in huge trouble. The football team would've been in huge trouble. It would've caused a huge rift in town.

Now ten years later, I realize that those are not good reasons to cover up someone's bad behavior, but again, I was a young girl who did believe that some of it was her fault.

Swallowing against the sick feeling in my stomach at the memories rushing at me, I follow Deanna as she leads us to an empty booth. There aren't many. It's busy in here, as usual.

Both Zach and I are greeted by nearly everyone in the building. We both smile, wave, and do the expected, "Hi. Good. How are you?"

Finally, we slide into a booth on opposite sides.

"I'll bring coffee for you," Deanna says to me, knowing my usual. "How about you?" she asks Zach.

"Hot tea, please."

Yuck. Right there I know nothing could ever happen between us again.

I pretend to study the menu, even though I know it by heart, and am absolutely getting French toast. I don't normally come to Dottie's for breakfast unless I'm with my parents and siblings. Dottie's is usually a lunch thing for me. But when I do come, it's her French toast and a side of bacon.

"You look gorgeous," Zach tells me, setting his menu down.

I'm wearing a basic green scoop-necked tee, denim shorts,

and sandals. My hair is pulled back into a loose, low pony, and I have no make-up on. I look up. "Thank you."

"Seriously. You've always been beautiful, but you're gorgeous now. The last ten years have been really good to you."

This is also stupid. It's not as if it's been ten years since he's seen me at all. His parents lived here in Sapphire Falls for the first three years after he graduated, and he was home for holidays. He even tried to see me during a couple of those trips. He's also breezed into town here and there over the years for homecoming, or the festival.

It has been a couple of years I guess, and I assumed he was busy with medical school and his residency, but I haven't changed that much.

Maybe he's fishing for a return compliment. That's not going to happen.

"Thank you. I feel good. I'm really happy."

Deanna returns with my coffee. Black, straight up, a little cinnamon on top. She sets hot water and tea bags next to Zach. "You want lemon or honey?"

He shakes his head. "I'm good."

"I know what Harlow is getting, what can I bring you?"

"Denver omelet, wheat toast."

Deanna doesn't bother writing it down but says, "I'll get it out as soon as I can."

The moment she's moved off, Zach leans in and says, "I don't want to beat around the bush."

I sit back and brace myself. "Okay, good idea." Let's get this over with.

"I want you back. I've thought about you constantly over the past ten years. I've changed. I am successful, settled. I know what I want. And it's you."

I stare at him. That is...appalling.

Even if I was interested in him, how the fuck does he know that he wants me? It's been ten years. I *hope* we've both changed a lot in ten years. He doesn't know me anymore. And I'm insulted that he thinks he might.

"I'm not interested," I say simply, hoping that's enough.

"I know that things in the past were...complicated."

I tip my head. "I'm not sure that's the word I'd use," I tell him. "I think it was pretty simple really."

He frowns. "I know there was a big gap in age. And experience. I think that made it complicated."

"Which part?" I ask. "The part where you didn't take 'I don't want to have sex yet' seriously, or the part where you thought that my youth and inexperience meant that you could emotionally manipulate me with guilt and the threat of other girls who *would* give you what you wanted. Or was it the part where my inexperience also meant that I hadn't ever drunk alcohol so getting me wasted was really easy, which made getting a lot further physically also really easy. Or the part where because I was young and in love for the first time you thought that it would be easier to get me to forgive your cheating?"

I stare at him across the table. There is humiliation and regret washing through me for sure, but there is also anger. So much anger. And pride that I can stand up to him now, say these things, admit these things, and not let him sweep it all away the way he did before.

"See?" I ask, my voice amazingly calm. "That's a whole lot of use of the word 'easy'. Which is the opposite of complicated."

I cross my legs and rest my folded hands on the table. "Or was the complicated part that I had something to hold over your head for the rest of your senior year that could have ruined everything for you and you had to constantly think of ways to keep me in check so I wouldn't tell anyone about the time you roofied my drink and tried to rape me?"

His face has gone pale and he sits back as well. "That is *not* what happened."

"Hmmm, I'm pretty fucking sure it is. And I think you know there are some people who would back that up."

"Harlow, I was...young. Stupid. Desperate to have you back."

"Jesus Christ, Zach. You have to know how horrible that sounds."

"I was in love with you."

I laugh. I didn't back then when he'd say that. My poor little in-love-for-the-first-time heart would cry every time. But now, I can laugh. "I *really* hope in ten years you've learned what love actually is."

"I was a dumb kid. I'll admit that. I didn't treat you right."

My eyes go wide. "You think?"

"But I don't think we remember those days the same way."

"It's not my fault you've justified it all somehow in your head, Zach. I know what happened."

He leans in, dropping his voice to a loud whisper. "Why would I drug you? We'd already had sex. It's not like I *needed* to force you."

I lift an eyebrow. "Because I'd changed my mind about ever doing it again after you cheated on me? Because you were an entitled asshole who couldn't handle being told no?"

"Be honest. You'd stopped saying no and it wouldn't have taken me much to persuade you," he says.

And there's a little smirk pulling the corner of his lips that makes me want to slap him.

I'm *not* a violent person. I'm not. I don't slam doors and throw things and yell.

Very often.

I'm cool and calm. I know that you catch more flies with honey than vinegar. I work fucking hard on my honey.

But this guy... I wish I had a fly swatter right now.

"I'd told you never, *ever* again after I found out that you had sex with Madison."

We'd been at a party after I'd given him my virginity thinking that would keep him with me forever, believing that was the last thing we needed to really cement our commitment. Because that's what he'd fucking told me. Over and over. And yes, I was younger, inexperienced, and madly in love with this fucking asshole.

I'd found out two days before that party that he'd cheated on me *again*, and that us sleeping together had done nothing to strengthen his commitment to me.

I don't know if he'd thought forcing me into sex again would make me more amenable to getting back together, or if it was just a control thing, or what.

I don't care.

I do know that he gave me a red solo cup, I'd drunk half of it, started feeling weird, and told Graham.

I don't remember anything after that, but I was at Graham's house, in *his* bed when I woke up, and Graham assured me that Zach hadn't touched me.

And I hadn't been alone, or really even near, Zach Nelson again.

My friends had been like little bulldogs, protecting me. Any event where Zach and I would both be present—and in a town like ours, there were many—there was always someone with me.

But I didn't really need them. Zach kept his distance. He didn't try to get me alone. He didn't call or text or email. We would make eye contact from time to time, but he'd look away quickly.

I'd stupidly thought maybe he was regretful.

But slowly, over the years, I'd started caring less and less about how Zach Nelson felt about...anything.

"I've thought about you so much over the past ten years, Harlow," he says, starting again with a new tone of voice. "I made mistakes, I'll admit that. Can't we try again? What we had was special."

I actually feel a shudder go down my spine. I was special to him, I believe that. Because I was submissive. I was easily manipulated. I put him on the highest pedestal. A lot of people thought Zach walked on water. Lots of girls thought he hung the moon. But no one believed *all* of his bullshit. Not like I did.

"Look, Zach," I finally say, feeling tired. "I'm not interested. *At all.* I'm not the girl you used to know. I actually don't think you'd like me very much now."

He sits forward again, looking serious. "I sincerely doubt that. I want to get to know you. I want to see how you're different. I want to fall in love with you all over again."

Fucking *yuck.*

Geez, he doesn't even have the decency to take five minutes to reflect on the huge, serious topics we just put out there between us.

"I don't care," I tell him. "I've moved on."

I totally have. I never think about Zach.

Well, almost never. I do have kids on my caseload that make me think of the really poor decisions I made, the people I *didn't* tell about them, the help I didn't get. I had so much love and support around me, and I still didn't tell my parents or lean on my friends' parents, or my teachers, or counselors. I didn't even tell all of my friends. But the friends who did know were solid. They got me through. I don't know what would have happened if Graham hadn't been there for me that night. If I hadn't been able to let him take care of me.

I assume Graham told Sloan and Margot what happened because they were the soldiers around me after that. But we never actually talked about it. Still, I knew I *could* tell them. They'd love me anyway. They'd believe me.

The kids I work with often come from situations where they have no one. Or feel like it anyway. They don't have the support network I had and so I'm very empathetic to the choices—and yes, mistakes—they make. And I do everything I can to make sure they know I'm a safe space for them, someone they can tell anything.

"*Please*, just give me this week. Just spend some time with me. I think you'll see that I'm an even better version of the guy you fell so hard for before."

God, he's so full of himself. I actually used to find that confidence attractive.

Remembering how easily and fully I fell for all of this makes me sick now. That, along with the confident look on his stupid face makes me *certain* I could stab him with a fork.

I can *absolutely* say no to this guy. No question in my mind. But...

I want him to suffer.

Just like Jefferson said last night.

I want Zach to be miserable.

I want him to not only know he has *no* chance with me but to be sad.

I *totally* get where Jefferson is coming from.

It might be one of the very few things Jefferson and I have in common, but yeah, I'm on the same page with him here.

"I'm so not interested in getting to know you again," I tell Zach. I should just leave it at that. I should just lean on my own self-confidence and willpower. I can do that. I can resist him. For sure.

But...what would make Zach even more miserable than just my ability to say no to him?

Me being with someone else. Someone he hates.

"I think I can convince you otherwise," Zach says, giving me a smile that I'll bet works for him ninety-nine percent of the time.

I really like being the one-percent exception.

One thing I do know about Zach that has always been true, he's very used to getting his way. Things fall into place for Zach Nelson. He's very rarely wanted something he hasn't gotten. And he's not above lying, cheating, and manipulating to get it.

This could be a very long week.

I don't worry about succumbing to his "charms"—at the end of this week I will *not* be back together with Zach—but avoiding him is going to be impossible and having this conversation over and over is going to be exhausting.

"I'm with someone," I say.

Jefferson will still go for this. I know it. It was his idea, and he was disappointed I wouldn't go along with it last night. Sure, when he first opened *his* stupid mouth, it was with the idea Graham and I would fake it. But our friends seem to think that Jefferson and I can make this believable.

I can fake being with Jefferson for a week.

I could do *anything* for a week if it makes Zach Nelson sad.

And Jefferson deserves it. Zach was a huge dick to him too.

Did I ever think I'd care if Jefferson got his revenge? No. But it will make this all the sweeter.

Zach frowns. "Someone told me that last night, but he didn't say who it was and no one in town seems to know anything about you dating anyone."

Of course he's asked around.

And of course they've all said they don't know.

"We've been keeping it under wraps," I tell him. "We're both from here and everyone knows us. We wanted a little privacy as we were figuring out if it was going to go anywhere."

"But now you're willing to tell me?" Zach asks, clearly suspicious.

"Seems that you have a direct interest." I shrug. "I'm not interested in you. I wouldn't be anyway. But no, I'm not willing to spend any extra time with you and I don't want any attention from you this week. My boyfriend and I are happy, and I don't want you messing with that."

"Who is it?"

I shouldn't say before I talk to Jefferson again. There are maybe a couple of other guys I could talk into faking this with me if he decides to be a jerk and *not* do this now.

"You'll figure it out soon enough."

"Zach!" someone calls from the back of the diner.

He looks over and his face lights up as he lifts a hand. "Be right back." He slides out of the booth to go say hi to whoever it is.

I take a deep breath and slump in my seat as he leaves. I didn't even realize how tense I was.

I pick up my cup and take a long, fortifying draw of Dottie's coffee. It's way stronger than what my mom and Adrianne serve. The farmers who come in for breakfast and gossip—heavy on the gossip and light on the eggs and toast—demand "real" coffee. I grin as I take a second drink. I agree with them.

I look out the window at the town square across the street. Preparations are already starting for the festival.

The festival is an annual event. Carnival rides and games roll into town. Booths for everything from food to crafts will outline the square. The two biggest being the dunking booth and the kissing booth, both of which raise money for local projects. There's also a petting zoo and any number of other crazy, fun, whatever-we-can-come-up-with-and-stuff-into-this-square activities.

Sapphire Falls' summer festival is famous and people plan their entire summer schedules around it.

It's why Kaelyn and Carver decided to put their wedding on the Saturday of the festival. Everyone will already be in town and there will be plenty for everyone to do around the wedding. The ceremony will be a simple thirty-minute diversion, in the gazebo right in the center of the square so that everyone who wants to be a part of it can be. Then everyone will have fun at the biggest wedding reception ever. There will be one booth where wedding cake and other wedding themed treats will be served, and they're sponsoring the street dance this year as their wedding dance. But it will look just like every other year with the portion of the street right outside Dottie's blocked off, picnic tables pulled out, lights strung up from the fronts of the buildings to poles in the square, and a live local band.

The games and rides and everything will continue to run during the dance, and everything will just blend together into one big party.

It will be perfect.

As I'm imagining the whole scene, Jefferson walks by, blocking my view.

And I find myself leaning over and knocking on the window before I even think through what I'm doing.

He stops and looks in. He's clearly surprised to see me waving at him. But as soon as I mouth, 'Help me', he pivots toward Dottie's front door.

A minute later he arrives next to the booth. "Hey."

"Hey."

"What's up?"

"I need you."

His brow lifts. "Oh?"

"Yeah, we've got a little prob—"

Zach returns just then, before I can finish my sentence.

So I do the only thing I can—I grab Jefferson's hand and pull him into the booth next to me.

CHAPTER 5

JEFFERSON

I MAY NOT BE the brightest of the Riley siblings, but I'm pretty sharp. It takes me only the time from when Harlow grabs my hand to when my ass hits the seat to figure out what's going on.

Harlow Hansen and I are now accomplices.

I slide my arm along the booth behind her, my palm resting on her shoulder, and I pull her close.

I feel her body stiffen. I'm sure in surprise. But if we're gonna do this, we're going to *do* it.

Zach's eyes narrow as he takes the seat across the table from us.

Deanna shows up just then, delivering plates. She puts the French toast and bacon in front of Harlow. Of course she does. And an omelet with a ton of vegetables in front of Zach.

I steal a piece of bacon from Harlow's plate and lift it to my mouth, feeling stupidly smug.

I don't know what Harlow has told Zach, I don't know how long they've been here, I don't really know what's going on at all, but from this moment on, Zach Nelson is going to think that

Harlow and I are crazy about each other. And that she is so far over him, she barely remembers the days of looking at him with puppy dog eyes and writing him little love notes that she'd slip into his locker.

Sudden tension wraps around my ribs. I remember those stupid notes probably better than either of them do. I also remember Zach showing them off to the football team and making fun of them.

Harlow doesn't know about that. And as long as I am breathing, she won't.

That's essentially what I told Zach and the rest of the team when I heard them joking about the notes ten years ago.

My stance hasn't changed.

I force myself to relax, hug her a little tighter, feel her squirm against me—obviously trying to put some space between us—and grin. Zach can think I'm grinning at him. I'm actually grinning about the extra perk of this whole thing: driving Harlow nuts. That's always been fun. This next week is going to give me all kinds of opportunities for that particular entertainment as well. Win-win-fucking win.

"Morning, Zach," I finally say.

I reach for Harlow's coffee cup, and lift it to my mouth. I'm prepared for it to be straight black and strong, but I'm not prepared for the taste of cinnamon, or just *how* damned strong it is. My mother, candy-maker extraordinaire and co-owner of the best bakery in the state, has spoiled me with lattes since I was in high school. I'm man enough to admit that I like my coffee a little sweet and frothy. I'm not ashamed of that. And if you want to put a swirl of chocolate in there, I'm not gonna be mad.

I work on not coughing as I swallow and set the cup back down.

"What are you doing here?" Zach asks.

He seems annoyed. Perfect.

"Was walking by and saw my girl in the window. Of course I had to come in."

Zach's brows slam together, and he looks from me to Harlow, back to me, then back to Harlow. "*Him?*"

Now she leans into me. "I told you you'd find out soon enough."

He looks back at me. "Why didn't you just say so last night?"

"Honestly?" I ask. "Because it's really none of your fucking business."

"Why doesn't anyone in town know the two of you are together?"

"Just because the people you've asked don't know doesn't mean no one knows," I say.

Lying my ass off is not something I'm good at, especially on the fly. But that's something I'm generally proud of. Guess I'm going to have to get a little better at it.

"I told you that we've been keeping it under wraps since we're both from here and everyone knows us. We wanted to be sure it was turning into something before we let everyone in on it," Harlow tells him.

Awesome. She's already come up with a story and smoothly let me in on it. And that's a pretty good one. Honestly, if I was going to date someone within our little friend group, or within the group of kids that came out of my parents' friend group, that's exactly how I would do it. The relationship would have to be well established, and pretty serious before we let everyone in on it. If it wasn't going to work out, or it was only going to be a short term fling, there'd be no point in pulling everyone in. There'd be potential for a lot of broken hearts actually.

Fuck.

We're going to have to let everyone in on this.

Our parents and siblings absolutely cannot think this is something serious or real.

"So how long has this been going on?" Zach asks.

I take a breath. "Zach. This really is none of your business. We've chosen not to tell a lot of people who are closer to us than you've ever been. We're not gonna discuss our relationship with you. But I am going to tell you, Harlow is absolutely, one thousand percent, still off-limits."

I feel Harlow's gaze on the side of my face. Probably that use of the word *still*. She has no idea that Zach and I have had previous conversations about her and his involvement in her life. Nor does she need to.

Now I get to play the part of protector to Harlow, and antagonist to Zach Nelson with a much better reason—even if it's fake—while he's in town. This is definitely going to be fun.

"In fact, I was coming to find her. Need you for something," I tell her, making eye contact for the first time since I sat down.

As our eyes meet, I become acutely aware of the fact that our bodies are pressed up against one another. She fits against me nicely. She's warm and soft and... I stop myself right there. None of that matters.

"Oh?" she asks. But she seems eager for the excuse. "Then let's go."

"You're not hungry?" Zach asks.

"I told you I was on the way to the bakery anyway," Harlow tells him. "I wasn't planning on French toast and bacon."

"Guess I'll take it home. Think of you later." He gives her a smile.

I want to punch him.

It's juvenile, but I slide out of the booth, go up to the counter and reach behind it for a to-go box. I come back, dump the contents of Harlow's plate into it, close the lid, and toss a twenty-dollar bill on the table. "That should cover her."

Then I grab Harlow's hand, tug her out of the booth, tuck her under my arm, and press a kiss to the top of her head.

"See ya' around." I say to Zach, wishing that wasn't true, but knowing that's too much to ask for.

He sits back in the booth, watching us carefully. "Oh. For sure."

We step out onto the sidewalk, and I say, "Admit it, I was smooth."

She nods. "I will admit that. Thank you for just going along with that." She pauses and then says, "Of course this was all your idea in the first place so really *I* was the one going along with it smoothly."

I chuckle. "Obviously it was a great idea, right?"

"Well, it's better than letting him be happy and confident."

I touch her on the tip of her nose, partly because it feels right and partly because I know it will make her nuts. "Exactly."

She frowns but does not swat me away. Probably because we're standing on display outside of Dottie's huge front window.

"We need to tell our moms," we both stay at the same time.

I chuckle and she smiles.

"Everyone needs to be in on it," I clarify.

"I know. They're going to think it's nuts."

"But they'll have our backs."

"Yeah."

We turn toward the bakery together and start walking. I grab her hand and entwine our fingers.

She tries to pull away, almost instinctively. "What are you doing?"

I tighten my hold on her. "The entire diner is watching us. We just announced we're together. For sure Zach is watching. We have to act like we like each other now, Harlow."

She huffs out breath. "Yeah, I don't think either of us thought this through."

Maybe not at the moment it was first suggested and it hit me that it was a great idea, but since then? Oh, I've thought about it. More than I should have.

I pull her in closer and kiss the top of her head again. She elbows me. I chuckle. "Oh come on, it's a week."

"About six and a half days longer than I think I can pull off liking you. "

"Look," I say, glancing side to side and then stepping behind the gazebo so that we're blocked from the diner. We're in the middle of the town square so it's not like we're totally hidden, but I can make this look good. I turn her and back her up against the side of the gazebo, then brace a hand next to her ear. "We *have to* pull this off now. We told Zach, word for word, to his face, *together* that we're a couple. It would be way worse for both of us if Zach figured out we're faking it."

She's staring at me with wide eyes. Maybe because this is the closest Harlow and I have been in years. And she doesn't remember the last time we were this close. Considering she was blacked out and I was carrying her into Graham's bedroom, I'm not surprised.

"We can pull this off," I tell her firmly.

She wets her lips, and I can't help it when my eyes drop to her mouth. It's just instinct. Or something.

Whatever. She has a nice mouth. At least when it's shut and not snarking at me.

"Yeah. I'm sure we can," she says.

"Maybe I'll ask your dad for tips on how to deal with brats."

"What's that supposed to mean?"

"Your mom pokes at your dad just like you do to me."

Harlow shakes her head quickly. "My mom *likes* my dad.

When she pokes him, it's teasing and...flirting." She frowns as if she doesn't really like using that word in reference to her own parents.

I grin. "Yeah, it is," I say thoughtfully. "Interesting."

"That is *not* what it is when I poke at you."

"But other people might think so."

"Wait, are you calling my mom a brat?"

I nod. "Totally."

She seems to be thinking that over. Then she frowns. "Don't talk about my parents like that.

I chuckle. "Okay."

"What do you know about brats? Your mom is super sweet. She never pokes at your dad."

"No, she doesn't. My mom has other ways of flirting with my dad."

"They do flirt?"

"All the time." I never really spent time thinking about it before but yes, there's no question that my parents are very much in love and that they have their own language that is flirtatious at times. "But I do know brats. My sister is one. Of course I blame you for that."

Harlow lifts her chin. "Good."

"Carver and I are the nice ones. And we're older than you and weren't really influenced by you. I don't think that's a coincidence."

She narrows her eyes. "You really want to start talking about your siblings with me? That's not really the way to make me happy and compliant with trying to like you."

"You're still mad at me about Graham." I don't phrase it as a question. I know she is.

She looks like she can't believe I just asked that. "Yes. Always and forever."

"Going to Colorado was good for him."

"He would've been just fine, great even, if he'd stayed here too."

"Agreed to disagree."

"I don't agree to that. I *do* disagree with you. But I'm not agreeing to put this aside. I still hate you for forcing Graham to leave. I still hate you for making him doubt our friendship. I still hate you for not trusting me and for questioning my place in his life. I was here for him at times and in ways you never were. You do *not* know everything, Jefferson, and you butted in!"

Her cheeks are flushed and I believe the anger in her eyes is real, even after all of these years. She believes I stole her best friend from her. That I ruined their relationship.

She's not totally wrong.

But I don't regret it.

"I know you don't forgive me, Harlow," I finally say.

"We still approach life very differently," she tells me. "We still look at relationships very differently. We don't look at home and family the same way. Those are big things to me. I can maybe pretend to like you for a week. But this is only because I hate Zach more than I dislike you."

I tip my head and look at her. Really study her. It's too bad she hates me. We actually do have a lot in common. Though I'm sure she would hate to hear that.

"Let's go tell our moms before this rumor about us gets spread around town," I tell her, stepping back. "And before you slap me in the middle of the square and go stomping off, ruining any chance of us selling this."

"We will be about ten seconds from that all week," she warns me.

"I know, Harlow. I know."

But she lets me take her hand as we turn toward the bakery.

CHAPTER 6

JEFFERSON

THE LITTLE BELL above the door jingles happily as I push open the door to Scott's Sweets and let Harlow pass in front of me.

Her mom, Peyton, one of my favorite people despite her hardheaded, feisty, smart-mouthed offspring, is behind the counter.

Her face lights up when she sees us. "Well, hi, you two!"

"Hi, Mom," Harlow says, her entire countenance changing as she crosses the shop and rounds the front counter to give her mom a hug. "I'm in desperate need of coffee and an orange scone."

"Your wish is my command," Peyton teases. "I've got nothing else going on."

Harlow laughs. "I know you're slammed in here. I can serve myself."

Peyton glances at me then back at her daughter who is already at the coffee pot. "Are you going to get Jefferson anything?"

Harlow doesn't even look at me. "Jefferson knows where everything is in here too."

Peyton props a hand on her hip and looks between Harlow and me. "You know we have windows on this shop, right?"

Harlow turns with her mug and leans her hip against the counter. "What do you mean?"

"That I saw you walking up the sidewalk holding hands."

Harlow doesn't react. She sips from her cup. "Yeah, we have something to tell you."

Peyton's brows arch.

I continue to just stand in the middle of the shop, my hands tucked in the front pockets of my jeans. I'm happy to let Harlow take the lead here. It will be amusing to see how she explains this to her mother. Of course, I'd been shocked that she'd asked for my help. But a simple *help me* from Harlow and my body automatically turned for the front door of the diner.

But now we've got a situation, and our moms are just two of the many people that need to be brought up to speed.

I wouldn't call Peyton Hansen laid-back. Not at all, in fact. Peyton is a hot-blooded, protective, feisty woman. Her temper flares hot and fast. There are many stories about young Peyton smashing headlights and even noses when needed. The best story-teller is her husband, the guy who was the cop back then too, as a matter of fact. She was a hellraiser. Though it seems she always channeled her ire and vengeance on people who deserved it.

Peyton is extremely protective of her inner circle. But I'm not worried that she'll turn any of that on me. I'm in that inner circle.

I was on my way over here to the bakery when Harlow waylaid me. I'd planned to chat with both of our moms and just enjoy one of my summer mornings off. Football practice doesn't start for a couple of months yet, and I'm not teaching any summer classes this year. I also got out of driver's ed and they didn't need my help with baseball this year, so I have a relatively low-key June and July ahead. I'm looking forward to it.

"I'm all ears," Peyton says, nudging her daughter's foot with her own.

"Is Adrianne around?" Harlow asks. "We might as well tell you both at once."

"Did you kill someone?" Peyton asks her.

Harlow doesn't actually act as shocked as you might expect. She laughs. "That's your first guess?"

Peyton shrugs. "That you would kill someone, and Jefferson would help you bury the body? It's in the top three."

I chuckle. I'm not offended by the assumption that I'd help Harlow cover up a crime. We don't get along, but that's because we approach life very differently. She's completely right about that. We love people differently. But we both love big and hard. So our people feel it. We are both pretty big influences in the lives of the people we care about.

And, because we share a lot of people and our lives overlap, we've butted heads. Graham is the main one she's pissed about, but he's not the only one. And, by the way, she's influenced some of our mutuals in ways that piss me off too.

No, we do not see eye to eye on things like what support and encouragement mean, but...do I think she's a good person? Yes. Do I think she truly does care about the right things? Yes. Would I help her bury a body? Yes.

And is it possible there would be a body to bury?

Yes.

Peyton's protectiveness has been passed on to Harlow. Harlow fights for the people she loves. But she seemingly lacks her mother's fire. Seemingly. On the surface, Harlow seems to take after her dad—the laid-back, rocksteady, even-more-stubborn-than-Peyton town cop who ended up smitten with the bad girl.

Scott and Peyton are quite a pair.

One of the most fascinating things for me about Harlow Hansen, however, is that I think there's more of her mother in her than she likes to let on. In fact, I think she squelches those tendencies. And sometimes I think that's difficult for her.

So do I believe there could be an instance where someone pushes her too far?

Yep.

And I know it would be because that someone did something to someone she loves.

So yes, I would help her cover it up. No question in my mind.

"And you think I would come tell you about the murder over scones and coffee?" Harlow asks her mom.

"Yes," Peyton says. "You wouldn't be able to keep it quiet and you wouldn't tell Mia or Austin. And you definitely wouldn't tell your dad."

I agree that she wouldn't tell her sister or brother. She protects them. She'd never want them to know something that might burden them somehow.

For some reason that annoys me. Who does Harlow lean on? I don't know why the question suddenly goes through my head, but I can't ignore it.

Probably because the answer is Graham.

Or was.

Before he went to Colorado.

I blow out a breath. *Do not let her get to you. Not already anyway.*

It could be a really long week if I start feeling things for Harlow. Like soft. Or sorry.

Harlow's eyes find mine across the shop. "I don't think I'd need to tell anyone else if Jefferson was in on it."

Peyton tips her head and looks at me as well. "Oh really?"

"Nope," Harlow says. "I'd have my partner in crime. Why would I need to tell you?"

"To assuage your guilty conscience?"

She snorts. "You'll always love me no matter what. And you would totally believe that whoever it was deserved it. But I would definitely make sure Jefferson's hands were just as dirty as mine, so I'd be able to hold that over his head forever. He'd have a direct stake in keeping it quiet. And that would be way more fun. He'd start being an ass at some family picnic and I'd just say, 'anyone know how to get blood out of cashmere?' and he'd shut right up."

I just shake my head, but she smirks. Because she knows she's right.

Peyton laughs, then raises her voice, "Adrianne, come out here!"

My mom emerges from the back, wiping her hands on a towel. Her eyes widen with pleasure when she sees Harlow, then she notices me, and her grins widens. "Hi."

"You should know that we are pretending to be madly in love for this week," Harlow says without preamble.

Our moms both just look at us for a couple of seconds, letting that sink in.

Then my mother says, "Sounds good."

Peyton nods. "Okay."

Harlow frowns at both of them. "You don't want to know why?"

My mom laughs. "Well, it's the two of you. I assume there's a good reason."

"Same," Peyton agrees.

"Don't you think it's weird?" Harlow asks.

I'm enjoying this far more than I expected to. I'm not sure what I thought our mothers' reactions would be, but calm acceptance wasn't it. I approach the counter and cross my arms on top of the bakery case, settling in.

"You don't think people will think this is strange and sudden?" I ask.

My mom shakes her head. "You've known each other forever. You've spent a lot of time around one another. You're about the same age. I don't think anyone will think it's strange that you'd date at some point."

Harlow snorts and I grin instead of taking offense as some men would. I can't help it, she cracks me up. Her seeming distaste for me is over-the-top.

I believe that she's mad at me. I believe the grudge she's holding, that she's held for years, is real. But I don't think she actually thinks I'm a horrible person. I think she enjoys telling herself and acting as if I'm a horrible person, though.

"I would never date him."

"Then why are you pretending to this week?" Peyton asks as she turns back to frosting the cookies laid out on the counter in front of her.

They're shaped like Ferris wheels and she's adding shiny icing that fills in the tiny seats and spokes of the wheel. Obviously, these are for the festival rather than the wedding. Then I shake my head. They actually could be for either. Or both. I love the way Kaelyn and Carver are combining their wedding with the festival. It's really turning into just another festival activity at this point.

"Zach Nelson is back in town," I say. "He thinks that he's going to win Harlow back. We decided to torture him a little bit. Harlow telling him no will upset him, but we want him to be *really* miserable."

Peyton is nodding as if she's fully on board with that. But then again, Peyton has a mean streak.

The amusing and mildly surprising part is that my mother is also nodding and smiling. My mother is very sweet. She's not the revenge type.

Unless, of course, someone hurts someone she loves. She won't smash headlights, but she'd definitely be up for some conspiring.

"Good for you. He doesn't deserve your time or energy," my mom tells Harlow.

My family loves Harlow. That's not in question whatsoever. And of course, they feel protective of her. Even if Zach was just your run-of-the-mill ex-boyfriend who had hurt her mildly. But he isn't. He was her first love and broke her heart badly. So they automatically don't like him. That's pretty amazing.

And they don't even know the half of it. Most people don't. Harlow doesn't even know that I know the whole story.

"While Zach's in town we need to sell the story that you two are together, madly in love, and we're all thrilled by it," Peyton summarizes. "That'll be easy."

Harlow narrows her eyes. "Yeah?"

"Certainly. We all love you both. Having you together will be great."

Harlow's gaze meets mine. She looks like she has questions. I just shrug. It's nice that our parents love us both and think it will be easy to treat us as a couple, I suppose. It will certainly make this week easier.

"You'll tell Dad?" I ask my mom.

My dad is an interesting guy. He loves us all, but he is very analytical. He might be one to dig more into why we're doing this, what is our expected outcome, is there another better approach, and what the effects will be afterward.

Those are all fair questions, and I'm not sure I can answer them. The best communicator with my dad has always been and will always be my mother.

She smiles. "Of course."

She'll also know when the best *time* to tell him will be. When he'll actually absorb the information and understand how he needs to act so that no one gets suspicious.

"Can I tell your dad?" Peyton asks Harlow with a grin.

We all laugh. Scott is protective. Of his wife and his children.

But I realize I'm not worried. Sure, Peyton will tell him that it's fake and why. I assume Scott will approve of me protecting Harlow to some extent from Zach. But I don't think Scott would have a problem with me and Harlow dating. Scott likes me. He knows I'm a good guy.

He also knows Harlow and my general vibe.

He might actually be worried about me.

"He's going to be out and about in town," Harlow says. "People might ask him about it. We should tell him sooner versus later."

"How many people know about this?" my mom asks.

"We were just down at the diner. So..."

"Everyone," Peyton fills in.

Not that the entire town was at the diner, but everyone at the diner has probably already told someone who has told someone. It's been about twenty minutes so...yeah, everyone.

Peyton pulls her phone from her pocket and presses a button.

A second later Scott's voice comes across the line. "It's early for trouble."

"That's not what you said in the shower this morning," Peyton tells him.

"*Mom!*" Harlow protests.

"I'm going to assume that Harlow is telling you what the hell is going on with her and Jefferson?" Scott asks, clearly having heard his daughter's voice.

"You already heard?" Harlow asks. She doesn't seem surprised.

None of us are.

"Well, Derek told me and Kyle that Jefferson announced to the bar last night that you're seeing someone and then walked out. Then just now Melissa Stevens asked me how long you and Jefferson have been dating so yeah, I've heard."

Derek Wright manages the Come Again and Kyle Ames is one of the town doctors. They're also Scott's best friends and the three of them get coffee every morning. Between the three of them, they hear as much gossip as the ladies at the hair salon and the old men at Dottie's.

"What did you say?" Peyton asks.

"That it's hard to keep track since we've known Jefferson all his life and he's always been around."

The four of us in the bakery all exchange impressed looks.

"That was pretty good," Peyton tells her husband. "Not a lie but you didn't give anything away."

"Thinking on my feet is kind of part of the job," Scott says.

"Makes you a good cop," Peyton says with a grin.

"I meant the job of bein' your husband, but yeah, it helps with the cop thing too," he replies.

She just laughs. "Well, for the record, Officer Hansen, this one is all Harlow's. Or Harlow's and Jefferson's. Not my idea."

"You're not discouraging it though," Scott says.

"Well...no."

"For the record," Scott says, "I don't like Zach Nelson either."

Harlow's eyes round in surprise. "Wow, you're like a detective or something."

"Damn right. You okay? Some reason you can't just tell Zach to fuck off?" Scott asks.

Harlow's gaze meets mine again. She smiles. I return it.

There is something about being partners in crime with her that gets my heart beating a little faster.

"It's more just for fun. Messing with Zach feels like revenge. I'm not too proud to admit that to you guys."

"In that case, I'm glad it's Jefferson," Scott tells her.

She looks mildly surprised. "Why is that?"

"Because he's probably the one guy who's not too tightly wrapped around your finger. He can keep you out of jail."

Her eyes are wide, and I cannot help my laugh.

"Thanks, Scott," I comment so he knows I'm here.

Scott chuckles. "Just remember that's my expectation, Jefferson."

"Duly noted. If she commits any crimes, cover them up."

Scott actually laughs a little harder. "Yep," he says. "That's exactly the energy I want from a boyfriend for one of my girls. I know it's a lot to ask to keep her from committing crimes entirely. Though if you could do that, I'd greatly appreciate it."

"Interestingly," Peyton says. "We were just talking about how Jefferson would help Harlow hide a body."

"I'm sure he would," Scott, the *cop*, comments calmly. "If for no other reason than to have something to hold over her head."

We all laugh at how closely his summation resembled what Harlow said.

And I'm not sure what that says about me, but I am looking forward to this week more all the time.

"So when people ask you about them," Peyton says to her husband. "You can't act surprised. You've known they've been dating for about three months," she says, talking without looking at either of us. "But they kept it under wraps because they wanted to be sure it was something worth coming out about. Since it's such a small town and they know so many people in common, they didn't want it to be a big deal if it didn't work out. But we, of course, have all known about it for at least two months. They successfully snuck around for about a month."

Harlow straightens. "You think we'd only be able to sneak around for a month before you found out? *Please.*" She rolls her eyes. "If I wanted to hide something from you guys, I could keep it hidden for way longer than that."

Peyton grins at her. "Oh, I have no doubt. But you fell madly in love with him in a month so you couldn't keep it inside anymore. You just had to tell us about it."

"I fell madly in love with Jefferson in a *month?*" She glances at me. "I don't think so. If anything, he fell madly in love with me. He was going to tell everyone, and I told him he had to keep it quiet and could only tell our families, if he just couldn't keep it inside anymore." She looks back at her mom. "And if we were madly in love, why wouldn't we tell everyone? Why just you guys?"

"Well, we convinced you to take it a little slower," Peyton says.

Then I laugh.

They all look at me.

"Really?" I give my mom a grin. "My parents fell in love in a weekend. And they're telling me that I would have to take it slower? No way is that believable."

My mom nods. "He has a point."

"Well, I know something about having a guy gaga over me *forever* before I gave in," Peyton says. "So I'm cool with the story that Jefferson fell really hard and fast, but Harlow made him wait to tell everyone."

Yes, we all know the stories of how all the parents in our

friend group got together. Scott apparently fell first and hard for Peyton and she made him work for it.

I shake my head. "No way. I want Zach miserable knowing that I have the girl he wants, but it doesn't help me out to make this look like I had to work extra hard to convince her."

Harlow crosses her arms and stares at me. "You don't think I would be hard to get?"

I chuckle. "In general? Absolutely. For me? No way."

"Really? Why is that?" she asks.

"Because I know you too well. I would be able to easily romance you. I know all your favorite things. I know all your friends. Your entire family. They all love me. In fact, if we ever decided to date, we'd go in knowing it was serious. We've already done all the get-to-know-you stuff. We already know all the good, the bad, the ugly. I know *all* the annoying things about you."

"And vice versa," she interjects.

I nod. "Exactly. If we ever decided to even go on a single serious date, it would be because we already decided we wanted to make this something more. So I don't think it would take us three months to come around and tell everyone. I'd say the story should be that we've been officially together for about a month. Our families have known for most of that time."

I can't pull my gaze away from Harlow's. I'm watching her digest everything I just said.

And she's not denying any of it.

I hadn't thought all of this through, I was just thinking out loud. But everything I just said is true.

"You're right," Harlow finally says. "That does make sense." She takes a breath and looks at her mom. "How's that sound?"

Peyton shrugs. "I'm sold."

I glance at my mom. "Me too," she says with a nod. "Makes total sense."

"Got it," Scott says from over the phone. "I'm keeping a tally of how many times I'm asked about this today. That's how many caramels I expect to get tonight when I get home."

My mom's caramels are famous. But Peyton laughs. "You can't have any extras. We're barely keeping up with the demand as it is with the festival and all the extra people in town."

"Then you'll have to reward me some other way. You know I'm going to get asked about this more than you are."

"I can't wait to talk about it," Peyton says, her eyes twinkling with mischief. "But you know I'm always up for a good *reward*."

"*Mom*," Harlow groans. "Please."

Harlow glances at me and I mouth 'brat'.

Harlow actually laughs.

"We need to go fill our friends in," I tell her. "They're going to be getting a ton of questions too."

She sighs. "Fine." She bends behind the bakery case and slides two orange scones into a to-go package.

"I want blueberry, not orange," I tell her.

She glances up. "I wasn't getting you one."

I shake my head. But watch as she slides a blueberry in with her two.

She also grabs a to-go cup of coffee.

"Vanilla latte," I tell her.

"You do not want me to make you a latte," she tells me, pouring her own coffee.

"You're not good at it?"

"I *will* spit in it."

I grin and move around the counter and in next to her to make my own latte. "See, there's no way it would take more than a month for us to get serious," I tell her, as I reach over her head, and very into her personal space, to reach the vanilla syrup.

"What do you mean?"

"I figure it would only take about thirty days for us to decide if we'd rather kiss or kill each other. Once we decide that, we'd be good to go. I would have no delusions about you being any kind of submissive, sweet, helpful girlfriend. You'd already know that I don't *need* a submissive, sweet, helpful girlfriend. There would be no learning curve. No disappointments. You'd just be you, I'd be me, and we'd already know it all going in."

She looks up at me, not trying to move away from me. I also keep my body very close to hers and just meet her gaze steadily, my arm still up.

Finally, she nods. "That's a very good point," she says. "Except..."

Of course there's an except.

"Except?"

"I don't think we'd need that long to decide on the kiss or kill thing."

"How long do you think it would take?"

She actually looks me up and down. Our mothers can't see the way her gaze tracks over me from the position we're in, but I do. Definitely.

"Probably about forty-eight hours. Some of it would depend on how good a cook you are." Then she turns away from me with her coffee and *our* scones and starts toward the door. "See you later," she says to our moms.

And I'm left frothing my milk and wondering if it's possible to decide in *one* day which of those things I'd rather do to her.

Or if it's possible to want to do both equally.

CHAPTER 7

HARLOW

I STEP OUTSIDE and take a deep breath.

I don't know what just happened, but standing close to Jefferson just now made my heart start beating faster.

He smells really good. And noticing that over all the amazing scents in our moms' bakery is saying something.

Maybe I'll just chalk it up to that.

But he sure seems comfortable getting into my personal space.

Starting with when he slid into the booth at the diner, right up against me, and put his arm around me. Or when he backed me up against the gazebo. And when he crowded in next to me at the bakery.

He doesn't seem to care who's around either.

Sure, in the diner it was for Zach's benefit. And I suppose at the gazebo, anyone could've been walking or driving by and he needed to look like we were friendly. Okay, more than friendly.

But at the bakery, the audience was made up of only our moms. We just told them the whole thing was fake. Still, he crowded right in next to me and stretched his big, long muscular body out, looking down at me as if in challenge.

No, I wasn't going to let him know it affected me.

I'm barely willing to admit that to myself.

But I can't escape replaying all these words from him and my mom. They're both right that it wouldn't take long for us to decide to be serious *if* this was real. It makes complete sense.

If, in some alternate universe, we *did* decide to date we wouldn't need anything near thirty days to know if it was going to work. We've known each other too long and too well. It would be clear quickly if we were in or out.

But not in *this* universe. The real one. The one we are currently living in.

He's number two on my shit list right after Zach.

I'm not going to forget that he encouraged Ginny to leave Sapphire Falls. I don't care if she's his sister. She's my friend. She's from here. Her friends and family and *home* are here.

He also encouraged my brother to leave. Austin almost never comes home to visit since he moved to Indianapolis and fell in love. My mom misses him so much. *I* miss him so much.

Jefferson Riley has been encouraging people to *leave* Sapphire Falls ever since *he* came back. His own bitterness over being stuck here bleeds over to all the people he "cares about" and he pushes them out as quickly as he can.

So he's the guidance counselor for the high school. He got to influence my brother that way since Austin was a junior when Jefferson took the job. But he wasn't Ginny's high school counselor. Or Graham's. He was just their meddling brother.

I won't forgive him for sending Graham to Colorado and breaking us up. Or for the things he said to Graham about me holding him back, about how much better off he'd be without me.

Graham and I have stayed in touch, of course. We're still

friends. But things between us have not been the same since Jefferson messed up the most important relationship in my life.

And then last fall he encouraged Alex Fallon, someone Jefferson and I literally lost sleep over *together*, to go to school in another state after he graduated. And, of course, Alex listened. Everyone always fucking listens to Jefferson.

Now, I'm constantly worried, still losing sleep, and upset because I can't be there if Alex needs me.

God. Jefferson is such a jerk.

Jefferson was the one driving around with me for *four hours* trying to find Alex two years ago when he was having nightmares and got suicidal. Jefferson was the one sitting up with me for twenty hours straight talking with, pleading with, and holding the grief-stricken kid who was plagued with survivor's guilt. Jefferson was the one sitting with me beside Alex's bed when his foster mom found him unresponsive on his bedroom floor. Jefferson was the one sitting in the waiting room of the doctor's office when Alex finally agreed to more intense counseling but would only go if *we* took him. Both of us. Together.

Of all people, Jefferson should have known that Alex needed to stay closer to us. Closer to *home*.

So no, I won't be forgetting or forgiving Jefferson Riley for always thinking he knows best, for getting people to trust him and listen to him, and for sending people away from Sapphire Falls. Away from home. Away from *me*.

And now, I'm stuck not just having to get along with him but having to pretend to date him. Pretending to not just like him, but to be falling for him. Or to have fallen, I guess.

My phone vibrates in my pocket, and I pull it out, grateful for the distraction.

But then I see my sister's name on my screen and I know immediately what this is about.

So much for being distracted from thoughts of Jefferson and my new fake, very serious relationship with him.

"Hey," I greet.

"What the hell is going on?" Mia asks.

"I assume someone has asked you what is going on with me and Jefferson?"

Mia wasn't at the house last night. If anyone there is asked about Jefferson and me, I trust that they'll think on their feet and assume we decided to go with the fake dating story.

Mia wasn't in on all of that, but she is in a position to run into a lot of people and I should have thought of that. I was too focused on getting to my mom and dad.

Mia's the town librarian. The library was her favorite place once she moved to Sapphire Falls, and the librarian at the time, Lucy Geller, allowed Mia to come in any time, go off by herself into a cozy little corner, check out any book she wanted, and lose herself in those fictional places and lives that were so much happier than the real one she was dealing with.

Lucy ran the library for a few years, but she fell in love and married famous best-selling mystery author, Michael Kade. Now she travels with him and handles a lot of his PR. But the Kades privately fund our library, including Mia's salary, now. So, Mia has the perfect job where she gets to spend her days surrounded by books and book lovers.

The library happens to be a popular spot in Sapphire Falls, which says a lot for the intellectual habits of our citizens, I guess, but it also makes it, like every other public place in town, a gossip hub.

"Who asked you about it?" I asked, legitimately curious at this point.

I didn't do a full roll call of who was in the diner this morning, but I scanned the room. I have a pretty good idea.

"Four different people," Mia says. "Summer reading program is going on."

"Right," I sigh. "I should've called you. We just got done telling Mom."

"So you *are* dating Jefferson?"

"Fake dating. Zach is back in town. He wants to get back together, so Jefferson and I have teamed up to make Zach miserable."

Mia is quiet for a moment.

While most the town knows that Zach is my ex, only a very few people know the entire story of what happened.

Mia is one of them.

She knows that Zach was my first, that he took my virginity, and knows about the cheating. She also knows that he slipped something into my drink one night after we broke up when he was trying to convince me to 'just talk things out'.

Mia had a rough childhood. Until she was ten she lived in a house where people fought constantly and things got physical on a regular basis. She isn't afraid to throw a punch. Or more. And once she came to live with my family she became *very* protective of us.

The night after I told her what Zach had done, she was missing for about three hours. I was very afraid for Zach. And for our dad. Because he would have been the one who would have had to arrest her for whatever she did.

"Well shit, "she finally says. "You know you can resist him, right? You're strong. You know he's a dirtbag. Don't let him intimidate you."

"Oh, no. It's not that," I assure her. "Especially after talking to him this morning. There is nothing there. But the idea of me dating Jefferson really annoys him. He and Jefferson have some old history too. We figured we might as well have some fun with this."

"Well, okay," she says.

I frown. That was way easier than I expected. "That's it? Just okay?"

She laughs. "Far be it from me to question you or Jefferson. Jefferson has always known how to handle Zach. If you guys decided this was your plan, I'm sure it's great."

I frown. *Jefferson has always known how to handle Zach.* What does that mean exactly?

Then I sigh. It's probably nothing. Jefferson is like me— we're problem solvers. And the thing about being the one who fixes everyone else's problems all the time is that they assume you don't need help with *your* problems.

"Thanks for the vote of confidence," I tell her. "I think it will be fine. It's just for this week until the wedding."

"Well, when people asked me about you today, I just asked what they heard. They said that you and Jefferson were together at the diner and said you were dating. I just asked them why they thought I would tell them anything different."

I laugh. "That seems like a perfect answer."

"Yeah," Mia agrees. "Seriously. Why would they think that they could come to me and get any kind of other story?"

My sister has a lot of residual trauma, not the least of which is trouble trusting. But she is loyal, protective, and amazing.

"Thanks, Mia."

"Of course." She pauses. "Let me know if there's anything else you want me to say or do."

I smile. My sister is also one of the most loving people. It takes a long time to get close to her, but once you're there, she won't let you go. "I love you. "

"Love you too."

We're disconnecting when Jefferson steps out of the bakery with his stupid froo-froo coffee.

"We need to tell our friends," I tell him. "Group text or something. People are already talking."

He shakes his head, swallowing mouth full of coffee. "No texts. I don't want that all in writing. Zach might see somebody's phone. We'll just tell everyone in person. Or they can tell each other. We have a very efficient grapevine. Oh, and we're having dinner tonight."

"You're asking me out to dinner?"

"You're my girlfriend. Of course we'll be eating dinner together tonight."

"If I was actually your girlfriend, you would still have to ask me out," I inform him. "I wouldn't be a sure thing."

He steps in close. "If you were my girlfriend, you *would* be a sure thing. You would be at my house every single night, where I could cook for you, make sure you were happy, cuddle your ass on the couch, and then carry you into bed where you would *for sure* spend the night." He leans in. "You'd be more than a sure thing. You'd be begging for it."

My breath sticks in my throat as heat and shock hit me in equal measure.

What the hell is that?

You should shove him back. And laugh. You should definitely laugh.

But wait, is Jefferson sexy?

I don't want Jefferson making me feel those things.

I stare at him. "I...um—" I clear my throat. "Begging for dinner? You'd try to starve me? That tracks."

His grin is slow. "To hear you beg? I do just about anything, I think. And I'm an excellent...cook."

That pause before 'cook' feels very innuendo-ish and I don't like it.

I also don't like the way it makes me think that I might need to see what gossip I can find about his past girlfriends. Then he straightens. "But dinner tonight is at the Spencers'. It's the whole family. Pre-wedding get-together. I'll pick you up at six-thirty."

CHAPTER 8

HARLOW

I IMMEDIATELY TURN on my heel and start down the sidewalk. I can *not* stand outside our moms' bakery and stare at him while wondering if Jefferson is actually an amazing boyfriend who's really hot and dirty in bed.

I Do. Not. Care. It doesn't matter to me *at all*.

Jefferson's love life has never been a topic I've cared about in the slightest.

I have never heard girls talk about him, but I'm certain that if I had, I would have immediately blocked it out.

Besides, where would I have heard about it? He hasn't dated a lot of women from Sapphire Falls. Sure, in high school he dated a couple, casually. But the only girls he was with for any length of time were from other towns and he was never serious about anyone. Sapphire Falls girls weren't good enough for him, I'm sure.

I remember Adrianne talking about a girlfriend in college, but he never brought anyone home for holidays or anything. Probably because he was embarrassed of his hometown.

I try to concentrate on our immediate issue of telling all of our friends, quickly, that we're fake dating so no one messes our story up. But I can't stop thinking about what Jefferson said. *Any* of what he said.

"Are you really a good cook?" I finally ask. Is there an underlying meaning there? Sure. But I honestly didn't know he could cook either.

He gives me a cocky grin, the look in his eyes telling me he caught the extra meaning. "I can make a beef stroganoff that would make you cry."

I narrow my eyes. Does he know that beef stroganoff is my favorite or was that a lucky guess?

"Cry because it's terrible?"

"So good you would never want to leave. And that's not even my specialty."

"Well, I'm sure I would want to leave because of something you would say regardless of the food."

He just chuckles and it hits me that one of the things I like best about sparring with Jefferson is I don't worry about actually offending him.

We've been doing this for so long, he expects me to say snarky things.

I also know that he can tell when I'm serious and when I'm not.

When we were younger, Jefferson would tease Graham and me, but it was in the older brother I-like-you-even-though-you-annoy-me way. I did feel like a younger sister to him. And I'm sure I did annoy him.

Graham and I would often be camped out in their family TV room when he wanted to be there watching sports or playing video games with his friends.

I'd also been known to borrow things from him. Without permission. Like shirts of his to act as swimsuit coverups when I was over at their house and Graham and I decided to head to the pool. I know I've lost at least two pairs of Jefferson's sunglasses, a cap, and I broke a flashlight that for some reason was very important to him.

But as we got older, Jefferson had started trying to get Graham to hang out with him and the guys and leave me behind. He wanted Graham to go out for sports, to go fishing and swimming with the guys, do almost anything on the weekend as long as I was not included, and things between Jefferson and me got more seriously tense.

Graham would confide to me that he felt pressured by his brother to fit in and be more social. Jefferson made him feel like his lack of interest in sports was a shortcoming. Jefferson encouraged him to ask girls out and asked Graham at least half a dozen times if he was in love with me.

Nobody messes with my friends, not even their older brothers, so I let Jefferson know how I felt about all of that. Often. And loudly.

Jefferson Riley is still one of the few people who can get me to raise my voice and even swear. I like to think I can keep my cool in almost any situation, but Jefferson has long been able to push my buttons.

Growing up with an older sister who had been in the foster care system, abused, and neglected, and was back-and-forth between that abusive home and ours for almost two years before her adoption was official, I had learned to be patient, calm, and quiet.

There were many times when I wanted to yell and cry about Mia's situation. But she was shy and timid and easily overwhelmed, and I needed to be a safe, comforting space for her.

So I squashed my impulses to lash out and be loud, learning to be a calming person who listened and gave quiet, positive encouragement.

I am a fucking Susie Sunshine as far as everyone knows.

Everyone but Jefferson. And Graham, who occasionally got to witness my outbursts with Jefferson.

That always frustrated Graham, though, so Jefferson and I got to the point where we would save our arguments for when Graham wasn't around.

"I'm not gonna make my baked manicotti for you though," Jefferson says as we step onto the path that leads across the square.

"Because you're the most annoying person I know?" I ask thinking that stuffed manicotti sounds pretty fucking great.

"Because mine is *amazing*, and I'm pretty sure that would make you start taking your clothes off. And that could get complicated."

I laugh.

I wasn't expecting him to say something like that and I definitely wasn't expecting it to make me laugh, but I do.

He grins. "Then again, that would make this whole week even more fun."

"You think baked manicotti is what it takes? Please. That's such an easy recipe. You have to at least sauté something before any clothes come off. *And* I need dessert."

His grin grows and I have a feeling he expected me to say something snarky instead of teasing back.

"Oh, we don't even want to get into dessert," he says. "You'll take your clothes off, beg me to take mine off, and never leave my house if I make dessert for you. I mean, yeah, it would be fun, but what do we tell our families when we're only supposed to be faking this for a week?"

I don't know how to respond to this. I have never, ever, in all the years I have known him, flirted with Jefferson Riley.

But that's what this feels like.

And he's pretty good at it. Because my skin feels a little tingly and I want to keep going.

And the fact that no one else is around, so this is not a part of our little show, is confusing.

"Good thing this week is going to be full of funnel cakes, wedding cake, and caramel apples, then," I tell him.

He winks at me, and I'm *shocked* to feel my tingly skin get warmer.

"Yeah, good thing."

I force my thoughts away from what kind of dessert Jefferson might be good at. His mother is an amazing baker and candy maker. He'd come by it naturally.

"So, you tell your friends, I'll tell mine, as quickly as possible," I say, turning the conversation back to the *plan* for the week. The only reason we'd be spending any time together. The only reason we'd be eating any meals together.

"Sounds good," he agrees.

We're not holding hands as we cross the square this time, and I think for a moment about being the one to reach out and take his. He might fall over from a heart attack. Which would be interesting. Maybe I could play the part of a sad-pseudo-widow instead of a girlfriend.

I'm pondering Jefferson's demise, which feels a lot more comfortable than thinking about eating dessert with him naked, when suddenly there's shouting and a bang, and we both turn toward the commotion on the other side of the gazebo. The swearing is coming from Travis Bennett, who is working with his brother Tucker and two of Tucker's sons, seemingly trying to put together the dunk tank for the upcoming festival.

Jefferson takes off at a jog without a word.

I follow behind slower.

By the time I get there, Jefferson already has a big piece of sheet metal braced with both hands while Travis works to move another piece into place.

A couple other guys from town have also come over from whatever they were doing. There are now seven men working to wrangle the pieces of the very old, well-used dunk tank.

"Just brace that part there," Travis calls.

Jefferson shifts, moving one hand to pull a piece of metal into place. Travis moves in beside him with a power drill.

"Okay, go!" Tucker yells from the other side.

The guys work for about five minutes, putting more pieces together. When his panel is screwed into place and he can let go, Jefferson straightens.

Then he whips off his shirt and tosses it in my direction.

On instinct, I reach out and catch it.

He sends me a smirk, but I don't even have time to work up a frown before he's turning back to the job at hand.

Which is just as well. I do *not* want him to catch me studying all that bare skin, those muscles, and the ink on his left shoulder.

He's an athlete. It's been a few years since he played football, but he still works out with the team. He's lean but his arm, shoulder, and back muscles are chiseled with tan skin stretched over all of those firm ridges. His hands suddenly look bigger, and his forearms ripple as he works.

And I don't stop there. I follow the taper of his back to his waist and then his hips down to his firm ass in the worn blue jeans he's got on, and over his muscular thighs.

I've seen him without a shirt many times. Swimming, working around his house, working out at school. I've seen the tattoo before too, though he adds to it periodically. It covers his left shoulder blade then wraps over his shoulder and down his upper bicep. I know it's a combination of symbols including a tree, his football number from high school, the M from his college logo, some other numbers, and a swirling design I think just fills in the spaces. But I've never asked.

"You are doing a really good job of seeming into him."

I turn and look at Margot, who somehow sidled up next to me.

I sigh. "Shut up."

She laughs. I now notice my sister crossing the square toward us as well.

"I don't need to like him to recognize and admit that he's good looking," I say. "It's an objective fact that Jefferson is hot. Lots of women think so."

That I am aware of, even if I don't know who he has dated and how they feel about him post-break-up. Or what they've said about what it was like to be with him.

Margot crosses her arms and juts one hip to the side as she studies the men in front of us. "He's not the only hot guy here."

"No. He's not."

She leans in and lifts her hand and covers my eyes.

"Hey," I protest.

"What color shirt does David have on?"

I think for a second, but I barely noticed that Tucker's son was there. I puff out a breath. "All right. Point taken."

Laughing, she drops her hand. I look over and note that David is also not wearing a shirt. But no, I hadn't noticed that before.

Mia has joined us by now.

"I take it that you and Jefferson decided to do the fake dating thing after all?" Margot asks.

"Yes, we were on our way to tell all of you."

"What changed since last night?" Margot asks.

"Ran into Zach." I sigh. "He got to me and I caved."

Margot frowns. "Well, I say make that fucker sorry. I'm all for this plan."

"Yeah. Strangely, it seems everyone is," I say, watching my sister nod her head.

"It's not really that strange," Mia says. "If you weren't fighting over Graham all the time, you might've actually dated in real life."

Nope. We fought over Graham for sure. That's how the antagonism started. But it was just the beginning of learning how differently Jefferson and I see things. Big things. Life, family, relationships. We would have never fit. Not long-term anyway.

I guess we might have dated short-term before we figured all of that out.

And I might know more about this happy-cuddling-and-begging thing.

Ugh. He is the *most* frustrating person I know. I do *not* want to be thinking about that stuff. That is not helpful at *all*.

"Well, we'll never know," I tell her. *Except this week you'll be able to see what it would have been like,* a voice in my head reminds me. *Maybe you'll get some cuddling-and-begging.*

Oh my god. This is so not good.

This is all fake and we're going to be on our best behavior because it's a show. It's *not* how we'd really act if we were dating.

"You just taking a break?" Margot asks Mia.

"Yeah, I came downtown to get something..." Mia comments, her eyes straying to the group of men working. "But I don't remember what now."

We all laugh.

We stand and watch the men work for a while.

And I can't deny that my eyes go to Jefferson often. I suppose he's just on my mind right now. I'm going to have to pay more attention to him this week than I usually do.

The guys are laughing, joking, and the dunk tank is now

almost entirely put together, and Jefferson is clearly a part of the community. All of these men obviously like him. He's completely competent, comfortable with every tool he picks up, taking direction but also giving some instructions.

He stops, puts his hands on his hips, says something I can't hear to David, and then throws his head back and laughs.

My stomach—I'm calling it my stomach even though it definitely feels a lot lower than that—clenches. "Ugh," I groan.

Mia and Margot both laugh.

"I don't think this week is going to be so bad," Mia says, nudging me with her elbow.

"I just have to remember that I hate Zach more than I hate Jefferson," I tell her.

Margot rolls her eyes. "Do you really *hate* Jefferson?" she asks.

"Yes," I say quickly.

"You *love* to fight with him," Mia says.

"I fight with him because we disagree about everything and everyone else in this town thinks he's so amazing and wonderful and I think it's important to remind him that there *are* exceptions."

Mia laughs. "So you're *helping* him by keeping his ego in check?"

"Yes. That."

"But that's not really *hate*," Margot says. "You disagree sometimes. So what?"

"We disagree on *big* things," I insist. "I hate that he thinks Sapphire Falls isn't good enough for most people and he's always trying to talk people into leaving."

"Well, that's pretty harsh," Margot says. "He just encourages people to go after what they want."

I gasp. "You're not going to defend him to me, are you?"

"I'm trying to make this week easier on you—both of you—by pointing out that maybe he's not the devil."

I frown.

"I agree," Mia says. "When he came to me a couple weeks ago and asked if I'd be open to helping some kids, he was really positive and very encouraging. He knew a lot about me and really emphasized my strengths. And he seemed to really care about the kids."

I turned to face her. "He talked to you about helping some kids? What kids? How?"

"Yeah, there's a couple kids over in Briarville. Their dad just got sentenced to a long prison term. He won't be out until they're well into adulthood. It was some pretty terrible abuse charges. Jefferson was talking to their counselor, and it just came up that maybe someone who's been in that situation would be a good listener."

I frown at her. "Are you sure you want to do something like that?"

She shrugs. "I've never really thought about it. I mean, obviously I'm not licensed for something like that professionally. It would purely be a volunteer mentor situation. But maybe just having someone they could talk to who wouldn't be shocked by what they might say, could help." She says it matter-of-factly, but I still feel my chest squeeze and my stomach twist.

I was only five when Mia came to live with us, and my mom and dad don't love talking about it, of course, but I've pieced things together. And now with my work as a child advocate and social worker, some of the things I've seen and heard from other kids in the system, kids who were in similar situations, I have a pretty good idea about some of the things that Mia has been through.

I can't think about it too hard, or I want to curl up and not leave my bed.

And that's just *knowing* about it. Not experiencing it myself.

I love her so much. I feel so protective of her. The fact that she's come out of all of that, and that she can be a happy, positive, loving person is amazing to me. Her parents hurt her. Her *parents*.

I don't think she should have to relive all of that. I don't think she should have to dredge all of that up.

"I know Jefferson can be very charming," I say. Just because *I* don't find him charming doesn't mean I don't know the effect he has on other people. "But you don't have to do anything he suggests. Don't let him talk to you into anything that you don't want to do."

She brushes her hair back over her shoulder. "No, I won't. But I'm flattered that he thought about me."

"Flattered that he might make you want to relive some of the horrible things of your past?"

She frowns. "I didn't think about it that way. What if I could help those kids?"

I reach out and squeeze her hand. "There are lots of people who can help the kids," I tell her. "I'll even talk to Jefferson and make sure they get help. But *you* don't have to take that on. You have a right to be happy. You don't have to dwell in all of those old memories."

She takes a breath and blows it out. "I know. Thank you. I'm only thinking about it."

Just then Jefferson joins us. His shirt is back on, but even if it wasn't, the coldness I'm suddenly feeling wouldn't be going anywhere.

"Ladies," he greets with a big smile. "I take it you've heard the news? Harlow and I are madly in love."

I growl softly and start across the square.

I hear Margot laugh. "Yeah, good luck with that."

CHAPTER 9

HARLOW

HE CATCHES up with me after only about three steps, of course.

"What the hell is going on?"

I whirl around and ask, "Why can't you just leave the people in my life alone? I know you like to mess with me but it's getting old."

His brows rise. "What are we talking about?"

"You're just not going to be happy until you drive away everyone I care about, right?"

His eyes go from me to Margot to Mia and back to me.

He shakes his head. "We're not doing this here." He grabs my hand and starts walking, tugging me along.

I dig in my heels. "You're not just going to drag me around."

He turns back. "Fine." Then he bends over and sweeps me up into his arms, bridal carrying me.

"Jefferson!"

He's heading for his truck, parked along the curb of the square. He grins down at me, but says tightly, "We're in love, remember?" He leans in and kisses my cheek.

I hate him so much.

I want to fight with him. I am mad at him. But, he's right. This is day one—actually we're only a few hours in on our plan —and I can't ruin it all by throwing a fit in the middle of town.

I stop squirming and take a deep breath.

"Good girl," he murmurs.

I growl.

He chuckles.

At his truck, he walks around to the passenger side, somehow pulls the door open, even with me in his arms, and deposits me on the seat.

"You're kidnapping me now?"

"Duct tape over your mouth sounds very appealing," he comments before he slams the door.

I sit on the seat, arms crossed. I don't know where he thinks he's taking me, but I do want to have this conversation, and bursting out of his truck and stomping up Main Street is also not the way to convince anyone that we are in a serious romantic relationship.

He gets in the driver's seat and I look past him to see Margot and Mia watching us. Both grinning.

Well, I'm glad that everyone's enjoying this. Including the two women who suddenly think Jefferson is such a great guy.

"You need to leave Mia alone," I tell him before he's even pulled away from the curb.

"I'm not messing with Mia."

"Why can't she just be happy? Why can't she just forget about the past? She doesn't need to get involved with those kids that you want her to talk to."

He grips the steering wheel. "Then she can tell me no." He looks over at me. "But she hasn't done that, Harlow."

"Everyone in this town, for some reason, has a hard time saying that word to you."

"Present company excluded."

I shift on the seat to face him. "Damn right. At least someone around here realizes that you don't actually have the ability to turn water into wine."

"You're so dramatic."

"And you're such a meddler!"

"Hi, pot, I'm kettle. "

"I don't meddle! I support people. I help them. I comfort them. I help them find homes and families and love and support! You're the one who's always trying to push people away. Trying to find them something *else*. *Somewhere* else. It's like you think going somewhere bigger, far away, *alone* is some badge of honor. That being stuck in this little town with people you know and love is weak and sad."

I see his hands tighten on the steering wheel. "You don't really think that's how I feel."

"That's how you act."

"Jesus Christ, Harlow, *I* live here. I came back here. I love this town. I teach here. I see my family every damned day. What the fuck are you even talking about?"

"Then you *are* only targeting people I care about?"

He pulls into a driveway and I realize we're at his house. He slams the truck into park then turns to me. "Get in the house."

I glare at him. "No way. "

"It is beyond time for us to have this out. But we're not doing it in my driveway where anyone could drive or walk by or look out their front window and see and hear the whole damned thing. Let's go inside and fight."

Fuck. I have been pretending to date this man for about two hours and already it's a pain in my ass.

I blow out a breath, open the door, and get out. He stops at the end of the path, letting me pass in front of him, the gentleman in case anyone's watching, and I stomp up his front porch steps. I shove the door open, knowing he didn't lock it, and head into his living room.

Jefferson took the job as guidance counselor and science teacher along with football coach right after college six years ago. In that time, I've been to Jefferson's house with Ginny and Graham a few times, once or twice with my own brother, and with my mom a couple of times.

We share an annoying number of people in common.

He shuts the door behind him, then leans against it crossing his arms.

"You're accusing me of some pretty big bullshit," he says.

"None of this is new. You know how I feel."

"And you have to know that none of that is true. I'm not targeting people that you love in some crazy attempt to try to get them away from you. I'm helping people, Harlow."

"You wanted to get Graham away from me."

He sighs. "Okay, in the case of Graham it was more about you," he admits. "But that's a specific situation."

I cross my arms as that familiar hurt makes my chest feel tight. I will *not* cry in front of Jefferson Riley. "Just because you're not content with your life here, doesn't mean other people can't be."

"What the fuck makes you think I'm not content with my life here?"

I squeeze my arms tighter against my stomach, mimicking his pose, though I'm not leaning against anything. My feet are braced, and I'm sure I look like I'm ready for a fight.

I am.

I don't fight with people. I'm calm, supportive, always the voice of reason. I talk things out. I look at all the different angles. Though I am steadfastly on the side of whoever has come to me for help.

Except with Jefferson. I *really* want to fight with him.

I'll admit that I'm not always totally rational when it comes to him. He makes me nuts. But I can yell at him. And the pounding adrenaline, the flushed cheeks, the heat I feel, is exhilarating.

I'm not proud of it, but I'll admit it.

"Fine," I say. "What makes me think you're not content with your life here? How about the fact that you didn't actually get to play in the big championship game that everybody still talks about to this day? Oh sure, they talk about what a big stud you were, what a star you were, how we'll probably never have a team that good again. But you weren't actually a part of that three-game series.

"And then you didn't get to go play for the University of Nebraska. You had to go to Minnesota instead. And no one really liked that, did they? They didn't really cheer for you once you left the state. You weren't the same Golden Boy then."

He doesn't say anything. He just clenches his jaw and waits.

He's letting me have my say.

Well, okay then.

"*And,*" I go on. "How about the fact that your whole family is rich, kind-of-famous scientists who are making the world a better place. Except you. You're stuck in your tiny hometown *teaching* science and coaching football. You can't seem to move beyond high school. You are in the same building, basically doing the same things you did your whole life. You spend time with the same people, in the same places, your days looking pretty much like they've looked since you were about five.

"You love your family, but being here in the same town makes it really easy for people to compare you. Anywhere else you could be an amazing teacher and coach, but here, it's kind of not-quite-as-impressive.

"But you got out for a little bit, right? You escaped. And now you think everyone should get the hell out of this place that *should* make you happy but makes you feel not-quite-good-enough. *You're* stuck but you can try to push as many people out of here as possible."

He's just watching me. He waits a beat, then asks, "You done?"

I take a deep breath. I can't believe I said all of that. I don't actually know that any of that is true. Those are the reasons I've come up with to explain how he behaves. But I've always wondered. I've wanted to ask him. So I nod. "For now."

"*You're* the one who thinks that Sapphire Falls is a fucking haven. Everyone should live here. If someone can't be happy here, they're done for, right? Sapphire Falls makes everything better. All you have to do is live here, eat a few pot pies at Dottie's, have some frozen lemonade at the stupid town festival and your life is sunshine and fucking rainbows."

I narrow my eyes and step forward. "Yes. I do believe that Sapphire Falls can be a haven. It is the epitome of home and family, and people deserve that, Jefferson. The fact that you look down on it, that you feel stuck here, and your entire mission in life is to make sure everyone gets the fuck out of here, is *your* problem."

He pushes off the door and steps toward me. "And the fact that you think everyone should come here, and never fucking leave, never think about anything bigger or better—yes, Harlow, I said better than Sapphire Falls—" He spreads his arms wide. "Am I going to be struck by lightning? Is the god of Sapphire Falls going to smite me?"

I'm breathing faster and my heart is pumping. "If you hate it here so much, why did you come back?"

"Why can't you believe that I don't hate it here?"

"Because you keep trying to make people leave."

"Just because Sapphire Falls is where *I* want to be, where *you* want to be, where a lot of people should be, doesn't mean it's right for everyone."

"Just because a place is bigger, glitzier, has fancier restaurants and higher paying jobs, doesn't make it *better*," I insist.

"And just because people have to travel a few hours to come home and see their family, doesn't mean they love them less."

I just stare at him. If anyone else were saying these things to me, I would probably agree. I am a grown woman. Mature, intelligent, even rational most of the time.

I have made my life's work finding people, especially kids, homes and families. It is important to me that people feel like they belong and that they find a place where they can be safe and happy.

Has Sapphire Falls been that place for me and the people I love most? No question.

But I am aware of the fact that Sapphire Falls cannot shelter everyone.

Still, there's something about Jefferson that makes me incapable of being rational and admitting all of that.

At least at this moment.

"Look at your dad," I say. "He's a world-renowned scientist. He meets with world leaders. He is literally on the front lines of helping cure world hunger. And he came to Sapphire Falls, fell in love with your mom, realized that this tiny little town had what he wanted to be happy and moved his whole company here. He brought a whole bunch of people here who also fell in love with this town and who consider it home and who count all of these people as their family."

Jefferson rolls his eyes. "You know that not everyone can

stay in Sapphire Falls. You know that that is not actually best for everyone. I don't know why you have to be such a brat."

"Leave Mia alone," I say, going back to my very first point. I'm about to lose the thread of this argument, and I know it, so I dig in.

"So now Sapphire Falls is also a mental and emotional haven? The pot pies, and festivals, and barbecues, and sweet town square aren't enough? We're not even supposed to *think* about sad things?" he asks.

"Not...Mia." I realize that sounds silly, but I can't stop.

"What if she can help someone? What if she can be that friend, that support system for someone, that you talk about being so important?"

"She should get to escape from what she went through."

"That's not how this works and you know it."

"You're a school counselor. You're supposed to help kids apply to colleges and work study. Quit acting like you're some kind of mental health expert."

That was a low blow. I've seen Jefferson in action. He was amazing when Alex was going through everything. He was amazing for *me*. Having him there with me while we were searching for Alex, while we sat in the waiting room at the hospital, while we listened to the kid sob his heart out, made me stronger.

But, as always, Jefferson doesn't even flinch at my insults. He studies me for a moment, then he says, "I know she was your first case. But just because Mia might get sad sometimes, or scared, or even relive some hurts, doesn't mean you've failed her, Harlow. You *have* helped her. No matter what still lingers or what's ahead."

I feel like he just slapped me.

How does he know that's how I feel? How can he tell that

I'm afraid that I haven't done enough? That what my family has built around her won't be strong enough?

I frown and squeeze my arms tighter against my stomach. "I don't know what you're talking about."

But holy shit, I definitely do. And I'm reeling from the idea that Jefferson might know this about me.

He takes a step closer. "Mia coming into your life is when you first realized that home and family and love and support are not givens. You were *five* when you first realized that not everyone automatically gets to feel happy and safe and loved. Then, also at a very young age, you got to experience giving her all of that. And you got a rush from it. You became addicted. And now, that's what drives you. You *need* to give everyone you get to know and care about that feeling of love and safety and happiness. And if anything would happen to the idea that you fixed Mia, your sense of who you are and what you do would crumble."

I pull in a shaky breath.

He is... absolutely right. On every single one of those points. I have never heard anyone put those things into words like that, not even the counselor of my own who helped me work through that realization in college.

It seems obvious where my interest in social work and child advocacy came from, but it's so much deeper than just placing kids with good families. It truly is about who I envision myself to be.

And I am shaking with the realization that Jefferson sees this in me.

"Mia is a grown woman," he finally says firmly. "If she wants to help, I'm grateful. I think she'd be great at it, and it could give her an important sense of self-worth. The idea that everything she went through could produce something good could be really powerful. But if she doesn't want to get involved, I absolutely will not pressure her."

I finally find my voice. "That's what you don't understand," I tell him. "You're this person, who is so..." I make a frustrated noise. "Perfect. Everyone respects you. Everyone likes you. You're good at everything you do. So, when you ask someone to do something, they want to please you. They're flattered. They figure if Jefferson picked them, then they have to say yes."

He looks thoughtful. "I don't think that's how people see me. I am, after all, the one who didn't play in the championship game or go to my dream college. I'm just a teacher and coach. I ended up back in my hometown living a life like I've always done, right?"

I blow out a breath. That was all really bitchy of me to say. Not only is he an excellent coach and teacher, I know that he's inspired several kids to go into fields that could easily lead them to do amazing things just like his family is doing.

Great teachers matter. Great coaches matter. Great role models fucking matter.

And Jefferson Riley is all of those things.

"You know damn well that's just how I see you," I tell him. "The rest of the town thinks you're fucking amazing for coming home and for coaching the team. Every kid loves you. All the parents love you. You're also the best science teacher that school has had in years. And I know your dad just hired someone who credits *you* for him going into science and wanting to help cure world hunger."

The corner of Jefferson's mouth curls up. "Pretty ironic that the thing that annoys you most about me is that I came back to Sapphire Falls, your favorite place, the town you think is perfect and where you think everyone should aspire to live."

"It's very annoying that you moved back and are the one blight on my haven," I agree.

"See," he says, his smile spreading. "We should start looking at all the ways we're the same. I think it would be startling."

I shake my head. "Our general life philosophy is completely different. I believe in home and family. I believe in keeping my loved ones close and supporting them no matter what. You believe in kicking everyone out of the nest. That's a pretty huge difference."

He shakes his head. "We both believe in loving our people hard and getting what's best for them. It's just that you're soft and squishy about it, and I'm tough and encouraging."

I gasp. "I am not *soft and squishy* about it."

Now he laughs. "You so are. You are a pushover. You bend over backward to make sure everyone is happy and comfortable *all the time*." He pauses, almost as if he's not sure he should go on, then he says, "Usually it's very sweet. But that was the biggest problem with Graham and you."

I draw myself up taller. "You really want to talk about this?"

He looks around. "This seems like a good time. We're here alone. We have some privacy. And it's probably a good idea to hash this out so that the rest of the week goes well."

I relax my arms but prop my hands on my hips.

My heart is still pounding, but now it is less about yelling at him and more worry about what he's going to say to me.

I do not like being criticized, and I know that Jefferson won't hesitate, but there's also a part of me that does want to hear this once and for all.

"Okay, tell me all the ways I was so terrible for Graham."

"You were too soft on him."

That's all he says. I stand blinking at him. "What?"

"From the moment you met Graham when you were five years old, you coddled him."

"Right, I sometimes forget that Graham's biggest sin in life was not being tougher and not wanting to hit other guys with his body."

"This isn't about football. Though your disdain for how I make my living is also maybe something we need to go over at some point," Jefferson says dryly. "But it was about how Graham never wanted to try anything hard, to never be outside his comfort zone. *You* were his comfort zone. And you loved that. You got a taste for helping, loving, supporting someone with Mia. And then you found Graham. Graham needed a protector as far as you could see. And you loved that. You loved being that mama bear. So you took Graham under your wing. And you never let him out."

That is *not* accurate. Jefferson was four grades ahead of us in school. He doesn't know what it was like day to day for Graham. He just wanted to be left alone.

"Graham is an amazing person," I say. "He's brilliant, he's caring, he's funny as hell, and he knows exactly who he wants to be. Carver always had his head in the clouds and was wrapped up in Kaelyn. You were always the social butterfly, the golden boy on the football field. Graham had nothing in common with either of you. Ginny was... Ginny. She had her girlfriends, she was definitely more social, and she was trying to find her place and didn't have time to worry about Graham. So yeah, Graham needed me. And we were a great pair. I don't regret helping Graham and protecting him."

"He never had a girlfriend because of you."

"Graham never *wanted* a girlfriend," I say, exasperated. "And you would know that if you ever talked to him. Also having a girlfriend is not the epitome of success or accomplishment."

"No. But it is a huge social milestone growing up. It's a normal part of socialization. One that he skipped."

"Is this about you thinking he was in love with me all this time?"

"He was for a while. Come on." Jefferson rolls his eyes. "At least he thought he was. But it wasn't that. It was that all the girls knew they could never measure up to you for Graham. So no one would even consider dating him. And he was shy enough that he would've needed a girl to express the interest."

"I am not having this fight with you again about how I was bad for Graham's love life."

"Fine, then let's just talk about everything else. He wouldn't go away to camp because of you. He wouldn't work a summer job outside of town because of you. He didn't want to socialize with any groups of people that didn't involve you. He took a lot of classes because of you."

"We were in the same grade! It's a very small school, and a very small town. Of course we were together a lot."

"You and Graham were joined at the hip, Harlow." Jefferson looks as frustrated as I feel right now. "He needed to have his own experiences. His own life. Friends outside of you. And when I realized that he was going to go to college wherever you went, I couldn't let that happen. He needed to cut the ties. Especially when Colorado wanted him, specifically for their engineering program."

"He could've done engineering here in Nebraska," I say stubbornly.

"And you and I both know that he would've spent every minute studying with you at the library, going out with you on the weekends, probably would've wound up as your roommate at some point, not dating. Hell, if I had looked away, he may have ended up with a social work degree."

"Fuck you. Social work is an amazing and important profession."

Jefferson scrubs a hand over his face. "Of course it is! It's the perfect fit for *you*. Not for Graham. Engineering is perfect for Graham. And since he's been in Colorado, he's made a ton of friends, dated, come out of his shell, and learned that he can stand on his own two feet. He's confident, even funnier, and is blossoming as a person."

I feel tears stinging the back of my eyes. Because he's right. I'd be an idiot to not see all of that.

But if I cry in front of Jefferson, *I'm* going to have to move to Colorado.

Of course, Jefferson would *hate* that.

"I love your brother," I say, trying to keep my voice steady. "He is one of the most important people to me. I can't believe that you think the way I feel about him is so damaging."

"And I hate to tell you that," he says, and I think he's actually sincere. "Graham leaving you for Colorado was the biggest step he's ever taken in his life, Harlow. You are incredibly important to him. I was shocked actually when he agreed. I didn't know if I'd ever get him away from you."

My mouth drops open. "Holy shit, Jefferson. How am I supposed to feel about the fact that you think I'm terrible?"

"I don't think you're terrible. I think that you and Graham's relationship was way too codependent."

"And you think the way that I hold my friends back is terrible."

"Harlow," he finally says with a deep breath in and out. "Honestly... you love people so hard."

I feel my heart thump. "What?"

"You think I'm so charming and whatever that people can't say no to me, but you are so loving and giving, no one can say no to *you*."

My eyes sting even harder, and I blink rapidly. That shouldn't be a bad thing.

"So loving people is terrible."

He steps forward. "You love people who are very vulnerable. And that's awesome when they need that protection. When they need that person to pull them in and hold them tight because everything else is spinning around them and they don't have anywhere else to go. But you need to learn to let them go when they get stronger."

I swallow hard. "I don't like letting people go."

"I know."

"They could get hurt."

He nods. "Like Mia did when she left your family to go back with her parents."

I press my lips together and nod. He doesn't need a psych degree. This is all very obvious.

"You have a lot of love to give. A lot of passion. But..." He stops and studies me, clearly trying to decide if he should go on.

I lift my chin. "But?"

"That can be overwhelming for people who aren't able to give it back to you in equal measure. They feel like they don't deserve it. Or they feel like they'll never truly love *you* enough."

"I don't need that," I argue. "I'm not expecting anything in return."

He nods. "But you should. You need to be loved and supported and safe too. I think that maybe there's a space inside that you need to fill up. You keep trying to put more people into it. People who *need* you. But maybe, what's missing is the love and security that *you* need. Maybe you need to be held tightly sometimes instead of always doing the holding."

Now my heart is pounding so hard. I'm having a hard time taking a deep breath. "You don't think that Mia and Graham love me back?"

"They both definitely do. But it is really hard to love as hard as you do. Not many people do. It's just so much."

Well great. So I am kind of unlovable because I love too much.

This man makes me nuts.

I think he brought me in here, just so he could say things like that, twist my mind and heart up, just to torture me.

"Jefferson Riley," I bite out. "There is no way I am going to be able to fake liking you for another six days."

Then I march past him, shove him out of the way, yank open his front door, and stomp down the stairs.

"Do you want a ride?" he calls after me.

Jefferson does live a little further away from downtown, but I have enough pent-up emotion coursing through me right now that a walk will probably do me good.

I simply raise my hand and flip him off over my shoulder.

CHAPTER 10

JEFFERSON

I'M relieved when I show up at Harlow's door at six-thirty to find that not only does she open it for me, but she is ready to go to dinner.

After that morning in my living room, I wasn't so sure she'd still go with me tonight.

I'm glad we cleared the air. She is under some very specific misunderstandings about my goals and motivations, but at least we've started the conversation. And it's not over.

But we're going out tonight and she's not just ready to go, she looks absolutely fucking amazing.

She clearly got my text that the Spencers and my parents decided to move the dinner to the Blue Stone Grill, the steak-house out on the highway.

The Blue Stone has only been open for about five years but gives us a little bit more upscale dining experience than Dottie's.

Dottie was thrilled with the idea of a place more geared toward a dinner crowd. She pulled back to offering breakfast and lunch only, opening at six a.m. and closing at four p.m.

every day. The Blue Stone opens at four-thirty six days a week and offers a fantastic prime rib and salad bar. It's the perfect location for dates and fancier family dinners celebrating things like upcoming weddings.

"Wow, you look beautiful," I say. I'm not buttering her up, it's true.

Her dark hair is curled and falling loosely past her shoulder blades. She's wearing a silky blue sundress that brings out the color of her eyes. It's a sheath that fits against her petite frame and curves perfectly. She's wearing heels that lift her about two inches off the ground, still putting her well below my chin, but making her legs look amazing.

"Do you like the dress?" She steps back and spreads her arms, then does a little twirl.

Well, if she wants me to look, I'm gonna look. I sweep my eyes over her from head to toe.

"I like it *very* much."

She turns and props a hand on her hip, looking at me over her shoulder. "It makes my ass look great, don't you think?"

I am not sure what she's doing, but I let my gaze drop to her ass. And I say honestly, "It really does."

Harlow has a great ass, and this dress clinging to it the way it does—if I was her boyfriend, of course—would make it very hard for me to keep my hands to myself tonight.

"I wore this just for you," she says turning to face me again.

And now I'm suspicious. "Really? And why is that?"

"Because if I was your girlfriend, this would probably be your favorite dress. I know blue is your favorite color. And I know you're an ass guy."

Blue is my favorite color. I especially like this specific color of sapphire blue. Call me sappy, but I spent years wearing this color from Little League, through high school football. "I'm an ass guy?"

"Aren't you?"

"I am. It's not the only female body part I like, of course, but it is one of my favorites. But how do you know that?"

Her hand is still on her hip, and she's watching me with a combination of amusement and exasperation. "The first summer you were home from college, you had been out drinking with your buddies, and you all came home and crashed in the basement where Graham and I were watching movies. You were talking about how great Whitney Bennett looked since she had started doing kickboxing. You were all being super gross. But someone commented that he'd always thought Whitney had a great body and you agreed that she had one of the best asses in town." Harlow shakes her head. "You were all such pigs."

I do not remember this conversation, but it absolutely sounds like something I said when I was young, immature, and a little tipsy. And yes, Whitney Bennett is a gorgeous woman and always has been.

"Whitney's beautiful," I say with a shrug. "You can't really blame us for thinking that."

"I will admit that at least you and your friends have gotten a lot better about not saying your stupid thoughts out loud."

"So you don't want me to say out loud that you look hot as hell and that your ass is amazing?"

She looks up at me. "If I was really your girlfriend, would you tell me that?"

"No. I think I would *show* you that," I tell her.

Her cheeks get a little pink, but she gives me a smile. "Good answer."

"Yeah? You would want me to express my feelings that way? If I was really your boyfriend?"

She runs a hand down the front of the dress. "What woman doesn't want her man to like how she looks?"

"Noted."

She steps forward and I turn to let her pass in front of me. As she steps out onto the porch, and I move to pull the door shut behind us, I smack her on the ass. She looks up at me. "Really?"

"You're my girlfriend this week."

"Fake girlfriend."

"I can't fake-slap you on the ass."

"There's no one around to see you do that, so you can keep your hands to yourself, Coach."

I laugh. "You don't think we should practice? Make sure we're both in the right mindset before we're in public?"

She gives me a wide-eyed look. "I do not."

"Okay. But you're giving me permission to do whatever I want in *public*? Is that right?" I ask with a smirk as we start down the porch steps.

"I really hesitate to give you wide-open permission for anything."

Smart girl. "But I need to act like you are my girlfriend. People have seen me with women before."

"Treat me like you would a real girlfriend in public. When people are watching who we are not related to or close friends with. But when it's just our inner circle, you can back off."

"I'm just a little worried." I stop beside my truck and open the door, giving her a hand up since her skirt is fitted and she's wearing heels.

She rolls her eyes and climbs up by herself.

I almost laugh. If she was my girlfriend, or we were in public, I would've grabbed her waist and helped her up anyway. And maybe slapped her sassy ass again.

"What are you worried about?" she asked.

"Just that there's a risk you're gonna get addicted and you

might be asking me to do some things in private even when no one else is around."

She snorts and reaches over for the door. "Please, hold your breath for that." Then she slams the door.

I laugh as I round the front of the truck. I know she doesn't like me and that irritates me. No, that's not true, I correct mentally. I think she likes me. But she doesn't *get* me. So this week, I'm going to work on that too. But I do love sparring with her. I love poking her. I love the way her eyes flash and her cheeks flush when I piss her off. I love that I can piss her off more than anyone else can. I really think this is going to be a very fun week.

As we drive toward the Blue Stone, I'm relieved that things seem okay between us. As okay as they ever are. At least she's not freezing me out or yelling at me.

I wonder if I'm supposed to apologize for anything that I said earlier, but I've been over and over our conversation and I'm not sorry. Everything I said was the truth and everything I've done, from talking Graham into going to college in Colorado to mentioning the kid who might need someone like Mia to talk to, was something I stand by.

I don't like hurting Harlow though. And it's weird that it's been bugging me. I mean hell, I told her she's a loving, supportive person. Though almost to a fault. Still, in the past, it hasn't bothered me that she knows that I'm a critic. Possibly her only one.

Now suddenly it does bother me. A lot.

I look over at her as we drive to the restaurant. "Are we okay?"

She shrugs. "We're...the same."

I think about that.

I don't want us to be the same.

It's a strange thought and it seems to hit out of the blue, but

I want us to be better than the same. Maybe this is hitting me because of everything I finally said out loud. I've never done that before. We've just bickered and been sarcastic with one another. She's tossed out things like *you made Graham leave* and I say things like *you coddle him.*

Today I let her know that I'm aware of the reason that she's so intent on helping people find homes and families. Which means I've given it some thought. I also admitted that I've paid attention to how protective she is of the people that she loves, especially the vulnerable ones. I told her that I see the way that she puts herself in front of people she feels need to be protected. But then she wants to shelter them from every tiny possible thing.

Our disagreement felt deeper today. More meaningful. It wasn't just us fighting over Graham's attention. This had real thought and understanding behind it. It's one thing to want to keep the people you love from the major storms. I do the same. I would throw myself in front of anyone I love if life tried to rip through and turn things upside down. But she wants to be the umbrella even for the lightest sprinkles. Sometimes people need to get wet. People need to learn how to dry themselves off.

I hurt her today more than usual *because* I showed that I understand her. And I still disagree with her. But I want that to bring us closer. I want her to see that I can disagree with her but still like her, respect her, and want her.

That hits me and I squeeze the steering wheel tighter.

I can still want her even while I disagree with her.

Because I do want her.

Well... dammit.

I clear my throat. "We're gonna have to act like we're a little better than usual," I remind her after a moment.

"I've got this," she tells me. "I understand the assignment."

But does she? Because suddenly this assignment feels a little different to me.

I think I need to help *Harlow* understand a few things before I worry about what everyone else believes.

We pull up the restaurant five minutes later.

Harlow, of course, lets herself out of the truck without waiting for me, but I take her hand as we walk toward the front of the restaurant.

For a split second she starts to pull away, then sighs. "You're a hand holder, huh?"

I'm actually not. To me holding hands is something couples do when they've been together for a long time. My mom and dad do it. Phoebe and Joe Spencer do it. Kaelyn and Carver do it. But I don't know any of my friends in newer relationships who do.

It indicates a long-time connection and comfort to me for some reason.

But holding Harlow's hand feels natural. So I intertwine our fingers and say, "Yup."

I think I do it to annoy her. But when she curls her fingers against my hand, I realize the truth—I like touching her and this is one of the only ways I get to. And I've got a limited time to do it.

I hold the door, letting her step in before me—resisting the urge to tap, or squeeze, her ass as she does—and simply give Cindy, the hostess a smile as we walk past. Our family table will be easy to find. It will be one of the biggest in here tonight, and probably the loudest. It will also be in the best location. We're sitting with one of the owners after all.

Levi and Joe Spencer own the place. Neither of them is a chef or even really a foodie. We've converted them both to fried chicken, chili, great steaks, and other classic Nebraska food. They both love runzas. But they grew up in the hospitality business in Las Vegas and when they were discussing business endeavors that would help the town, a restaurant seemed like an obvious choice.

The Blue Stone is much less glitzy than anything the Spencer family owns in Vegas. It is a small-town steak house and event space, providing a place for big parties, anniversary celebrations, even wedding receptions, and the annual prom dinner for Sapphire Falls High School. But it is as warm and friendly a gathering place as Dottie's is. The Blue Stone serves everything from steaks and seafood to gourmet burgers and a fancy grilled cheese.

My whole family is already here as is Kaelyn's. They occupy a long table near the windows that overlook the rolling hills to the west where the sun is beginning to dip closer to the horizon making the summer sky a pretty pinkish orange.

Phoebe and Joe and my parents have been friends for years. My dad and Phoebe went to high school together. My mom and Phoebe became friends almost as soon as my mother moved to Sapphire Falls. Phoebe Spencer is a bright, friendly, funny woman who everyone loves.

Joe first showed up in Sapphire Falls actually pursuing another woman. Nadia is one of the lead scientists for my father's company. She and Matt Phillips have been married as long as all of our parents. I don't know all of the details, but Phoebe was supposed to help Joe get Nadia back. Instead, Phoebe and Joe fell in love.

My mom and Phoebe are sitting at one end of the table with Joe and my dad. My mom and Phoebe are acting as if they haven't seen each other in years, heads huddled close together, laughing and talking. The truth is, they've probably already talked three times today.

They are thrilled that they are soon to have their children as in-laws.

Graham, Ginny, and Kaelyn's two brothers, Elliot and Noah, are also already here. Her sister Gillian won't be home for a couple more days.

Everyone is talking and laughing. Our families have always been close. Which is what makes it interesting that as soon as Harlow and I arrive at the table, everyone stops talking and turns to face us.

I don't think I have ever made an entrance like this with these families.

I give them all a look. "Hey, everyone."

Phoebe gives us a sparkling smile. "Hi, Jefferson. Harlow."

Okay, so my mom has filled everyone in on the situation I take it.

I pull the chair out next to Ginny and nudge Harlow into it. I sit next to her. "Are we late?"

Of course we're not, they just showed up early, so everyone would be here when we walked in.

"You look gorgeous," Ginny tells Harlow.

"Thanks. This is the first time I've worn this dress," Harlow shoots me a little grin. "Thanks for letting me come," she says to Kaelyn.

"Of course," Kaelyn laughs. "This—" She waggles a finger between me and Harlow. "—is way more interesting than us getting married."

Harlow shakes her head. "We're not trying to upstage you. But thanks for going along with it."

"Trust me, we're enjoying it," Carver says, giving me a grin.

I sit back in my chair, resting my arm behind Harlow. With my index finger, I trace a wiggling line over her upper back. Goosebumps erupt over her skin, and she turns to look at me quickly.

I just lift a brow. Everyone at this table might know this is fake, but the rest of the restaurant has to buy it. And if she were my girlfriend, I would definitely be touching her every chance I got. All this bare skin in this dress? I would absolutely be running my finger back and forth along her smooth, creamy skin, reminding her I'm right here, that she is leaving with me later, and that there will be a lot more touching to come.

At that thought, I have to shift in my chair.

It's going to be very important that I remember this is all fake too.

That won't be hard. No one knows better than I do that Harlow Hansen is not generally my type.

I tend to like women who like me.

As Harlow settles into an easy conversation with my sister and Kaelyn about wedding plans, I look around the restaurant. It's busy tonight, but I know everybody in the room, including the group that pulls my attention with raucous laughter. They're at a table near the bar, and the loudest one is none other than Zach Nelson.

I look at my brother. "Coincidence?"

Carver lifts a shoulder. "Joe and Phoebe decided we should come down here for dinner instead of their house," he says. "That's all I know."

Kaelyn overheard me though, and she shakes her head. "Of course it's not a coincidence. Adrianne told my mom about your situation, and they decided this needed to be public right away."

"And she knew Nelson had a reservation tonight?" I guess.

Kaelyn just grins.

That is absolutely something Phoebe would do.

"Well," I say. "I'd rather have your mom on my side than the other."

Kaelyn laughs. "You know my mom loves some good, fun drama," she says. "Especially fun drama she can be a part of."

"Especially fun drama she can help stir up," Carver says.

I move my hand up Harlow's back, dragging the pads of all four fingers up her spine. I love the little shiver I feel go through her. I rest my hand on the back of her neck, stroking my thumb up and down the side of her throat. "Well, we'll take all the allies we can get. The fun of torturing Zach isn't something we would selfishly keep to ourselves."

From here, Zach can clearly see our table. Harlow's and my backs are to him on this side but that gives him an even better view of how we sit and touch each other. And it doesn't take a genius to realize that these chairs were left open by our friends and family on purpose.

I grin. Having a team is going to be fun.

I'm surprised a moment later, when Harlow's hand lands on my thigh. She runs her palm up and down, then squeezes.

I give her a little side eye, but she continues to talk with Graham.

Anyone looking on would see two people dating, casually but lovingly touching one another.

I give her neck a little squeeze, and she runs her hand up a little higher.

I am struck by how much I like her touch.

That could be problematic.

For one, there's no sense getting used to it.

For another, letting Harlow too close to the family jewels could end up being a mistake. This is an act after all—she's not *actually* fond of me and that's a particularly vulnerable body part to be letting a wild card like my pretend girlfriend get too friendly with.

"You should come over after this," I hear Harlow say to Ginny and Graham. "We can watch it and make popcorn."

"Do you mean spicy popcorn, or chocolate marshmallow popcorn?" Ginny asks.

I already know the answer.

Harlow rolls her eyes. "We could compromise with just regular popcorn I guess," she says, her tone indicating that is the most boring thing she's ever heard.

"Yes, let's do that," Ginny says, laughing.

This all catches Phoebe's attention.

"You're not going back to your place, are you?" she asks Harlow.

Harlow leans forward slightly to look down the table. "Well, yeah. I didn't think we were partying here until the wee hours."

Phoebe shakes her head. "You have to stay at Jefferson's this week."

I feel Harlow tense under my hand. "What? No way."

Phoebe drops her voice, making it softer. "You're supposed to be dating,"

"I don't have to be at his place every night." Harlow glances at me.

"Of course you do," Phoebe insists.

"Why?" Harlow asks.

I snort.

Harlow looks at me, eyebrows arched.

"Well, you wouldn't be just having quickies in the truck or even at his house and then leaving," Phoebe says.

Harlow chokes. I grin.

"Serious girlfriends stay all night," Joe agrees.

"Maybe we're not *that* serious," Harlow insists.

"You would be," my mom says. "We talked about this. It wouldn't take long."

"So everyone is just assuming we'd already be sleeping together?" Harlow asks, keeping her voice down but clearly a little outraged.

That's hilarious.

"Obviously," I say.

She swings to look at me again. "What?"

I shrug. "If we were dating, we would definitely be sleeping together. Sooner versus later."

She narrows her eyes. "Not necessarily. I might not want to."

I squeeze her neck. "You would want to."

I'm gratified when her gaze drops to my lips before bouncing back to meet my eyes.

I just grin.

"Some people—" Phoebe tips her head in Zach's direction. "—need to think you are."

Harlow lets out a breath. "*Every* night?" she asks.

"Yes," I say as Phoebe answers, "Definitely. The two of you would be together constantly."

I feel the tension leave Harlow's body, but it feels less like relaxation or relief and more like defeated resignation.

She looks at me. "You agree?"

"That you would be unable to leave me alone?" I grin and nod. "Absolutely."

"This week is going to be such a pain in the ass," she mutters.

I just chuckle.

"I don't know why you're all making this so complicated," my dad says.

Everyone turns to look at him. My father is quiet, almost always preferring to let my mother do the talking. And when he does talk, he's often blunt. Okay, he's always blunt. You never have to wonder what he's thinking.

"We're making it complicated?" Adrianne asks. "You don't think Harlow should stay at Jefferson's?"

"I'm talking about the entire premise," Dad says. He looks at Harlow and me. "You're trying to convince everyone that you're dating. Instead of worrying about getting the details right and everyone being on the same page, why don't you just actually date?"

I watch him. But he doesn't go on. He lifts his drink to his lips and sips.

"But..." Harlow starts. But then she stops and frowns.

My mom starts nodding. "That makes sense." She turns to look at us. "Don't you think?"

"It does," Joe agrees. "You've known each other a long time. You've been friends—"

Harlow snorts. I squeeze her neck again. More to let her know I heard that.

"When it turned into more doesn't matter," Joe continues. "Only that it's more now. Just date for this week. Don't pretend. That would be simpler."

"It would seem too new," Harlow insists.

"I don't know," Joe says. "Is there a magic specific moment when a friendship goes from that to more?" He looks at Phoebe and it's clear something passes between them. "Or does it happen all along until you just finally admit it?"

I'm fascinated.

"When did it happen for you?" Ginny asks him, smiling at him and Phoebe. "You were both intending to date other people. When did you decide *you* were in a relationship with one another?"

Joe grins down at Phoebe. "The first time she kissed me. I was done for. I fought it. *We* fought it. We tried to lie to ourselves. But yeah...kissing changes things."

Phoebe giggles. "We were so dumb."

"*So* dumb," Joe agrees, watching her with so much adoration it actually makes my chest squeeze.

"Well, if kissing is the catalyst, I started dating your mom the first night I met her," my dad says, grinning at my mom.

It always jabs me in the gut when my dad smiles at my

mom like that. He doesn't grin with pure joy and unrestricted emotion very often. He's pretty serious. And even grumpy at times. But with her...he's different. Every time.

"You kissed the first night you met?" Harlow asks.

I look at my siblings and we all smile. We know this story. We've heard my mom and dad's love story dozens of times.

"I did. Couldn't help it," he says.

"You don't..." Harlow trails off, pressing her lips together.

I chuckle. "Go ahead and say it. He doesn't seem like the type of guy to lose control like that, right?"

"You really don't," she tells him.

"Things got a little out of hand," my dad admits. With a big grin.

My mom is blushing. "Yeah, we were pretty...involved from the very start."

Phoebe laughs. "God, that was fun."

Phoebe was very involved in concocting the plan to keep my dad away from Hailey Conner, the then-mayor and my dad's sort-of ex. My mom was Hailey's assistant back then and Mom was the decoy, tasked with distracting my dad for the weekend of the summer festival. And it definitely worked.

Hailey is now married to Ty Bennett and they are close friends with my parents, and hearing them all tell the story, years later, with laughter and embellishments, is very fun.

"So, honestly, it's an easy sell to tell people that you two started dating," my mom says. "Just...try it out for a week. What would really be the difference between what you've always been and dating?"

"We'd *like* each other," Harlow says.

"Kissing," I say at the same time.

She looks up at me. "You don't think we need to like each other?"

"I think we like each other just fine," I say, meaning it.

"And I think if we spend more time together, we'll like each other more."

I've been thinking about this a lot today. I think I'm someone in Harlow's life unlike any other. I'm someone she can be angry and loud and rude and messy with. And I do think she likes that. Or she will once she really realizes it.

But I decide to give her an out here. I lean in. "And I promise if I kiss you, you'll like that too."

She growls. "I need a drink." Harlow shoves her chair back, causing my hand to drop away from her neck. "Anyone else?"

Ginny and Kaelyn give her orders.

Harlow looks at me. "Order me...some chicken thing."

"You got it, babe," I tell her.

As she stands, I put my hand on her hip and pull her in close. "Harlow," I say.

She leans over. "Yes, dear?"

"You need to dial back the eye rolling and sarcasm."

Again, her eyes drop to my mouth, then she nods. "Fine."

I pinch her ass and let her go.

She swallows and I know she is fighting the urge to glare at me or slap me.

I thought this week might be fun before. Now I *know* it's going to be.

"Shouldn't you go with her?" Graham asks. "Zach has already noticed her, and that she's alone."

I nod. I've been keeping my eye on Nelson. "Part of the plan. I want him to dare to talk to my girlfriend when I'm not around."

Graham shakes his head. "For the record, I'm not as convinced you can pull this off."

I focus on my brother. "Why is that? You don't think we have chemistry?"

They have both assured me several times over the years, as

have our friends, that there are no feelings—at least romantic ones—between Graham and Harlow. But old habits die hard, and I feel a twinge of...something at my brother's words.

If I didn't know better, I'd call it jealousy. If it was anyone else that's also what I would call it.

"Oh, there's chemistry," Graham says with a chuckle. "It's more the constant, will they-won't they."

"Will they or won't they fall into bed with each other?" Kaelyn asks.

"Will they or won't they claw each other's eyes out," Graham corrects.

"Nah, it's more will they or won't they tear each other's clothes off," Ginny says.

"Shouldn't that be a little disturbing to you?" Elliot, one of Kaelyn's brothers, asks.

Ginny hums thoughtfully. "You'd think so. But I'm used to it. This is how they've always acted."

I look at her with surprise. "You've always thought that Harlow and I have chemistry?"

She shrugs. "I don't think I would have labeled it that, but now that I think about it, yes. I mean, you've always been the same. And now that people have pointed it out, that does seem to be what it is. I wonder if some of the irritation she feels about you is irritation that she can't act on the chemistry because she doesn't like you."

I frown. "You do think she dislikes me? For real?"

"I think you can have chemistry with someone who you dislike because of their actions. I mean it's not like you kill puppies or steal from children's cancer charities or something. You just see the world a little differently. You have a lot of people in common, and what you think is best for them is different."

"And you don't think we can get past that."

Ginny laughs. "Of course you can."

"Yeah?" I note the way that makes my heart rate speed up. But I shouldn't.

"Yeah. You both need to mind your own business. Our lives —" She motions between her and Graham. "Aren't really either of your concern."

I prop my forearm on the table and lean in to pin my sister with a look. "You *are* our concern. We both love you. We want you to be happy. Safe. Loved. Just because she does that differently than I do doesn't mean I disagree with her doing it at all."

Ginny shakes her head. "Yes. And that's all lovely. It's a fantastic thing for the two of you to have in common. But the fact that you're both constantly trying to tell us how to make those things happen, is the problem. You don't see eye to eye on that. So what? Neither of you should be so concerned with our lives anyway. You both need to work on your own."

I frown. "Harlow and I have great lives. We're both very well adjusted and happy."

"Then why do you both fight with such an awesome person who could be a really good friend? And maybe even more?"

I look around the table for some support. Turns out everyone has been listening. And no one is jumping to my defense.

I glance over in the direction where my girlfriend—fake girlfriend, dammit—is waiting for her drink to be mixed. I know she didn't get a simple beer or glass of wine. It's not something fruity and blended. It's probably a Jack and Coke, light on the Coke.

Dammit. I even know how to mix the perfect cocktail for her.

And, sure enough, Zach Nelson is right next to her.

"Excuse me. I'm needed at the bar."

Everyone at the table smirks.

Hey, Harlow and I might not see eye to eye on everything, but being mean to Zach Nelson is something we do agree on.

As I'm standing, our waitress arrives with four platters of appetizers. One in particular catches my attention. Grinning, I load a little plate with bacon and brie brussels sprouts.

A chance to wound Zach and ruffle Harlow at the same time? How can I pass up that temptation?

CHAPTER 11

HARLOW

"DAMN, YOU LOOK GORGEOUS," Zach says, as he comes up next to me at the bar.

The bartender just pushed my Jack and Coke across the bar to me. I take it, lift my glass for a sip, then turn and look at my ex.

"Thanks."

"I've been thinking," Zach says.

"Uh oh."

"I'm not surprised about you and Jefferson."

I sigh. It seems that Jefferson and I are the only ones who are surprised. That's annoying.

Even Jefferson's very practical father isn't surprised. In fact, Mason Riley thinks we should just date for real. Even if it's only for a week.

Good lord, if someone told me I'm in some kind of alternate reality right now, I'd believe them.

"Okay," I tell Zach. I am not really sure why he thinks I need to know this.

"I mean, you've known him forever. He's a good guy. Successful, for Sapphire Falls," Zach goes on.

Oh, got it. I see exactly where Zach is going with this.

I turn to face him fully. "Please, tell me everything you think about everything."

"Don't be like that," he says. "I just want to lay this out for you. Because no one else will."

I take another sip of my drink. "Lay out what?"

"You have choices, Harlow. I know it probably doesn't feel that way. People in this town see the world a little differently. You've grown up here. You're still here. So it makes sense that you would gravitate toward the guy who is also still here. I mean it really does make sense, on paper, to everyone here, that you would end up together."

I sip again then swallow. Then I set my glass on the bar. "So what you're saying is that Jefferson and I are together because we ran out of options. It was just a process of elimination, right? Everyone else left. You left. So what else would I possibly do?"

Zach just studies me for a moment. He nods. "I wouldn't have put it exactly like that. But yes. Jefferson is definitely your best option. Here."

"Here. In my hometown. The place I love. The town that's full of people that I love. The place where I do a job that I love."

"You can have more."

I take a deep breath.

This should be funny. Or at least seem ironic. A few hours ago I would have thought Zach and Jefferson have this in common. I would have believed that they both look down on Sapphire Falls, and feel the people who stay here are unimaginative, lazy, or stuck in a rut.

But... Jefferson and I talked.

Okay, we fought. Argued. Whatever.

But I've been replaying our conversation ever since I stormed out of his house and...I believe him. I believe that he loves Sapphire Falls. That he *chose* to come back and make his life here. He could have gone anywhere. He's charming and intelligent and talented. He was also a star in Minnesota. So it was a step "down" for Nebraska fans. That doesn't mean other people see it that way. At all. He could have gone anywhere to coach and teach.

He chose to come home.

That means something.

And I'm not an idiot—or *that* much of a bitch—to not admit that.

"I have what I want right here, Zach," I say, feeling not only irritated with my ex-boyfriend, but a strange camaraderie with Jefferson now that I've realized, or admitted, that he's here because he wants to be. Like me.

I *could have* left. I've never truly considered it, of course, but in my rational brain I know I could have. I could have gotten a job somewhere else. I just don't want to.

"Harlow, I am through my residency. I have a fantastic position with the practice locked in," Zach says.

"So you're going to whisk me away from all of this? Give me a new lease on life? Show me everything I've been missing?"

"I'm giving us a second chance. We've both grown up. We're different. I want to try again."

I look at the guy that I was such a fool for at one time in my life. I feel *nothing* for him. Except a true desire to make sure he knows that. "If you're such a big deal, so successful, so good looking and amazing, how come you're back here, digging through your past? Why not find some hot new girl, who will appreciate the city life?"

"I've never stopped thinking about you."

"It's because I'm the one that got away. It's because I'm the one who broke up with *you*. Am I the only one?" I study him. "Oh my God, is that it? Am I the only girl who's ever broken up with you?"

He doesn't confirm or deny. "I just miss you."

"Well, let me tell you something," I say. "Jefferson Riley has something that you never had and I very much doubt you've developed in the past ten years. Integrity.

"He is generous, kind, self-sacrificing, funny, And, *so* much hotter than you. The orgasms are..." I take a deep breath and make myself concentrate on what I'm saying instead of thinking about Jefferson and orgasms. "I can't even describe them. So... I absolutely am not settling. I'm lucky he was still available."

I am really trying hard not to pay attention to the way my stomach is flipping as I say these words. I'm just trying to piss Zach off. That's all. I'm trying to take him down a peg.

But...dammit, they're all true.

I don't know about the orgasms but there's no way Jefferson isn't good at that too. There's no way the guy is good at literally *everything* else he does and he's not good in bed.

Having his hand on the back of my neck, having his finger dragging over my upper back, having him just *say* the word 'kissing' made my body temperature rise.

There is no way Jefferson Riley couldn't make me very hot and bothered if he tried.

And while Jefferson Riley is also a know-it-all, cocky, and frustrating as hell, *I* can criticize him, and talk about what a pain in the ass he is. Zach Nelson can *not*.

I don't know the women that Jefferson has dated very well. He's only had a couple of girlfriends from Sapphire Falls, and they are both enough older than me that I've never heard them spill anything about him, good or bad.

But while Jefferson is a lot of things, a lying, cheating scumbag is not one of them.

And as I think about it, it *is* kind of amazing that he's still single. And it's maybe even more amazing that he's willing to pretend to date me. Because I am a pain in his ass too.

"How's everything going over here?"

I am a little appalled by the relief that sweeps through me at the sound of Jefferson's voice and the feel of his big body behind me. He moves in close and rather than flinching away as I did at the house, now I'm tempted to lean into him.

Not because I'm afraid of Zach. I'm not intimidated by my ex.

It's more that I just feel comforted by Jefferson. And all of these realizations that I've finally let really sink in.

Jefferson is a good guy and would make a great boyfriend.

There, I said it.

And thought it.

Gave it actual conscious thought and let myself acknowledge it without any qualifiers.

It's not that any of this is a huge shocking revelation. If anyone had criticized Jefferson to me in the past, there's a chance I would have defended him the way I just did. The thing is...no one would've criticized Jefferson. Everyone truly likes the guy. He's fucking likable. He is a good person.

"Actually, Zach and I were just realizing that we have nothing to talk about," I say, meeting Zach's gaze.

I feel Jefferson's hand on my hip, and I reach for it, linking our fingers and pulling his hand around and over my stomach. He moves closer, spreading his fingers so that even more of his hand is covering me. It is a very possessive gesture and I fucking like it. Probably because it makes Zach's eyes narrow. That has to be why.

"Well, you've been gone a little bit, and I was missing you," Jefferson tells me as he presses a kiss to the top of my head.

That's sweet. I know, in truth, he was watching and came over because Zach was talking to me. He's here to help.

See? Good guy.

"Here, you said you were hungry," Jefferson says. "I brought you some appetizers, so you weren't drinking on an empty stomach. Don't want you getting sick."

That's nice too. I am actually very hungry.

He brings a small plate up in front of me and my gaze drops to...Brussels sprouts. I carefully school my features.

Jefferson knows me really well. And he loves to give me a hard time.

He knows I fucking hate Brussels sprouts.

Asshole.

I dig my nails into the back of his hand as Zach's eyes drop to the plate then come back to mine.

"Harlow doesn't like Brussels sprouts," Zach tells Jefferson with a bit of smugness.

"She didn't used to," Jefferson agrees. "But she's changed since you knew her. In lots of ways." He withdraws his hand—the one I'm not sorry to see tiny nail imprints on—and moves slightly to the side so he can look at me. "Isn't that right, Lily?"

I get it. I wore the blue dress to drive him a little crazy, so he's going to make me eat Brussels sprouts in front of my ex. We might not be outwardly fighting right now, but there's still a battle of the wills going on.

I pluck one off the plate. "That's right."

"Lily?" Zach asks.

Jefferson watches me wet my lips in preparation for biting into the disgusting green orb in my fingers.

The corner of his mouth curls and it does look affectionate, but I know it's because he can't wait to see me eat this damn thing and pretend to like it.

I am so getting him back for this.

I don't give a fuck how much bacon and cheese and balsamic glaze someone put on these little fuckers, they are still disgusting.

"Oh, that's my little nickname for her. She didn't really like lilies, but I gave them to her on our first date."

"I know she doesn't like lilies," Zach says, as if it's the most obvious thing in the world.

I push the Brussels sprout past my lips, bite into it—oh my god, that's horrible—and hide my grimace with a forced smile up at Jefferson. He lifts a hand and swipes his thumb over my bottom lip. Apparently, there was a smudge of balsamic glaze there. He lifts it to his mouth and sucks it clean.

And for just a second, I forget the bitter green blob in my mouth.

Damn, why was that hot?

"She still doesn't really like them," Jefferson says to Zach, still looking at me. "But it's kind of our little joke. I gave them to her on our first date, not knowing she didn't like them. She smiled, thanked me as if she was delighted, then brought the bouquet with us and handed flowers out to people as we went along all night. Now I bring her a lily for each date. She always gets rid of it as soon as she can. I started calling her Lily." He shrugs. "It's just our thing now."

I'm blinking at him, the Brussels sprout nearly forgotten.

Wow. That's a good story. Adorable even.

I almost wish it was true.

"I see," Zach says.

Now he looks really frustrated.

And that is probably worth having a Brussels sprout in my mouth.

But we need to wrap this up. Because now I've remembered it's there and I'm starting to feel a little like gagging.

I look at Jefferson, willing him to read my mind.

He leans in, kisses my cheek, then says, "We should get back to the table."

Thank God.

Zach says, "Sure. See you around."

"Maybe," Jefferson sighs.

"I'll wave from my front porch," Zach tells him.

Jefferson stops mid-turn.

I almost groan. I need to get back to the table where I can spit this thing out.

"What front porch?" Jefferson asks.

"I'm staying in Mrs. Dixon's house for the week," Zach says.

Jefferson frowns. "Since when?"

"About three hours ago. I was renting the Kastenbaum house, kind of an Airbnb thing, but the AC went out. Fortunately for me, the Dixons are out of town visiting their daughter and grandbaby in their RV. Of course, someone knew that instantly, and was able to get a hold of them. They said they were happy to let me stay in their place."

I want to growl. The Dixons live across the street and down one house from Jefferson. That means Phoebe's suggestion about me staying with Jefferson is an even bigger deal. Zach will be driving right by Jefferson's place all the time, and he'll see if my car is in the driveway or not. Hell, he'll be able to look out his living room or kitchen window and keep track of us coming and going. He'll know exactly when I'm there, when I'm not, and how often Jefferson and I leave or return together.

Well, fuck.

What's Ray doing? He's the heating and air-conditioning guy in town. Can't he go over and fix the AC at the Kastenbaums?

"Okay then. Let me know if you need a cup of sugar or anything," Jefferson says.

"Yeah. Ditto," Zach says. His eyes land on me. "I guess I'll be seeing you too. "

I nod. "Yep." I hope it doesn't sound like I'm holding a piece of food in my cheek.

Jefferson turns and guides me back to the table, his hand on my lower back, in clear view of Zach, who I am sure is watching us walk away.

As soon as we get to the table, I step in front of Jefferson, quickly reach for *his* napkin and spit the Brussels sprout out.

Jefferson chuckles.

"I will be getting you back for that," I tell him.

"Can't wait, Lily," he says, pulling my chair out for me.

Then he looks at the end of the table with the parents. "And what's going on at the Dixons? They weren't gone as of yesterday."

"They just decided to go visit their daughter this afternoon," Adrianne says. "Isn't that such great timing?" Then she looks at Phoebe and they both start laughing.

Joe just smiles. Mason shakes his head.

Great. The parents 'broke' the Kastenbaums' AC and then made the Dixons leave town?

Well, if I wanted help pulling a fake dating scheme off, I've got it. Maybe more help than I want, in fact.

CHAPTER 12

JEFFERSON

I HAVE my hand on Harlow's low back, escorting her out of the restaurant after dinner when I see Zach and a couple of friends lingering by their cars.

I don't know what they're doing. It doesn't matter.

I lean in and say near her ear, "Just so you know, when we get to my truck, I'm going to kiss you."

She jerks to a stop and looks up at me. "Excuse me?"

I smile down at her, playing the part of adoring boyfriend, having an intimate conversation with the woman he's madly in love with. I lift my hand and brush her hair back from her cheek. "Zach is out here. So I'm going to kiss you."

"We don't have to be kissing and all over each other every time he's around."

But I notice that she's breathing a little faster.

I cup her cheek. "Oh, but we do."

Suddenly, she gets a sly look in her eye, then flattens her palm on the lapel of my jacket and runs it up and down. From a distance at least it looks like we're discussing something friendly. "Why is that?"

"Because if you were my girlfriend and your ex was in town and interested in getting you back, I would be doing everything I could to show him that you are very taken." I slide my hand from her cheek down her neck, then skim it down her back, still loving all the bare skin this dress shows off. When I get to her ass, I cup it and bring her closer.

She takes a quick little breath in.

"Though, if you were my girlfriend, and you were wearing this dress to dinner, I'd be touching you a whole lot anyway."

"Wow, I was really right about my ass in this dress, wasn't I?" Her voice is a little breathless.

I love that.

"It's your ass, your legs, your breasts..." I take a breath. "Your smile, your sense of humor, the way you tease with our friends, the way you take care of our families."

Her smile fades and her mouth drops open.

I kind of hate that me saying I like all of that shocks her.

She swallows hard. "You think I coddle people and hold them back."

I take a breath. "I think you love people and...yes, you coddle them." I don't want to fight with her. I don't want to make her feel bad. So I go for light. "That doesn't change the fact that you have great breasts, and legs to go with that ass."

She clears her throat. "Careful, that all almost sounded like you might be attracted to me for real."

Is she fishing here? Is she joking? I don't care. "Well, let me make that very clear. I find you incredibly gorgeous, and I've been itching to run my hands all over you all night. Zach or not. Fake boyfriend or not. *That* is very real."

She stares up at me, those words hanging between us.

I wonder if she's also thinking about how much between us has been very real.

Like all of it.

The "dating" part maybe not, but our conversations, the emotions, the chemistry, even the laughter—and there has been some of that, dammit—has been real.

Finally, she says, "I hope I have garlic breath."

I chuckle. I would expect nothing less from Harlow.

I kiss her forehead, then turn her toward my truck and continue across the parking lot.

Because of the way the truck is parked, the driver's side is the side closest to where Zach and his friends are leaning against their cars, casually chatting.

So that's the side Harlow is getting in on.

"I don't have anything at your house," she says to me. There's no way they can hear us from here, but they can see us.

"I know."

"So we're going to have to swing by my house."

"You are staying tonight, then?"

She rolls her eyes and again I'm glad Zach is too far away to see it. "Phoebe thinks I should. Everyone thinks I should." She narrows her eyes. "Unless *you* don't think I should."

"Oh, I definitely think you should."

"Why can't *you* stay at *my* place? You know they manipulated everything so that Zach is staying in a house across the street from yours. We could mess with them and have you stay at my house."

"Why would we mess with them? They're trying to help us."

"They're enjoying it too much," she says grumpily.

"For someone who is so sweet and sunny all the time," I say, lifting my finger to rub right between her brows where there's a little wrinkle. "Why is it that you suddenly *don't* want everyone to be enjoying themselves?"

"I guess I can't get over how easily everyone is accepting us as a couple."

"Maybe they see something we haven't."

"Maybe there hasn't been enough drama around here lately, and they're bored."

I chuckle. In our parents' friend group, which has created our friend group, there are simply too many people with too many big personalities for that to be true. And that's not even taking into consideration the rest of the town.

"Harlow," I say as I lift my hand to the back of her head and slide my fingers into her silky hair. "Shut up and kiss me."

Her breath catches and she tips her head up. "*You* better not have garlic breath," she mutters as she goes up on tiptoe.

Neither of us kisses the other. Our lips meet right in the middle and we kiss each other.

At first, it's just a soft touch. And honestly, that would probably be enough. A guy, kissing his girlfriend in the parking lot, sweetly, romantically, before he takes her home makes more sense than what happens next.

But Harlow sighs, and her lips are soft, her breath is actually sweet. And feeling her hands slide up my chest along my neck and into my hair as her body arches into mine, makes every other thought disappear.

I don't care about garlic. I don't care about the chocolate cake and coffee she shared with Ginny. I don't care about Zach or anyone else who might be walking through this parking lot. Including our parents and siblings.

I just want more.

More of Harlow's mouth. More of her body against mine. More of the husky sounds she makes that shoot straight to my cock.

I tip my head, drop both hands to her ass, pull her closer, and open my mouth, sliding my tongue over her bottom lip.

If I'd really stopped to think, I would have realized in that moment that Harlow could've bitten the thing off.

But she doesn't.

Instead, she makes a soft moaning sound, opens her mouth, and meets my tongue with her own.

I wouldn't say the kiss is hungry or carnal, but it is definitely not simply a sweet just-for-show kiss.

It is a sexy, I-want-more-of-this kiss.

Eventually, the sound of car doors opening and shutting, and engines starting filter in.

She pulls back, blinking up at me.

I lift my head.

And we stare at each other for at least ten beats.

Then she closes her eyes and moans. But it's definitely a different moan than the ones when my lips were on hers.

This is a moan of frustration.

"Dammit, Jefferson," she mutters.

"What?" That was a damned good kiss and there is no way in hell she can convince me otherwise.

"That wasn't supposed to be *good*."

When she opens her eyes and meets mine, I laugh. "No?"

"Kissing Graham was like kissing my brother. Kissing *you* was supposed to be like kissing my brother, but a brother I don't like *at all*."

Several thoughts and emotions hit me at once. I'd assumed she and Graham had kissed in the past, but I hate the sharp stab of jealousy that follows that confirmation. I almost equally hate the surge of satisfaction I feel at hearing that it wasn't good. I kind of like the idea that they did try it, and nothing came of it.

And none of that is as strong as the smugness that I feel at her admission that our kiss was good.

It was great. I haven't had a kiss like that in a really long time.

"Look at it this way," I say, trying to keep my grin in check. "It'll make this week easier."

"I suppose you think we're going to do more of that."

Now I can't contain my grin. "Oh yes, Lily, we're going to do more of that."

She tips her head back with a long, "Uuuggghhh."

My eyes drop to the long smooth expanse of her throat. I very much want to press my lips there.

"You can't keep calling me Lily."

"I definitely can. Of course, I would have a pet name for you. And of course, it would be one that started out annoying."

Finally, she chuckles and tips her head to look at me directly again. "Started out?"

"As far as everyone else knows."

"And the fact that it still annoys *me* is just sprinkles on top, right?"

I squeeze her ass, then turn her toward the truck and lift her up onto the seat. "You got it."

I watch as she crawls across the console to the passenger side.

"And, girl, you were right. Your ass definitely looks amazing in this dress."

She doesn't say anything as I climb up into the driver seat. But I definitely hear her heavy sigh.

It only takes her two minutes to realize that we are headed for my house and not hers.

"I need to get some stuff if I'm staying at your place. Especially if it's for a week."

"You can get your stuff tomorrow. Zach is obviously going to be getting to the Dixons' soon. We're going straight home."

"I think it's okay for him to think that we occasionally go to my house. We're not living together."

"You don't need anything tonight. We're in a hurry to get home."

I feel her watching me. "We are?"

"That dress? My jealousy over your ex? That kiss? Yeah, we're in a hurry to get home."

"Are we gonna start tearing each other clothes off on the porch for him to see?"

I glance over. "I'm game."

She chuckles now. "Not fair. I'm like a zipper away from practically naked."

Heat and desire tighten my gut. "Noted."

She quickly looks away from my stare.

"I don't have anything at your house. Not even for a one-night slumber party."

"What do you need?"

"Pajamas. Toothbrush." She pauses. "I guess those are the basics. "

"I have extra toothbrushes."

"And pajamas?"

"You'd definitely be sleeping naked if you were my girlfriend."

"But I'm not. And Zach isn't going to be checking what I'm sleeping in."

I am resolutely *not* wondering about just how much—or how little—she has on under that dress right now.

If she's only a zipper away from 'practically' naked, does that mean no bra? There are definitely no panty lines...I would have absolutely noticed with how I studied her ass tonight and when I had my hands there...

Okay, maybe I'm not so resolutely not wondering.

I clear my throat. "You can borrow a t-shirt. It's one night. We'll get your stuff tomorrow."

I am not immune to what the thought of her sleeping in one of my shirts does to me either. It's probably the kiss. Or this fucking dress. Or maybe the fact that even playing her boyfriend for a day has already gotten me thinking about what it would be like to date Harlow.

Fun.

Sexy.

Easy.

Sure, I'd always have to be on my toes, but it would be easy to be around her, and to blend into each other's lives. Even when we're not getting along, my heart pounds and I enjoy myself.

And when we *are* getting along, I just want more and more.

Sure, she's a pain in my ass. She doesn't let me get away with anything. She does not think I am amazing. We would no doubt bicker just like this if we were dating.

But it feels fresh. Even though we've been doing it as long as I've known her. Our relationship is well established, but how we both approach things, how we live our lives, and what we bicker about has evolved. And I think it always will.

Harlow and I would never get boring.

She's not wrong when she says that I have it pretty easy around Sapphire Falls. People like me. It's not hard to be liked. My family as well liked, they contribute a lot to the community, and the local economy. Honestly, my siblings are all great. We have a big, influential friend group. And the group is influential because they are kind, generous, hard-working, *nice* members of the community.

I'd have to be a real asshole to be disliked in this town.

But Harlow keeps it real with me. She makes me actually think about the things I do. Like my job. She's not impressed with me as a coach. Football—the game itself anyway—is not impressive to her. The number of wins and losses on my record don't matter to her.

But the way I interact with the kids does make an impression.

And though she may not admit it, she notices.

Maybe not all of them though and I'd love to tell her more. Because I didn't become a coach just because I love the game. I did want to make a difference.

I am not going to become a Mason Riley who's curing world hunger and having meetings with presidents and prime ministers.

But I could be teaching someone who could become the next Mason Riley.

And Harlow has seen me in action. We spent a lot of intense time together when it came to Alex. She knows I care. She makes me think. She's like a constant niggle in the back of my mind asking if what I'm doing is important and if it's the best I can do.

Sometimes I hate it but most of the time I appreciate it. When I'm working with a kid, or even in front of my classroom or on the field, every once in a while, the thought will float through my mind, *what will Harlow think of this?*

For better or worse.

We pull into my driveway, and both get out. My porch light is on, so if Zach is looking out the front window of the Dixons' house—and yes, I've glanced over and noticed his car is in the drive—then he'll notice us coming home.

I move in close to her, putting my hand on her waist as I unlock the door.

She doesn't move away. She doesn't stiffen under my touch. She doesn't act surprised at all.

Good. We're already getting past all of that.

Once inside the house she kicks off her heels.

"Guess what number I'm thinking of," she tells me.

I frown. "What?"

"Just do it. What number am I thinking of?"

"Four," I guess.

"Nope. That means I get your room and you get the guestroom."

I laugh. "No way."

"Graham says that the bed in the guestroom here sucks."

"Ha. If you want to sleep in the master bedroom, you're gonna have to share the bed with me."

"Nice try."

"Well, you're not a guest. You're my girlfriend. No way would you sleep in the guestroom anyway."

"I am your fake girlfriend, and no one is coming over while we're sleeping to check what bed we're each in."

I shrug out of my jacket and start unbuttoning my shirt as I head for the stairs ignoring the way my body reacts to even the suggestion of Harlow sharing my bed. "Like I said, if you want the nice mattress, you're gonna have to share."

"Hey," she says.

I turn and look back.

"You're going to bed now? It's so early."

"Did you have something in mind?" And I can't help but think of all the ways I would be spending the next couple of hours if she really was my girlfriend and we had just gotten home from dinner.

"Well…" She looks around the room. "We could at least watch TV or something. It's way too early for bed."

She's not wrong. It is.

But that means Harlow and I are going to spend time alone together. Just us. I don't think we've ever done that. Not for hours anyway. Maybe five or ten minutes at the most. Except when we were out looking for Alex. Or sitting by his hospital bed.

Those were intense hours. Ones I'm sure neither of us want to repeat.

"Yeah," I say casually. "I'm just gonna change clothes. Come on up and I'll get you... stuff."

"I don't suppose you have any ponytail holders?" she asks, following me up the stairs.

I'm not sure what she wants to hear here. That I do because I've had women here before or that I don't because I don't date a lot.

"I think there are some in the second drawer in the bathroom," I say.

"Okay," she says noncommittally. "Are they Ginny's?"

I stop outside the bathroom. "They might be."

I watch her for a moment. Surely it doesn't bother her to think about women I've dated in the past. Women who might've spent the night here.

Then she surprises me and says, "I'm going to pretend they are."

"Jealous they might not be?" I ask.

"Worried about cooties," she says.

I snort. "Washcloths are in the cupboard. New toothbrushes should be in the same drawer with the ponytail holders. There might be other useful things in there too."

She tips her head, a tiny smile tugging at her lips. "Useful things like?"

"I think there are makeup wipes. Some bath salts. Tampons."

Her eyebrows lift. "You have bath salts and tampons?"

"I have things that...people...have brought over that I haven't thrown away. That drawer is kind of a catch-all. Feel free to dig through it."

"Well, I don't think I'll be taking a bath. And I don't need any tampons."

"That could potentially be filed under TMI," I say, but still have the urge to chuckle.

"If you were my boyfriend, you would totally know that," she says lifting a shoulder.

"Good point. I'd also know what kind of bath salts you like."

She wrinkles her nose. "I'm not really into baths. More of a shower girl."

"Oh, that's too bad. I do like baths, and I have an amazing tub. And if you were really my girlfriend, I'd make sure you liked them too."

Why do I keep saying stuff like that? She's not my girlfriend. We are not getting in that tub together.

Why don't you just actually date?

My dad's words come back to me in that moment.

Taking a bath together would be one thing that would definitely convince Harlow that dating me is a good idea.

"Gee, just one more reason we're not a good match," she says dryly. But her tone is less biting than usual.

"Yep. Guess so." I pivot toward my room before I spend any further time thinking about her in my bathtub. With me. I really do like baths, but not solo ones. "Let me grab you a shirt."

In my bedroom, I take a couple of deep breaths, then rummage in my drawer for one of my bigger shirts. Any of my shirts will be huge on her, but the bigger the better. I step back into the hallway with one of my Sapphire Falls football shirts, in part to annoy her. I toss it to her. "Here you go. I'll meet you downstairs."

She holds the shirt up, rolls her eyes, which is stupidly gratifying, and says, "Okay."

Ten minutes later I'm in the kitchen on my phone, pulling

up recipes for spicy popcorn when Harlow walks into the room.

Her hair is up in a ponytail, her make up is scrubbed off, and she's wearing my shirt. And only my shirt. Which, of course, I was expecting.

But I realize in that moment that my insistence on not stopping at her house and making her feel the fullness of being on my turf is very much going to backfire.

She looks hot as fuck.

She looks relaxed, ready for a night in, but despite the fact that my shirt is huge on her, I am acutely aware of her long, tan, bare legs, bare feet, and that there isn't much underneath that shirt.

She looked gorgeous in that dress tonight with her full make up on and those heels.

But this is Harlow. The Harlow I've known for so many years. The sassy small-town girl I've grown up with.

Looking at her, I immediately flash back to so many nights with her hanging out at my house with Graham, before they were old enough to drive and go out on the weekends.

She'd look a lot like this, lounging on the sofas in our basement, or cooking in our kitchen, or goofing around on our back deck.

It also reminds me of so many barbecues, hangouts at the Come Again, street dances, and football games with our friends and family.

And it reminds me of how she looked when we were scouring the county for Alex the night he went missing, how she looked sitting up next to his hospital bed. She'd been rumpled, tired, worried, not caring at all how her hair looked, or what clothes she was wearing. She'd been fully focused on him and what he'd needed.

She'd been so fucking beautiful that night. Her raw emotions exposed, leaning on me, letting me help her.

Harlow can dress up. She can pull off updos and high heels with seeming ease, but this is the real her.

Of course, she usually wears pants.

"I'm ninety-eight percent sure this scrunchie is Ginny's," she tells me turning her head so I can see the hunter green elastic that's holding her hair up. "Do not tell me if you know that's not true."

I pull myself together and grin at her. "I'm ninety-nine percent sure you're right."

She props her shoulder against the doorframe and crosses her arms, "What are you doing?"

"Trying to figure out what exactly spicy popcorn is."

She looks surprised for a moment, and I realize I just confessed that I overheard her comment to Ginny and remembered it. And that I am giving some effort to trying to give her something she wants.

But truthfully, if she was my girlfriend, that's exactly what I would do.

She doesn't comment on it though and just pushes off the doorframe and comes into the room fully. "You don't need a recipe. I know exactly how to make it. Where are your spices?"

I point to the cupboard next to the stove. She pads across the room on her bare feet and opens the door, then stretches to reach the higher shelves.

And that is a terrible idea. Heat slams into me as my shirt rides up on the back of her trim, smooth thighs. It still hits well below the curve of her ass, but the move pulls the cotton up against her curves and, a better man might be able to avert his gaze, but not me.

"Is there any chance you have ancho chili powder?" she

asks, flipping through the small plastic bottles of spices on the shelf.

I clear my throat. "I can't imagine why I would."

She turns holding three bottles. "I guess we'll make do with these."

I read the labels. There's onion powder and garlic powder but she's also got my chili powder out.

"But it'd be better with ancho and cayenne powder," she says.

"You weren't kidding when you said spicy."

She shrugs. "It's also best if you pop it on the stove top. Not in the microwave."

"And you have all of this at your place."

"Along with scrunchies I know don't have cooties and—" She glances down. "Pants."

"We already established that scrunchie is ninety-nine percent cootie free, and I gotta say, you're pulling off the no-pants look."

"Thanks, I guess," she says with a light laugh.

"But," I say pushing off from the counter. "Because I really am the best boyfriend, I'm going to your house to get the spices and the popcorn."

"You're going to leave me here?" she asks. "What will Zach think?"

"I'm going to sneak out the back door and then sneak back in." I hold out my hand. "House keys?"

"There's a spare tucked behind my front porch light," she says.

"Great. I'll be back."

"Bring the canola oil too," she says. "And some pants."

"Spices, popcorn, oil. Got it."

"And pants!"

I'm laughing as I pull the back door shut behind me on her, "*Jefferson!*"

CHAPTER 13

JEFFERSON

I JOG the distance to her house, easily find the key, and only need a few minutes of rummaging through her kitchen to find all the ingredients. I do glance down the hallway toward her bedroom. I could bring her pants. But I also know that she never wears many clothes when she's lounging around, and I would bet, if she were on the couch watching television by herself, she wouldn't have pants on. So she's not going to have them on at my house.

I'll give her a blanket, or even sweatpants of mine if she really gets uncomfortable. But if she were my girlfriend, we would definitely have a no-pants-at-home rule.

I am jogging across the yards, and up my back steps less than twenty minutes later. I let myself in the back kitchen door, but immediately stop when I hear voices.

I set the popcorn supplies on the counter and tip my head listening.

Motherfucker. That's Zach Nelson's voice.

"You should just go to Dottie's for coffee," Harlow is telling him. "Or the bakery."

"I just like having that first cup or two at home while I get ready," he says. "You can't spare enough grounds for one morning? I'll go to the store tomorrow."

"The Dixons really don't have any coffee?"

"They might but I can't find it. Wanna come over and help me look?"

Is this guy fucking serious? He came to *my* house to ask *my* girlfriend to come over to look for coffee?

"They don't have tea either? That's what you drank this morning," Harlow says.

"I'd already had my coffee for the day. I try to watch my caffeine."

"Well maybe tomorrow is a good time to start cutting back."

"Come on, Harlow. Be a good neighbor. Just loan me some coffee."

"The only thing I really want to give you, Zach," Harlow says, "is my middle finger."

I grin. Sounds like she's handling him fine. But I'm annoyed that he came over. Why? He couldn't borrow coffee from anyone else? He couldn't just wait until tomorrow?

He's checking up on us. He's suspicious.

I stop just out of sight and contemplate how I want to play this.

Harlow's at my house. It's late at night. And... I straighten, realizing how she's probably dressed while answering the door. On one hand I like that she's wearing my T-shirt and nothing else. That should send Zach a clear message. On the other, I hate the idea of him seeing her partially dressed. The shirt hits her the same place on her thighs that a pair of shorts would, but there's something about him seeing her in an oversized T-shirt that is a little too intimate for me.

I'm in a T-shirt and joggers, so I kick off my shoes, strip off my shirt, and head out of the kitchen through the opposite doorway, making it look as if I'm coming in from the back of the house.

"Hey, Lily, what's going on?" I ask.

Harlow looks back at me, and I notice how her eyes flicker with surprise when she sees me shirtless. She recovers quickly though and says, "Poor Zach here can't find the coffee at the Dixons."

"That sucks," I say, moving in behind Harlow and resting both of my hands on her hips.

She's standing in the doorway, blocking Zach's entrance to the house. She has one shoulder propped on the open door, her other on her hip.

"Thought you said I could come borrow a cup of sugar," Zach says.

"Do you want some sugar?" I ask.

Zach's eyes scan down Harlow's body. "Who doesn't like sugar?"

This fucker. I grab Harlow by the back of the shirt and tug her behind me. I step forward. "There's nothing here for you," I tell him. "And I absolutely want nothing to do with making tomorrow, or any other day, any better for you. That includes coffee."

"Does everyone know what an asshole their favorite coach is?" Zach asks.

"You haven't even begun to see asshole from me."

"Unless we count ten years ago, right?"

I lean in. "Unless you want a repeat of that, you need to go." Then I step back, shut the door, and lock it.

I immediately became aware of Harlow's hand on my back. My bare back.

"You okay?" she asks.

I turn to her. "He just showed up?"

"Yeah. It's kind of ballsy of him to show up at your house, when he knows we are here together alone."

"Do you think he knew I left?" I ask.

"No. I think he was checking up. To catch us together and see what we're like when we're alone."

"So he's suspicious."

"Or he thinks if he keeps showing up, he'll make me think twice about my choice?" she suggests.

"That's plausible too," I agree.

"Well, I'd say catching us half naked can't hurt," she says, letting her gaze travel over my bare chest and down my abdomen.

I feel my body heat, and the air around us suddenly fills with electricity.

I'm even more acutely aware of how sexy she looks wearing only my shirt. I lift my hand and brush her hair back from her face. For just a second, I am tempted to lean in and kiss her. I could say that I did it in case Zach was looking in my front window, but I acknowledge to myself that wouldn't be the full truth. Or maybe any of the truth. I'd be doing it because I just really want to kiss Harlow again.

I drop my hand instead.

But I can't seem to keep my dad's words from dinner out of my head. *Why don't you just actually date?* Instead of making this all fake, why don't we just date? Give it a try? While we're doing this, why not see if this could be something?

She takes a breath and turns toward the sofa before I can do anything else.

"So you found all the spices?"

"Yep, and the popcorn and oil."

She crosses to the couch and sits down, grabbing the

remotes off the coffee table and pointing them at the TV. "And pants?"

"Oops, I forgot."

But looking at her, sitting on my couch, one long bare leg tucked up under her butt, the other dangling over the edge of my couch, knowing she's got panties and nothing else under that shirt—my shirt—I regret nothing.

She rolls her eyes, but smiles, "I'm shocked."

I chuckle. "You know that I don't know how to make this popcorn, right?"

Her eyes widen. "Oh, that's right. I can't let you ruin my popcorn." She bounces up from the couch. "I'm on it."

"Teach me. "

She glances back as I follow her into the kitchen. "You want to learn?"

"Why not?"

She eyes me again, her hot gaze sliding over my torso. "You should probably put a shirt back on."

"Too distracting?"

"The hot oil could be dangerous."

"Especially in your hands."

"I should say that I would never throw hot oil on another human being," she says, taking inventory of the supplies laid out on the countertop. "But I feel like the threat of it could keep you nice and polite for the next few minutes."

I actually love her sass. She's rarely snarky with anyone else, but I think that's what I like the best about it. Besides the fact that she's just funny. I feel like she's more herself with me than most people. Even her family at times. It's like she has to be softer, more composed, patient, and calm with everyone else. But she lets it all loose with me.

"Do you have a deep pot with a lid?" she asks.

I start to move toward the low cupboard where my pots and pans are stored, then think better of it. I lean back against the countertop and point. "Down there."

She bends to get a pot out and I just appreciate the view.

She seems to realize that a moment later. But she stays in the bent over position and swivels to look at me, her hair falling over her shoulders and across her face. She blows a strand up out of her eye and looks at me. "You did that on purpose."

"Stored my pans down there in case you ever came over and took your pants off?"

"Made me bend over to get it."

"You're closer to it."

She's still bent over, clearly not shy or embarrassed by the position she's in or my ogling.

"I guess if I was really your girlfriend, me bending over in front of you would be a regular thing."

That getting-very-familiar heat hits hard. "Oh, for sure," I tell her. My voice is low and a little huskier than I intend.

She straightens slowly. "But if you were really my boyfriend, there would be one difference."

"Do tell," I say as she sets the pot on the stove and reaches for the oil.

"I wouldn't be wearing panties when I bent over in front of you. And I trust I'd be in that position for... a while."

I choke on... air, I guess. I cough and watch her smirk as she adds oil to the pot and turns the stove on.

I really like this side of Harlow. We've bickered, but we've never outright flirted until all of this started.

I won't go so far as to say that I am thankful to Zach Nelson for coming back to town this week, but this is all turning out pretty well.

We keep up the snarky banter, teasing, and yes, flirting, as

MAKE HER MINE   151

she heats the oil, adds the popcorn kernels, and covers the pot with a sheet of aluminum foil.

After all the kernels have popped, and while the kernels are still hot and oily, she adds the mixture of spices, shaking the whole thing so that they are evenly distributed. I notice she goes heavy on the cayenne. Of course she does.

"So are we gonna need beer with this or what?" I ask, watching her dump the popcorn into a big plastic bowl that I stretched up to retrieve from a higher cupboard.

"Beer is great with this," she agrees. "So is soda and hard cider. What do you have?"

I go to the fridge and pull out two of my favorite ciders.

I hold the bottles up and nod. "You're not really a beer drinker so how about this?"

She picks up the bowl. "Depends. Beer isn't my go-to, but it sometimes fits. Sometimes it's just really convenient too."

I follow her out into the living room. "And you tend to just go along with whatever the people you're with are drinking."

She sinks onto the sofa and looks up at me with a frown. "What do you mean?"

"You like to make whoever you're with comfortable and happy. If you're in a place where you can get what you like too, you will. Like at the restaurant. You'll go get your Jack and Coke. But if you're at someone's house, and they're making daiquiris, you'll choke them down. Or if your friends are coming over to your house, and everybody wants margaritas, you'll make that for them and drink with them."

She pops a spicy popcorn kernel into her mouth. "You mean, I'm laid-back and considerate."

I join her on the couch, taking the opposite end. "You are overly concerned with everyone else always feeling good when you're around."

"Overly concerned? How can you critique someone for wanting to make other people feel good?"

"I just don't think you should *always* make other people feel good at the expense of your own pleasure."

"I'm fine," she says rolling her eyes. "My life is great. I have it really good. If once in a while, my friends want to drink margaritas, even if they're not my favorite, I'd rather spend time with them and make fun memories than worry about having the perfect drink."

I hand her one of the ciders. "I understand that. I'm just saying, you deserve to have what you like too. Like tonight. What movie were you going to watch with Ginny and Graham?"

"It's a new romcom."

"But you prefer thrillers."

She narrows her eyes and I suspect she's a little surprised that I know that.

"Of course, *Ginny* loves romcoms," I add. "But the last time you got together I'm guessing you watched a romcom then too. Why can't they watch a thriller with you, especially at your house?"

"I'm fine, Jefferson," Harlow says, but her voice is softer now. "How do you know I like thrillers anyway?" she asks after a brief pause.

I honestly can't answer that. I think I've just noticed it over time. "I'm not sure. But you do, right? I know I've seen a lot of thrillers in your book collection."

She nods. "You are right."

"Why is that? You're such a Susie Sunshine. You always want everything to be happy and good for everyone. I would expect that you would prefer happy movies."

She sighs, then takes a drink of her cider. I'm not sure if

she's going to answer me, but eventually she leans to set the bowl of popcorn on the table and looks at me directly.

"The romcoms and the happy feel-good movies feel a little fake to me. Or I feel..."

She takes a deep breath and blows it out.

"I like books and movies about terrible shit that can happen in real-life because I can turn it off or shut the book." She takes another deep breath. "And I can remind myself they're actors and someone wrote the lines and it's all staged and all of those people like each other and probably go out to lunch and stuff when they're not shooting the movie." She shakes her head. "I know that seems so weird. But it gives me a sense of control and comfort that I don't get in real life with the real drama and real bad guys. I don't have assurances things will turn out. The people I run into are *truly* bad. I can't control when and how things happen. And I can't turn it off when it gets to be too much. I have to stay in there and stay with it until it's over."

I study her. This is not the first time it's occurred to me that I admire and respect what she does for a living. She helps kids. She helps families. She tries to create families and homes and security for people who don't have that. And she is successful. More of her cases turn out well than turn out poorly.

But they don't all turn out well.

I know she's had heartbreak. And even at the time, but certainly in retrospect, I realize that I was even more invested in things turning out well with Alex because of her. I would've wanted Alex to get happy and healthy, no matter what, but the nights when we didn't know how things were going to turn out, my worry and frustration were definitely doubled because I was worried about Harlow too. I knew if things turned out badly with Alex, it would affect Harlow deeply.

Sharing that experience with her made it even better when it turned out well. The way Alex grew and blossomed and accepted the love and support we were giving him, and his foster family gave him, was incredible to see. And watching Harlow do the good work she had done with him was gratifying. I'd been proud of her.

I've never let myself really think about that. I probably figured it didn't matter.

But now, with her sitting on my couch, dressed in my shirt, I have this urge to give her all the popcorn and the movie she wants, that she doesn't give herself when she's trying to make other people happy. And it makes me think about how it felt to partner with her in helping Alex and how happy I was that she was happy on the other side.

Why don't you just actually date?

My dad's words go through my mind again.

I lean over and take the remote off the table and hand it to her. Then I hand her the bowl of popcorn.

"You can watch whatever you want when you're here, and you can pause it or turn it off whenever you need to."

She looks at me and I prepare for a funny or snotty response.

Instead, she says, "Thanks."

Just thanks.

And when she points the remote at the TV and pulls up a movie I've never heard of, I settle into the sofa happily. I haven't sat and watched a movie with someone in a long time. Harlow and I have never sat quietly, just the two of us for two hours.

If nothing else, this will be interesting.

"Do you want a blanket or something?" I ask, eyeing her bare legs that are stretched out on the sofa cushions between us.

She looks over as the beginning credits start to roll. "No, I'm good."

"Pillows? Anything?"

"No, I'm good." She frowns. "Why?"

"You have a ton of pillows and blankets and shit at your house."

She grins and puts a piece of popcorn in her mouth. "You'll be shocked to know those are for everybody else," she tells me. "All of my friends like to be all cozy and cuddled up when we watch movies. I actually hate it. I get too hot and claustrophobic."

I sigh but keep my thoughts on that to myself. Of course, she has her house stuffed full of things for other people. Of course, she puts up with being hot and claustrophobic, so her friends can cuddle up on her tiny little sofa in her tiny little house with pillows and blankets on top of them.

She's all about making other people happy, creating comfort, and heartwarming memories.

But I find myself smiling and feel a little warm spot in my chest as I think about it.

Harlow Hansen is a very nice person.

And I wonder what it would feel like to be on the receiving end of her trying to make me happy.

And I immediately shut down the running list of things I would be very happy to have her do for me. To me.

I'm actually shocked by how quickly that list forms.

She pulls one leg up, her knee bending as she settles more deeply into my sofa cushions, and I catch a flash of bright blue panties.

I like the color blue.

I like bright blue panties.

I like spicy popcorn.

I like sparring with Harlow.

I like sassy, smart-mouthed brunettes who bend over backwards to make other people happy.

I like the idea of being someone who can make that sassy brunette happy in that same way.

"This is nice," she says softly.

I glance over. Her eyes are on the TV, but I heard her. I know she was talking to me. About all of this.

I nod. "It is."

She smiles and lets out a deep, contented sigh.

Fuck.

I might be in really big trouble.

CHAPTER 14

HARLOW

I WAKE SLOWLY, and happily, the next morning the way you do when you know you slept deeply and that you don't have to get up and rush around.

The sun is streaming in through the window, I'm the perfect temperature, the pillow is the perfect softness, the room smells good. Then I roll over, look at the clock, and, right after realizing I slept until eight-thirty—which is unheard of—I realize that is not my clock.

I look down and realize this is not my duvet.

I look at the ceiling. Nope. That's not mine either.

But I know whose it is.

It all comes flooding back.

As does the realization that this isn't the guest room.

I'm not really surprised to find that I slept well at Jefferson's.

I am very surprised to find that I slept well in Jefferson's *bed*, though.

I roll to my back, clutch the duvet—which is really, *really* comfortable—to my chest and think.

I do not remember coming up to bed.

I don't remember the end of the movie.

I lift the duvet and find I'm still in Jefferson's t-shirt and my panties and I do remember putting those on.

But deductive reasoning means that I fell asleep watching the movie and Jefferson carried me up to bed.

To this bed.

His bed.

I did not wake up once in the night, so I have no idea if I slept in here alone. He might have slept in the guest room. I told him I wanted this bed because Graham told me it's the most comfortable.

That doesn't seem like something Jefferson would do though.

Except...I frown. It does.

Strangely.

If someone had asked me a week ago, I would have said no way would Jefferson let me sleep in the most comfortable bed and taken the other, but now...

He's been doing little things like that ever since we started this crazy fake relationship. Things that should make sense since he's playing my boyfriend, but all of this stuff is behind closed doors.

Yes, he's held my hand and had his arm around me and kissed me in public.

But he also fed me Brussels sprouts and nicknamed me Lily in public.

The sweet stuff, the actual *nice* stuff, the stuff that would make me *like* him, has been in private. Letting me eat spicy popcorn. Going to my house to get the spices for that popcorn. Watching the movie I wanted to watch. Giving me a big comfortable shirt when he could have given me a tiny tank or something that would make me truly uncomfortable.

Yes, he ogled my legs in this shirt but...

I liked that too.

Telling me that I deserve to have things I like and want too.

Revealing that he really knows me and telling me that I need someone who can love me as hard as I love other people.

Nope, haven't been able to stop thinking about that.

I put my hands over my face and groan.

Fuck. Fuck, fuck, fuck.

I like Jefferson Riley.

Dammit.

Okay, to be fair I like *some things* about Jefferson Riley. Not everything. For sure.

But he's been easy to be around and fake-date so far.

I might be in really big trouble.

"It's been one fucking day," I remind myself. Out loud.

But he watched the movie you wanted to last night, on purpose. He did it because he knows you don't usually get to watch what you want to.

"It's been *One*. Fucking. Day," I say out loud again, trying to shut the quiet inner voice up.

But it doesn't help.

I haven't gotten to sit and watch a movie I wanted to with someone else in a long time. I do watch thrillers, but I typically have to do it alone. Which is definitely creepy.

Jefferson seemed to really enjoy the popcorn too.

His sofa is really comfortable.

And when Sloane texted me about thirty minutes into the movie to ask if I wanted to go down to the Come Again to hang out with a bunch of them, I said no.

I was really happy on Jefferson's couch.

In Jefferson's shirt.

With Jefferson.

Fuuuuuck.

I slowly turn my head to look at the pillow next to me.

There's an indentation.

My gaze runs down that entire side of the bed. The sheet is wrinkled, the duvet thrown back.

I sit up.

He slept in here.

In this bed.

With me.

And instead of being annoyed or even angry that he'd dare, I feel disappointed that I slept through that.

What does he wear to bed? Did we cuddle? Did we touch at all? Was his warmth and presence why I slept so well? How did he sleep? Oh God, how did I look this morning when he woke up?

I throw the covers back and swing my legs over the edge of the mattress.

Okay, I need to get myself together. I should ask him those questions. I should ask why he carried me to bed instead of waking me up. Or leaving me on the couch. Does that mean something?

Or maybe...

I narrow my eyes.

Wait a damned minute. I know what this is.

This is Jefferson and me.

That means this is a game of chicken.

He wants to see how I react. If I'll freak out. He'll act unaffected by the whole thing. It's fake, right? Why is it a big deal? Nothing happened. So I slept next to him half-naked. So what? And if I react, then that must mean I feel something.

So I can't react. I can't ask questions. I can't make a big deal out of it.

We watched a movie and slept next to one another last night. The way I've done with Graham a million times.

Is Jefferson trying to tell me that if we did try to date, he wouldn't even be tempted to touch me if I was sleeping, half-naked next to him?

Oh, okay, future ex-fake-boyfriend, I see what you're doing. I can play this game.

And it's my turn, I guess.

I put my dress from last night back on and make my way to the kitchen. I find a note by the single-serve coffee pot on the counter.

Had a morning work-out with some of the players, then have some festival stuff to help with. -J

He's set a little bottle of cinnamon on the note with an empty mug and a dark roast coffee pod.

I frown. That's nice.

So he doesn't want to cuddle me at night, but he'll make sure I have my morning coffee just the way I like it?

I start for the front door, intending to ignore all of that, but after I slip my shoes on, I get real.

It's already two hours past my usual first cup and I'm going to have to walk home in heels. I return to the kitchen, make the cup, get annoyed that the dark roast is really pretty good, peek in the little drawer of pods to find that he has more of them, then take the cup with me as I head out the door.

I stop halfway down the walk. I *could* walk home. But it's daylight, I'm in the dress and heels from last night so this definitely looks like a walk of shame, I didn't get to have sex last night to warrant this walk of shame and...I don't want to walk. So I borrow Jefferson's truck that's still in the drive.

I assume he jogged up to the high school for the work-out, but he'll probably need his truck for whatever festival stuff he's doing later, which means it will be inconvenient that I've got his truck.

Perfect.

When I get home, I shower, braid my wet hair, put on shorts, a tee, and tennis shoes, and then start loading Jefferson's truck with essentials.

I get a text about an hour and a half after leaving Jefferson's house.

Jefferson: *Do you have my truck?*

Me: *I do.*

Jefferson: *Am I getting it back?*

Me: *Just needed it for a couple of errands. Is that okay, pookie?* <heart eyes emoji>

Jefferson: *Did you wreck it? I feel like 'pookie' is code for you wrecked it.*

I laugh despite myself. *It's in perfect shape. But you need a nickname from your loving girlfriend.*

Jefferson: *I'm not sure I'm a nickname guy.*

I just smile at that. He's probably right. *Then you should have picked another girlfriend.*

He doesn't respond for a minute, so I get in the truck and point it toward my next and final errand.

My phone dings again.

Jefferson: *Do you need help with your errands?*

I hesitate. He's offering to help. And that's not just a fake-boyfriend thing. Jefferson is actually a nice guy and I think he'd offer no matter what. I think being his girlfriend would be a pretty easy gig. If you could get past the know-it-all-ness.

I'm getting a real taste of what being his actual girlfriend would be like and it's making me feel things I shouldn't.

Me: *I'm good. When will you be home?*

Jefferson: *About an hour. Miss me already?*

I smile. Not exactly but I am eager to see his reaction.

Me: *Can't believe you ate all the French toast before I woke up.*

I'll bet he actually makes really great French toast. He's annoying like that.

Jefferson: *Can't believe you sleep without any blankets on at all.*

I pause and read that twice. I really don't like blankets. In fact, it takes me until well into December in Nebraska to even wear a coat. I run hot and I prefer as few layers as possible at all times. But that comment, while seemingly harmless, could mean a number of things considering how I was dressed last night and the fact I was wondering where he spent the night. Did he get an eyeful?

Be honest, he adds before I can respond, *do you sleep in the nude at home?*

I do actually.

Me: *Wouldn't you like to know?*

Jefferson: *I would. A lot. And next time you try to take your shirt off in bed, I'm not going to stop you.*

I swallow hard. It's not difficult for me to believe that I tried to strip down to nothing even if I was asleep.

I swallow hard and contemplate my next question.

I shouldn't flirt. I shouldn't talk about last night. I shouldn't talk about nakedness with Jefferson.

But I send it even though I know it's dangerous.

Me: *Why did you stop me last night?*

Jefferson: *When you wake up naked next to me, I want you to remember everything.*

I read that three times.

And my body gets hotter with each read.

He uses the word 'when'. Not 'if'. It doesn't sound hypothetical.

I also realize that I'm thinking about where we're each going to sleep tonight.

Dammit.

Such a gentleman, I finally text back.

Jefferson: *Told you I wasn't giving up the good mattress. But I do like when you beg.*

My cheeks get hot. I begged him? For what exactly? To sleep with him? Oh, God. How had *that* sounded exactly? I wrack my brain but cannot remember anything after about an hour of the movie. Which is crazy. I never sleep that hard. I had two Jack and Cokes at dinner. And that hard cider at his place with the popcorn. But that shouldn't have knocked me out like that. Which means I must have felt completely safe with Jefferson.

That realization is not shocking.

But now I'm wondering about the begging. I really want to remember that.

He could be messing with me. I do not want to fall into the trap of asking about it. I need to be nonchalant. I need to act as if he cannot get under my skin.

But he can. And even just acknowledging that to myself is problematic.

Me: *Noted.*

I stick with that as my response, hoping that niggles at him a little. If I don't react then maybe he'll wonder about why I'm not reacting.

Jefferson: *Wanna go to the festival this afternoon? I have to do some stuff, but I'll buy you funnel cakes.*

One of the few sweets I really like.

Plus, the festival starts today. Of course I want to go.

And that will keep us from hanging out alone. Because if I was begging to be in his bed last night when I was half-asleep... or fully asleep apparently...God only knows what I might start begging him for when I'm conscious and we're alone and he's being...how he's been.

Me: *Yes. Duh.*

We can play the part of boyfriend-girlfriend but not be *alone*, and we won't have to worry about things like how comfortable we are together, and I won't have to dwell on the fact that he'd probably actually be a pretty great boyfriend if I didn't blame him for things like all of my best friends and one of my siblings leaving me.

Jefferson: *Wear that yellow dress.*

Me: *You're picking out my clothes now? Controlling much?*

Jefferson: *If you were my girlfriend, I would really like you in that dress. And you'd really like me liking you in that sundress.*

He has to stop saying—texting—stuff like that. This feels like flirting. For real.

But I can't help but think of other things that would happen if I was his girlfriend for real.

Like, if I was his girlfriend, I would wear my hair down loose and curled slightly, I'd wear my citrus-coconut body spray, and lotion.

Jefferson likes coconut.

CHAPTER 15

JEFFERSON

I GET HOME MORE eager to see Harlow than I should.

She didn't ask more about the begging that happened last night even after I teased her about it.

That's interesting. Does she remember it? Maybe. But if not, I will happily tell her *all* about it.

She was asleep, and I think actually dreaming when she asked me to lie down with her. But far be it from me to deny a beautiful woman with her mouth pressed against my neck, begging me to stay in bed with her.

Yes, we slept together.

I could tell her that we didn't touch all night, but that would be a lie.

Harlow might not be into blankets and pajamas, and I wouldn't exactly call her a cuddler, but I couldn't sleep in even a king-sized bed, *trying* to keep space between us, and not know she was there.

If she didn't have a hand on my arm or chest, she had a foot against my leg or wedged between mine. And there were about three hours where her sweet ass was nestled up against my hip.

She just seemed to want to have some part of her body against some part of mine at all times.

And she definitely doesn't like blankets.

I tried to cover her up, because she wasn't wearing much and I didn't want her to be cold, but also for my own sanity. Without a blanket, there was a lot of smooth, bare skin and sweet curves on display in my bed. But she almost immediately threw any coverings off.

And while the shirt covered a lot when she was upright, it did a pretty poor job of covering her when she was lying down and moving around on the sheets.

I not only know the color of the panties she was wearing, but I now know the exact shape of her thighs, hips, and ass, how smooth her stomach is, and that she has a tattoo on her left rib cage. It's a quote, done in a pretty script. It says, *be a rainbow in someone's cloud.*

I've already looked it up. It's a Maya Angelou quote.

I'm not surprised by the quote at all. Or that it's placed, essentially, under her heart.

I'm surprised by how fucking hot it makes me, though.

I didn't even have to stare and ogle her. There was just no escaping it.

Especially when she *did* strip her shirt off sometime in the night.

I put it back on her, but...how could I avoid taking a mental snapshot of a nearly naked Harlow Hansen in my bed? I'm no fucking saint.

She's gorgeous. Her body is toned and curved in all the right places. I would very happily spend hours running my hands, lips, and tongue all over every inch.

Not, of course, when she's asleep and unaware.

But were she ever fully aware and begging for it? It would take one *please* and I would be the happiest man on the planet.

The second I step through my front door I see what she was up to this afternoon.

There is now a plethora of colorful throw pillows covering my couch and chairs.

There are also house plants on every obvious surface. The coffee table is no longer the space solely for coasters and remote controls. Now there are magazines and books stacked haphazardly across the top. There's even a blanket draped over the back of the couch. Which makes me grin and roll my eyes. Who the fuck will be using that? She didn't bring that over for herself.

The air is scented with a light lemony vanilla scent, and I notice a candle burning on a new table. She brought an entire table over. It's a long, narrow piece that sits right behind the couch. Where there are more books and another plant.

"Harlow!" I call.

She pops her head around the corner from the kitchen.

"Oh, good, you're home. I have all the ingredients prepped."

"Ingredients?" I ask, kicking my shoes off by the door. "You're cooking for me?"

She laughs. "Don't be ridiculous. You're cooking for me. Well, us, I guess."

I should've known. I wait for a moment, but she says nothing about the new décor in the living room. She disappears back into the kitchen.

Still, she has clearly moved into my house.

Damn, that means she has pants here now.

"What am I making?" I call, refusing to say anything about the pillows and candles.

I don't hate them. They're clearly not to my taste, but they're very Harlow. And it's interesting how they blend into what I've already got going on. My furniture is mostly dark gray, which goes with the dark hardwood floors and the colorful rug my mother insisted had to be put down if my interior decorating was going to be so dull.

I have the basics. That's all I need. I am a single guy, and I simply need things to sit on, put things on, sleep on, etc.

Taking in the room as a whole, with all the homey touches, I realize that I was maybe, subconsciously, keeping the slate clean for when someone else was around to add to it.

I've never assumed that I would stay single forever. Coupling up makes sense to me. I've been raised around couples. Happy couples who made families and homes. That feels normal to me. Just because it hasn't happened for me yet, doesn't mean that I've written off the possibility.

"Strawberry Jalapeño Chicken," she calls back.

I chuckle and start for the kitchen. "Did it occur to you that I might not know how to make that?"

"You caught on quickly with the spicy popcorn, so I figured you'd love to learn to make something new."

She's not wrong. I'm always up for trying something new. And how hard can it be?

"Do you like strawberry jalapeño chicken?" I ask.

"I've never had it, but I read the recipe and I think I will."

"Then I guess I would want to learn." I pause a beat then add, "If you were really my girlfriend."

I don't know when this little game shifted. But I like it. I am able to show her what it would be like for us to date without either of us having to commit to anything.

It's risk free. Even while I cannot forget my dad's words about us dating for real, this feels like we have a safety net. Anytime it starts to feel too real, we can simply fall back on the idea that while these might be real gestures, real thoughts, real likes and wants, we're just going through the motions.

Or at least that's what we're telling each other. And ourselves.

I study the ingredients that are set out on the countertop and then Harlow hands me her phone, with the recipe displayed.

I've just started to scroll when a streak of gray flashes past in my peripheral vision.

I frown and turn toward it.

Big green eyes blink back at me from my kitchen table.

I immediately look at Harlow.

"Why is there a cat on my kitchen table?"

She smiles and moves toward the animal. "We're fostering them."

"We're what? *Them?*" I ask the questions in quick succession as they occur to me.

"There are three. But the other two are a little skittish. One is under our bed and the other is *on* the bed but hisses when I go in there."

"Three? Fostering? *Our* bed?" Again, the questions tumble out in the order they flip through my mind.

"Well, I'm not going to the guest room now that I've slept so well in your bed. And I assume you're not." She shrugs and picks the cat up, nuzzling her face into its fur. "And yes, three. They lived together so we can't break them up. But we're just keeping them until Delaney can find homes for them. But it might take a while since Delaney and Tucker have the kids there and they've got a lot going on. These are Delores Landers' cats."

The cat blinks at me as I process the information.

Delaney and Tucker were taking care of these cats since Delores passed away about four days ago. But they are also helping one of their sons with his two kids, so finding homes for the cats is low on their list of priorities.

Got it. That all makes sense.

Of course, they need to focus on Jack and his kids. Jack was widowed about six months ago. He's moved back to Sapphire Falls to regroup and because he needed help with his two heartbroken children. Delaney and Tucker took him and his three brothers in when their parents—Delaney's sister and her husband—died when Jack was only six. It's a fucking tragedy that Delaney, Tucker, and Jack are all now doing this again. But of course this is where Jack and his kids belong.

Obviously, I'll help with Delores's cats. I would have even if there weren't extra kids at the Bennett farm.

But...

I study Harlow, who is now softly cooing to the cat in her arms.

I think about the pillows, candles, and books in my living room. I think about Harlow saying she's going to be sleeping in my bed with me from now on.

I like that part *a lot.* I also realize there is a very good chance that my bed now has new sheets and pillows. I'm ninety percent sure my bathroom has new towels and shower gel and lotion that now smells like Harlow. I am also cooking something for her I've never done before. And I'm now fostering three cats.

And I understand completely what's going on.

She's trying to annoy me.

That's...funny. And interesting.

Because she's failing miserably.

"I think you should know that I really like the way that candle smells."

Harlow looks at me. This was clearly not what she was expecting me to say.

"You do?"

"I do. And the pillows look nice."

She frowns. "You always say how cluttered my house looks."

I step closer to her and run my hand over the cat's head. It's purring. I'd be fucking purring if I was nestled against Harlow's breasts too.

"I do say that," I agree. "Because I'm kind of an ass sometimes. At least when it comes to you. The truth is your house is very cozy. Very comfortable. Very...*you.*"

Her frown deepens.

I grin. "You're disappointed that I'm not annoyed."

"Are you not annoyed just to annoy me?"

I chuckle. "No. I'm actually not annoyed."

She opens her mouth to respond, but then tips her head, and closes it.

"You don't believe me?" I ask.

She shakes her head. "No. I'm just realizing..."

"What?"

"I was thinking that if Zach ever comes over again, there should be signs that I'm here a lot. And throw pillows and candles would be signs of that." She shakes her head again. "But he would never know if I added lotion and towels to your upstairs bathroom."

I *knew* she'd added lotion and towels.

"Did you add lotion and towels to my upstairs bathroom just to annoy me?"

"I think in part, yes. But also...just to be more comfortable while I'm here."

"I want you to be comfortable while you're here, Harlow," I say.

She swallows and looks down at the cat in her arms. "And it just hit me...if I was your girlfriend..." She trails off, then looks up at me again. "This is something I've always wanted to do, but I can't at my house, because some of my friends are allergic.

I can't have cats and cat hair on my stuff. But if I had a boyfriend, I could foster cats at his house. Because I would only seriously date a guy who would let me do that." She takes a deep breath. "And you would be great about it. You're kind and patient. And you like cats. When you were a kid, you were the one that rescued Pixie. I'm just remembering that."

Pixie was a stray I had found and taken home, prepared to negotiate and battle with my parents over letting me keep her. But it hadn't been a battle. They'd been fine. Pixie had lived with us for twelve years. The rest of her life.

"You've always known that I like cats."

"Yeah. I did think about how it might annoy you a little to move all of this stuff in without asking but...I was actually just more excited about bringing the cats here. Tucker and Delaney love to have extra hands and homes whenever they can and I've wished I could help out before."

I nod. I'm very aware of Tucker and Delaney's animal fostering.

There's a strange warmth in my chest as I realize that Harlow and I have always had some antagonism between us, that we've definitely butted heads, but it's always been over important issues that really matter to both of us. It's never been trivial. And it's always made me like her because I like that she's passionate.

And there are a lot of ways that we would fit together really well.

I take the cat from her hands. "We can definitely foster cats here. Even after these guys find a home, there's no reason we can't keep doing this here."

I look into the cat's eyes instead of staring at the beautiful woman who's getting to me. Very quickly.

"Thanks," Harlow says softly.

"Of course."

Okay, so something going on between us is going to keep happening.

I wonder if other things are going to keep happening between us.

And I like that idea way more than I should.

CHAPTER 16

HARLOW

JEFFERSON'S strawberry jalapeño chicken is amazing.

Because of course it is. The guy really does seem to be good at everything he does.

I mean, I've never had that chicken before, but it's now one of my favorite dishes. I also enjoyed the prep and cooking stages. I'd perched on one of the kitchen stools, sipping iced tea and watching him cook as we chatted.

I didn't know a guy who can cook would be so sexy.

But it is.

And I'm telling myself it's *all* men who cook and not just Jefferson.

That should annoy me. Two days ago, it would have. Now it just makes me smile.

I can have his strawberry jalapeño chicken whenever I want.

Then I frown.

I can have it whenever I want *for the rest of this week.*

I sigh.

How did I suddenly just forget this is not only fake but it's also got a timeline? A short one at that?

"You *have to* tell us everything!"

I'm accosted by Mia, Ginny, Margot, and Sasha the second I set foot on the grass of the town square. They've clearly been lying in wait.

"What are you talking about?" I ask as they surround me and literally start herding me across the square.

Margot hands me a frozen lemonade, and Sasha presses a corndog into my other hand.

I hand the corndog back. "Thanks, but I already ate lunch."

"What?" Mia asks. "You did? Even knowing you were coming down here to festival food?"

Yes, that does sound suspicious. I love *all* festival food. Put something on a stick and deep fry it and I'll eat it.

Except Brussels sprouts.

"Uh." I eye the corndog. Could I fit it into my stomach? But my stomach immediately rejects the idea. "We had lunch before Jefferson came down here to…"

I trail off, wincing as I realize what I just said and take in the looks on my friends' faces.

That 'we' came out really easy.

"Uh huh," Margot says with a smile. "You and Jefferson had lunch together. At his house? Because you weren't at *your* house."

"And I didn't see you at the diner," Sasha adds.

"None of us have seen you at all since last night," Ginny says, grinning.

I frown. "It's not like I haven't left his house at all. I was at my house this morning. And I was out at Delaney and Tucker's."

"We heard. You now have three cats. I assume those are at Jefferson's, too?" Ginny asks. "Because Sloan is allergic."

"Sasha is too."

Sasha shrugs. "A little."

"And you hate having dog hair on your clothes," I say to Margot. "I assume the same would apply to cat hair."

She looks at me with clear amusement. "And now you have a boyfriend who will let you have cats. That's *really* sweet."

"He's my *fake* boyfriend," I say.

"But the cats are real," Margot says.

"And he's the guy you were *really* kissing the hell out of in the parking lot last night," Sasha says.

I look at her. "What? How do you know that?" She wasn't there.

"Ginny's video."

I turn wide eyes on Ginny. "Ginny's *what?*"

Ginny swipes over her phone screen, then holds it out.

I lean in, watching the video play of me and Jefferson next to his truck. Kissing.

It's...very hot.

I look up at her. "You *recorded* us?"

She grins. "Of course. Because I'm a very good friend."

"How is that being a very good friend to me?" I demand. "That was a private moment." But even as I say it, I hear a voice in my head telling me not to be ridiculous. The whole thing was *to be seen* by other people. Zach in particular.

Ginny laughs. "I'm a very good friend to Mia, Margot, Sasha, Sloan, Graham—"

"Okay," I cut her off, jabbing my finger at her phone screen to stop the video that started over.

I narrow my eyes. "It's not weird for you to watch me and your brother kissing?"

She gives me a genuine smile. "No. I love you both so much. Why wouldn't I want you to love each other?"

I feel a swirl of...something...ripple through my belly. Love? *Love?*

"We are *faking* this," I say on a sharp whisper.

"Uh huh," Ginny says.

"Yeah, that kiss was *very* real," Sasha says.

"The kiss was..." I blow out a breath, then relent. "Good."

"Good?" Margot asks.

"Okay, *really* good. And we're getting along better now. And yes, he made me lunch. And yes, we're fostering three cats. But, at most, this is becoming a we-don't-hate-each-other-every-second *friendship*. Don't be getting all weird about this," I tell them.

Mia is the one to finally smile, nod, and link her arm with mine. "Okay. Whatever you say."

"Are you being sarcastic?" I ask.

She shakes her head and shares glances with the other girls. "You and Jefferson are the most confident, self-aware people any of us know. If you say you're just friends, we believe you."

Ginny, Margot, and Sasha all nod.

We start off across the square again.

Jefferson is already here somewhere. Since he had to come down and help with some things early, I walked over by myself to meet the girls. He did tell me to come find him when I got here though. And, for just a couple of charged moments, I thought he was going to kiss me goodbye.

And then for a couple more seconds I was disappointed when he didn't.

But *then*, and now, I've settled on being glad he didn't. Kissing in public for show is one thing. Kissing in private is something else entirely.

We stop at a few tables to check out crafts, to sniff hand-made candles and soaps, and to sample baked goods. My mom owns a bakery, so I'm never without amazing carbs, but some of the ladies in town *really* know how to make sourdough bread, and banana bread, or strawberry rhubarb pie, and my mom forgives us for partaking from others this time of year.

Eventually we arrive at the dunk tank.

"Hey, ladies." Graham comes strolling over with a grin. He's holding a caramel apple.

"Hey, have you seen Jefferson?" Ginny asks her brother.

I hear the clang of the target at the tank being hit, the splash of someone hitting the water, and the cheer of the crowd.

"Yeah." Graham's gaze lands on me. "Your boy has single-handedly gotten them halfway to their goal just during his hour."

My boy.

Even Graham is in on this.

I just roll my eyes.

Of course, Jefferson is over there throwing balls. The dunk tank is raising money for some new equipment in the weight room that the high school sports teams use but that is also open to the public after hours.

There's plenty of money in our town. Jefferson, Graham, and Ginny's family for instance. Their father's company brings in hundreds of millions. Of course, Mason and his partner, Lauren Davis-Bennett, also spend a *lot* on research and development as well as funding a multitude of charitable projects around the world.

The Spencers, Joe and Levi, are also both worth millions. And any of them would give money to Sapphire Falls for literally anything. But the community feels strongly about raising money for projects and letting everyone contribute as much as they can.

And it works. Sometimes the more affluent members of our community chip in if things fall short of the final goal, but the town shows up for needs over and over again.

It makes me feel warm and fuzzy inside every time.

I don't even correct Graham on calling Jefferson 'my boy'. I shrug. "Well, it's no shock he's doing well. He's got a pretty great arm."

Graham laughs. "He's not dunking people. He's the one *getting* dunked."

My eyes widen. "What?"

Graham nods. "The first twenty people in line were his players. And they all dropped some pretty good money. Especially since he was trash-talking them from his perch. Even after he went under the first few times."

I laugh. That all tracks.

"But then he took his shirt off and the line got a little more... estrogen filled."

I take that in and work *very* hard on not reacting.

Because why would I react?

Just because I can easily flash back to last night in his living room when he came into the room without a shirt on when Zach was at the door?

Just because I can still feel the heat and firmness of his body against mine from our kiss in the parking lot?

So what? Like I said before, Jefferson Riley is good looking. It's simply an objective fact. It's not like I think I'm the only one to notice.

"Oh really?" Mia asks. "What kind of estrogen?" She slides me a glance.

I'm totally nonchalant. Totally cool. Not at all resisting the urge to jog over to the dunk tank.

I don't need to catch a glimpse of Jefferson without his shirt on.

Dripping wet.

Muscles rippling as he hoists himself out of the water.

Grinning, because of course he's grinning and having a blast.

I also don't need to stake a claim and I'm *very* annoyed that's also an urge I feel.

"It started out with some of the female athletes," Graham says. "And some of them have really good arms too. But then a couple of older women petitioned Hailey to move the line they had to throw from closer to the target. And she obliged." Graham laughs. "He's been going under almost constantly."

"Who? Like Susan and Linda?" I name two ladies who are probably in their late seventies.

"No. Like Allison and Lu."

That definitely makes me frown harder. Allison is a single mom who graduated in Jefferson's class and LuAnn is a year older than me. "Those are 'older women'?" I ask Graham.

"Older than the teenagers," he says lifting a shoulder.

"And that's who's dunking Jefferson now?" I ask.

"Among others."

I start forward. And I know how this looks. But...

Fine, I'm feeling a little possessive or something. But I don't like the idea that those women, and any others, are flirting with and ogling *my* boyfriend. They don't know it's fake and they need to back the fuck off.

Haven't they seen the video of us kissing in the parking lot?

I get through the crowd just as someone hits the target again. Jefferson plunges into the water and everyone cheers.

It's Allison. She high-fives Lu.

I roll my eyes.

"How much time does he have left?" I ask Graham.

"Only about five minutes."

As I come up behind Allison and Lu, Jefferson does the thing. The thing where the hot, muscular guy braces his hands and hoists himself up, water cascading over all of the hard planes of his body.

I freeze, my attention fully on Jefferson.

He stands up on the platform, his long, lean body now glistening in the sun as he lifts his arms and pushes his hair back, then shakes out his arms, causing water to spray in every direction. He's grinning the entire time.

I'm jerked out of my daze when Allison says, "I might have to sell my car, but I'm staying here until they kick me out."

The jab of jealousy or possessiveness—or stupidity—is sharp. I lean forward and say, "You should see him without the shorts on."

They both whirl around.

Lu at least looks embarrassed about talking about my boyfriend. Allison doesn't.

Her eyes go back to Jefferson. "I have a very good imagination."

I follow her gaze and agree that the way the athletic shorts he's wearing, soaked wet and clinging to every inch of him, do show off his assets nicely.

But no matter how well Allison and I have gotten along in the past, she doesn't get to talk this way about Jefferson to me. "Trust me. You can't *possibly* fully imagine"

Hailey Connor Bennett spots me just then. Hailey is running the dunk tank, and she raises her hand and waves. "Harlow. Step right up!"

Jefferson's gaze immediately jerks to mine and our eyes lock. He gives me a slow grin.

I shake my head. "I'm not in line." I'm terrible at these kinds of games and I definitely won't be able to hit the target with everyone watching.

Hailey laughs. "This is your last chance. He's almost done. Come on."

I dig for some bravado. "Why would I pay for something I can see anytime I want?"

There are low whistles and *ooohs* from the crowd.

Hailey laughs again. "Okay, fine. I suppose you want to save your money for the kissing booth, huh? But you can't monopolize him the whole time."

My eyes go back to Jefferson's. "Kissing booth?"

He grins as he settles himself on the perch again. "You know me, Lily, always happy to help out around here."

I don't even need to look in the direction of Lu and Allison to know that they are already heading toward the kissing booth to find out when Jefferson's shift starts and to be first in line.

I should not care. The kissing booth is harmless after all. It's an age-old tradition. It's fun and silly and raises money for causes. I don't know what the cause is this year, but it doesn't matter. Jefferson is a regular. He brings in a lot of money. And obviously he signed up for this before he and I were involved in this crazy plan.

But despite all of that, I don't really love the idea of him at the kissing booth, puckering up for anyone and everyone who comes along. Or really *anyone* else at all.

Dammit.

Well, I can convincingly play the jealous girlfriend I guess.

I dig in my pocket and hand my money to Ty Bennett, Hailey's husband. "On second thought," I say. "I think I will take a shot."

I hear Jefferson's chuckle as I walk to the line from which I have to throw the three balls. I glare at him, focus on the target, imagine Allison kissing him, and throw the first ball as hard as I can.

It hits the target dead center, and Jefferson goes splashing down into the water again.

He comes up laughing, and his eyes find mine immediately.

His gaze stays locked on me as he pulls himself up out of the water, and while he again stands, stretches, and pushes his hair back.

"I think that rounds out my shift," he says to Hailey.

She nods, grinning broadly. "It does. I don't wanna make you late for the kissing booth."

Jefferson climbs out of the tank and comes down the stairs. He heads straight for me.

I actually find myself glancing around, contemplating an escape route.

He comes to stand directly in front of me. "Nice shot."

"I know."

"I need to change."

I just nod.

He wraps a cold, wet hand around my upper arm. "Come with me."

I give in immediately. Can't have the town see us bickering. I fall into step beside him as he starts for the 'changing room' set up off to the side for this very purpose. It's essentially a tent made up of sheets draped from poles and clotheslines.

I don't even hesitate when he ducks inside. I follow him in. He's able to stand up inside and it's got four sides, but I know people can hear our conversation outside so when he lifts an eyebrow, I lower my voice to a whisper.

"I kind of made a big deal about having seen you without your shorts," I tell him. "So I can't really act like it's weird for me to come inside while you change, right?"

He grins. "You made a big deal about seeing me naked?"

"Shut up."

He grabs a towel and starts drying off, then reaches for a T-shirt, dry shorts, and boxers from a duffel.

I turn around, and he chuckles.

"So you can't do the kissing booth," I say, working hard not to envision what he's uncovering at the moment.

"I signed up before we were doing this thing."

"I figured. And I know you always bring a lot of money. But come on, it will look weird for a guy who's taken to be at the kissing booth."

"My shift literally starts in fifteen minutes. I can't bail. They do need the money."

I think about that. "Well, we'll just donate the money. Me making a big deal out of you not doing the booth will also look good for us, right?"

"Okay. But do you think you can afford to donate the money to cover what I'll bring in?"

I roll my eyes even if he can't see them. "How much do you think you're worth? Prices are a dollar for a hug, two for a kiss, and three for 'not dating their daughters'."

I smile as I think about the sign that has been on the front of the kissing booth for as long as I can remember.

The Bennett boys, including Tucker, who I got the foster cats from, and Ty, who I just paid for the balls to dunk Jefferson, used to be popular at the kissing booth from what I hear. But I can't imagine either of their wives letting that continue after they were taken.

"Well if it's two bucks a kiss, I can make thousands in the course of an hour," Jefferson says. There's a pause that he adds, "You can turn around now."

He's just pulling his shirt down over his abs, and I wish for a second that I had turned a little faster.

"Thousands?" I scoff. "I know these women are not getting a simple peck on the lips and running. No way can you get through five hundred women in an hour."

He steps closer. "How long do you think a kiss takes?"

I catch my breath in spite of myself. I'm staring at him,

replaying our kiss from outside the restaurant. "I've never timed one," I say, hating how breathless I sound.

"Start your watch," he says, reaching up to the back of my head and pulling me in.

I could lie and say that it happened quickly, but I realized what he was going to do with plenty of time to stop it if I wanted to.

I do not want to.

The kiss is as good as everything else he does. Maybe better. If the guy kissed me like this every day, he wouldn't have to cook for me. Other people can cook for me. It seems that Jefferson is the only person who can kiss me like this.

I feel myself melting into him, leaning into his body, opening my mouth for his insistent tongue, loving the way he uses the hand on my head to tip it back so he can kiss me more deeply.

When he finally lifts his head and looks down at me, I can see a heat and a slightly dazed look in his eyes as well.

"I could kiss you just like that for an entire hour," he says, his voice husky.

"But then you'd only make two dollars."

He gives me a soft smile. "I can't imagine kissing anybody else after that. How about we go over and just write a check?"

The kiss, the way he's looking at me, the memory of how he looked coming up out of the water, the fact there are three foster cats back at his house, all combine at once and I feel my chest tighten.

Uh oh.

I *more* than like Jefferson Riley.

And I was completely right about private kisses being a lot more dangerous than public ones.

CHAPTER 17

JEFFERSON

I DON'T KNOW what exactly happened, but something has changed with Harlow. But as a guy who's had a lot of things come along that feel like just good timing and good luck, I'm comfortable simply enjoying this moment.

We walk toward the kissing booth, holding hands. Lots of people notice, and we get a lot of smiles. No one seems shocked, and many of the smiles seem knowing.

I don't point that out, figuring Harlow would hate that. But I like it.

How can I convince her to keep this up past the end of the week?

"I was just coming to find you two."

All the happy warm feelings evaporate as Zach strolls up to us.

Fuck, I really hate this guy.

"Why would you do that?" Harlow asks, pressing against my side.

Okay, maybe a few warm happy feelings remain.

"I was just going to offer to keep you company while

Jefferson kisses the entire single female population of the county."

I open my mouth to respond, but Harlow beats me to it.

"That's not going to happen," she informs him. "They messed up the scheduling. There is no way I am letting Jefferson kiss anyone else."

Zach gives her a dubious look. "They messed up the schedule?"

"We told you, we haven't been public for very long. They've had Jefferson on the schedule routinely for years. They just didn't get around to taking him off after we let everyone know we were together."

"So you're going to rob some charity of a bigger donation?" Zach makes a tsk-ing noise. "That's so unlike you, Harlow."

"Actually, we're on our way over to donate right now. Believe me, I'm willing to pay a hefty price to keep this guy all to myself."

She hugs my arm and I enjoy the press of her breast against my bicep.

I like this possessive side of Harlow. I hate that it's fake, and I recognize the fact that wanting it to be real is problematic, but if Harlow ever felt possessive or protective of me, I would be immediately addicted. I have witnessed her feeling both of those things for other people. I have also been the target of her ire when she's felt I was the one threatening those people.

"Flat-out donation, excellent idea," Zach says. "I'll come with you."

"Why the fuck would we want you to come with us?" I ask him.

He looks around. "Probably because the Golden Boy Jefferson wouldn't want to cause a scene."

"I thought *you* were the Golden Boy," Harlow says. "Oh, that's right. You left. You barely come back to even visit.

Whereas Jefferson came back to be a teacher and coach here. To contribute to the community. To support the people he loves and give back to the town that was so important to him growing up. He's here in his hometown with his family and friends. And you are off doing what exactly again?"

"Oh, nothing important," Zach says we all start walking across the square like a happy little threesome. "Just healing people. Making their lives better."

"Strangers. Far away from here. In a city where you can make more money. Because that's more important than taking care of the people here."

I know that Harlow hates Zach. And I'm glad about that. But listening to her comparing the two of us and declaring that I've done something better, at least in her eyes, reminds me of all of the conversations she and I have had about people leaving Sapphire Falls and not coming home.

Is she finally convinced that I want to be here? That returning to Sapphire Falls was a *choice* I made and that I'm happy about it? Does she really understand that I did it because I love this town? And does she actually admire that?

We arrive at the kissing booth, and I'm greeted with several grins.

"There he is," Travis Bennett says. "The man we've all been waiting for."

I grin and shake my head. "Change of plans."

"Sorry, Travis," Harlow says. "His kisses are all mine. These lips are off-limits to everyone else."

Travis laughs. "Oh, come on, Harlow, what are we gonna do over here for an hour?"

She laughs. "Well, we're willing to make a three-hundred-dollar donation to cover what Jefferson would typically bring in. And then Zach's going to fill in for him." She looks at Zach.

"I know he can't raise three hundred, but every little bit helps, right?"

Zach bristles. "You don't think I can bring three hundred dollars?"

She shakes her head. "I really don't. But hey, step right up and prove me wrong."

I smirk. Not only is she going to get Zach off our asses for the next hour, but now she's challenged him publicly. He'll either double the donation which benefits the cause, or he'll be embarrassed when he falls short. Either is fine with me.

"What do you say?" Travis asks Zach. "People are going to be a little disappointed that it's not Jefferson but..."

I like Travis Bennett. And he's a smart guy. He said exactly the right thing to get Zach to say, "Yeah, of course I'll do it. Anything for the hometown." He looks over at me. "No worries at all."

And that's where we leave him as Harlow and I stroll off across the square to enjoy the festival.

And we really do. For the rest of the afternoon we play games, we snack, we go on rides, and we spend a lot of time talking to friends and family, some who we see every day and some who are back in town for the first time in a long time.

I haven't had this much fun in longer than I can remember.

Watching Harlow with the town is not something new for me. I've seen her interact with this community a million times. But doing it from right beside her, knowing that everyone assumes she's my girlfriend, feels different.

It feels really fucking good.

The lights around the festival have just started to blink on, the multicolored bulbs on all of the booths and rides twinkling, throwing a rainbow-colored glow over the square, when we hear, "Harlow! Jefferson!"

We turn to find Graham, Margot, Sloan, and Mia coming toward us.

"We're all going down to the river for a bonfire tonight," Margot says. She pins Harlow with a look. "You're coming out with us tonight. Both of you. Together."

Harlow looks up at me. "What do you think?"

What I think is I want to prolong being able to hold her hand, stand close, and maybe even sneak a kiss or two, and I can definitely do that at a bonfire. Some of our friends who will be there know about our situation, but not everyone does. We'll have to keep the ruse up. This is perfect.

"Sounds fun," I say. "We should definitely go."

She turns back to Margot. "We'll be there."

"Great. See you in an hour," Margot says. "BYOB."

They walk off to issue more invitations and I look down at Harlow. "How do you want to kill the next sixty minutes?"

"Maybe I should change," she says looking down at the yellow sundress she's been wearing.

The one I asked her to wear.

Okay, I *told her* to wear it.

I really, really like this dress. "Why would you need to change?"

"It might get chilly after the sun goes down."

"There will be a fire," I remind her. Then I slide my hand around her waist and pull her up against me. "And you'll have a boyfriend there. It's kind of his job to keep you warm, isn't it?"

She doesn't pull away, she doesn't even tense. She looks up at me from beneath her lashes. "That's a very good point. So, I guess we can just hang out here until it's time to go."

Fuck yes. Cuddling by a bonfire? Bring it on.

I look up at the one festival ride we have not done. "How about the Ferris wheel?"

The Ferris wheel is something of a special tradition in

Sapphire Falls. Everyone knows that when a single guy takes a single girl on the Ferris wheel, it's a sign to everyone else that their relationship has gone to the next level. If he kisses her on this Ferris wheel, it is a public announcement to the town that they are serious and exclusive.

"I don't know. Should we do that? We are still just pretending," she says.

I really want to kiss her on the Ferris wheel. I really want this to not be pretend. The next time I'll be able to kiss her on that Ferris wheel is a year from now.

I want things to be very serious by then.

That thought hits me and I'm not surprised.

"It will look strange if we don't," I say. "Zach has probably been watching to see if we do it."

Using Zach is probably unfair but I don't feel even a twinge of remorse when she says, "You're right. We should definitely ride."

We get in line, and I slip my arm around her, keeping her against my side. She slides her arm around my waist as well.

There are people in line with us, so I'm shocked when she looks up at me and asks, "So, you liked the begging in bed last night, huh?"

Heat rocks through me and I inadvertently tighten my hold on her. I look down, my brows up. She has a mischievous smile on her lips. That makes me glance around.

I realize that Allison and LuAnn are behind us in line. This little brat.

Okay. Fine. She started it. I don't even have to make this up. "I like it a lot," I tell her. "You know I love when you beg me to..." I make a point of looking around, then dropping my voice. "...do that thing you love." I don't drop it so low that Allison and LuAnn can't hear me though.

Harlow's cheeks get pink.

And she can't fake that.

I want to know what she's thinking *so* badly.

"And I will *always* deliver on that, Lily," I say, lifting my thumb and tracing it over her lower lip. "You don't really have to beg, you know. It just makes it hotter."

She opens her mouth, then shuts it.

I look straight ahead, grinning.

She is absolutely wondering what she begged me for last night.

And I'll happily tell her. But not with an audience.

We step up and take our seat in the next bucket. The attendant locks the lap bar into a place and then we are lifted into the air so that Allison and Lu can get on.

And as soon as we are dangling above the platform, Harlow asks, "Okay, what did I beg for?"

I look at her. "Do you really want to know?"

"I cannot believe I was so asleep that I don't remember this. But yeah, I need to know."

She looks like she's bracing for the worst. Honestly, I was surprised by her request as well. She was sound asleep on the couch, I nudged her and spoke to her, trying to get her to wake up enough to walk upstairs. But she simply curled up tighter and rolled over to face the back of the couch. I had debated leaving her there for the night, but in the end, couldn't do it. Not when I had two perfectly good beds upstairs. Of course, I had to debate myself over which bed to put each of us in. In the end, I'd decided to mess with her a little. Sleeping next to her had been torturous, but also worth making her wonder about.

"You asked me to touch you," I tell her. It's the truth.

Her eyes widen. "What do you mean? What did I say?"

"I tried to talk you out of it," I say. I will never not enjoy messing with Harlow Hansen. "I told you to go to sleep. I told you that you would not appreciate it in the morning when you found out. But you were insistent. You told me you wouldn't be able to sleep until I did it."

Her cheeks are bright pink now and her gaze drops to my mouth. That's interesting. She's certainly not acting disgusted.

"What exactly did I say?" she asks, her voice softer.

"There were lots of *pleases*. My name. How you totally trusted me. How you were gonna die if you didn't get my hands on you."

She narrows her eyes. "I didn't say that part."

I chuckle. "Okay, some of that might've just been how I heard it. There were a couple of pleases, and you said it was very important. And that I shouldn't be a prude and I should just do it."

She seems to think that over. Then decides that does sound like her. Which it does. That was exactly what she told me.

"Okay, what was I asking you to do?" she says.

"What do you think you were asking me to do?" I ask her as her gaze goes to my mouth again.

"No. No fair," she says. "Just tell me."

I lean in. "Actually, I don't think so. I would like very much to know what *you* think you might be willing to beg me for."

I see her breath hitch and make a note of that. Her gaze is on my mouth again and now not moving. "I suppose it's possible, that I asked you to..."

"To?" I ask, my voice dropping. "Because before you go on, or worry about going on, you should know that I would probably do anything you asked me to do. Especially anything you begged me for in bed."

Now the breath hitch is more of a gasp. Her eyes bounce up to meet mine. "Did I ask you for sex? Or to touch me..."

Her saying sex already has me tensing, but I have to hear how she's going to finish that sentence. I give her a half grin. "Touch you where, Harlow?"

Her voice drops to a whisper, and she leans closer. "Just tell me if I asked you to have sex with me or to...finger me."

Shock, lust, and gratification shoot through me. Gratification at the fact that she said those words, gratification at the fact that she thought she might possibly, in any world, in any circumstance, ask me for that.

I keep my eyes on her and say, "Unfortunately no."

She sighs with relief. "Okay." Then she narrows her eyes. "Unfortunately?"

"No, you're right, it's *fortunate* because if you *had* asked me for that, and I wouldn't have been able to—which I wouldn't have, since you were kind of out of it—that might've killed me."

Now her cheeks get even pinker, but I think it's from desire, not embarrassment.

"So what did I ask for?"

I lean in. And take a breath. "You smell so fucking good."

"Jefferson."

I grin. "Right." I whisper, "To put lotion on your feet and legs."

She pauses. She stares at me. Then she closes her eyes and groans.

"I did it too," I tell her. "You were very pouty, so I had to."

She leans over and runs her hand down her calf. "Wow."

I chuckle. "The begging started with, 'I *really* need lotion on my feet and legs before I sleep'. I said it would be fine to skip just one night. And then I got, '*pleeease*, Jefferson.' I tried to hand you the bottle but you just pushed it away and said, 'You do it.' I finally did, but only to your knees. Then the begging got worse. Because you had to have lotion, 'all the way up to my panties,' I say, making my voice high, mimicking hers terribly. I grin. "That was exactly what you told me. All the way up to your panties. Both sides."

She has her hands covering her face, but she's laughing.

"Oh my God. I'm so sorry. "

I chuckle, but I reach up and tug her hands away from her face. "You were asleep. And trust me," I tell her. "As pervy as it sounds, I enjoyed it."

She nods. "That does sound pervy."

I shrug. "What can I say? You have great legs and very smooth skin. I guess now I know why."

She's still grinning. "I am very diligent about my lotion routine."

I laugh. "You did also try to take your shirt off. That I wouldn't let you do. Even when you whined about being hot."

She grins. "I'm surprised I didn't strip off in the night when you weren't looking."

I clear my throat and shift on the seat. "You did."

Her eyes fly to mine. "Seriously?"

I nod. "I made you put it back on. Or rather I put it back on you. You sleep like the fucking dead."

She gives a little laugh. "I don't."

"Well, you did last night. I put the shirt back on you without you even waking up."

She looks at me through one eye. "Did you take a look first?"

"I have no idea what you mean."

She laughs. "Before you answer, just know, that if you had stripped your boxers off in the night, I totally would've looked before I made you put them back on."

I smirk at her. "Of course I looked."

She tips her head. "And?"

"Are you seriously asking me how I liked my glimpse of your breasts?"

"I am," she tells me. "Now that it's out there between us, I have to admit I'm curious."

"You have to be kidding," I tell her. "You know you're beautiful, right?"

She gives me a look. "I'm okay. I know you like my ass. But I'm specifically interested in what *you* think of how I look naked."

I lean in. "Harlow, I think you're fucking gorgeous. Of course I looked at your naked breasts. And I enjoyed it very much. And have thought of them several times today."

She smiles. "That's better."

God, this is all so easy with her.

We've been around the full rotation twice now, since all the cars got unloaded and reloaded. I look out over the square below us, the lights twinkling, people filling the streets and sidewalks. I take a long, contented breath. I love the festival, but this year it feels even better than usual, and I am not stupid. I realize it has everything to do with the woman next to me.

"Margot and Graham have been hanging out a lot," I comment as I notice my brother and Margot walking across the square, just the two of them now.

Harlow looks over at me. "Graham has a crush on her. Has for a long time. You know that right?"

"Really?" How had I missed that? And that makes a few things more interesting.

Harlow nods. "Yeah. Since sophomore year of high school."

Yes, very interesting.

Should I tell Harlow that Margot has asked me what I think about a job opportunity that has come up for her in Colorado? Specifically in Denver? And does it have anything to do with Graham? Margot didn't mention *that* when she asked for my opinion.

That was about a week ago and we were talking casually. The company is actually going to be contracting with my dad's company. They are opening an office here in Sapphire Falls so they can be closer to the IAS headquarters, but they are based in Denver. Margot interviewed for an executive assistant position with the office here, but she's thinking about asking them about openings in Denver.

I'll admit I was surprised. Margot is a hometown girl. But if she wants to give Denver a try, I am, of course, supportive. I know our friends come to me with these ideas because they know that I'll tell them to go for it. I assume it means that they've already given it a lot of thought and actually want someone to nudge them. That's always been my role.

"Have they been in touch while he's been in Denver?" I ask Harlow.

"I don't think so. At least not anything out of the ordinary. They see each other when he comes home to visit. She went out there with me that one time," Harlow says. "But no, I think they're just kind of reconnecting this weekend. Maybe he'll finally get the nerve to say something to her."

"Does she have feelings for him?"

"If she does, she's never told me but I'm definitely going to ask tonight at the bonfire," Harlow says.

Would one of her girlfriends tell her if they had feelings for Graham or would that be awkward?

But maybe the Denver thing with Margot doesn't have anything to do with Graham.

Should I say something to Harlow?

But no. This is Margot's story to tell. And she might decide not to take it. There's no reason to upset Harlow for no reason.

"Wouldn't it be awesome if they got together?" Harlow asks, grinning as she watches them cross Main Street together. She looks up at me. "I get what Ginny said about how she loves both of us, so she loves the idea of us together."

I return her smile. That's really nice. I'm so glad Harlow's not weird about a close friend being interested in Graham.

"If they get together, Graham will move back here, and we can all be together again."

My smile fades. Oh. Yeah. Right.

Of course, Harlow would assume that Margot and Graham getting together would mean that Graham would move back to Sapphire Falls.

Fuck.

I need to say something to Margot. She needs to bring this up with Harlow if she's serious about Denver.

Just then our car comes to a stop at the top of the Ferris wheel.

I look over at Harlow. She looks so damned happy. Beautiful. Relaxed. I'm not going to waste this opportunity. "You know what this means," I say.

Harlow feigns innocence. "What?"

"We have to kiss. Everyone's gonna be watching."

Surprise and pleasure zips through me as she leans in. "Oh darn."

And then Harlow is kissing me.

But only for a couple of seconds.

I quickly slide my hand into her hair and tip her head back so that I can deepen the kiss.

But she definitely initiated this, and I'm not going to forget that.

Yes, this is for sure my favorite festival to date.

CHAPTER 18

HARLOW

EVEN THOUGH THEY invited most everyone, Graham and Margot are the last ones to show up to the bonfire.

Jefferson and I are standing on the far side of the fire pit, drinks in hand, chatting with Ginny, Sasha, and Carver when I see them walk into the circle of light from the outer perimeter of parked vehicles.

"Be right back," I tell our little group as I beeline for Graham.

He sees me coming and pulls up, saying something to Margot. She nods and continues on toward the fire. "Hey," she greets me as we pass.

"Am I stealing your date?" I tease.

"Not if you don't keep him all night," she says with a grin.

I lift a brow as I turn to watch her walk away. That almost sounded as if she agreed that Graham was her date.

Well, okay, then. Very good.

I turn back toward my best friend and cross the grass quickly. "Okay, spill."

Graham tucks his hands into his pockets. "I have no idea what you're talking about."

"Bullshit. You can't lie to me. What's going on with you and Margot? Did you finally tell her how you feel?"

"Well, not exactly."

I narrow my eyes and look up at him. Graham is a very straightforward person, especially with me. "What does that mean?"

"We haven't really talked about it, but I think kissing her last night probably gave her an idea of how I feel."

My mouth drops open, and I swat his arm. "You did? You just grabbed her and kissed her?"

He laughs, then gives me a goofy grin. "I didn't *grab* her. But we were saying goodnight, and I said, "there's just more thing" and she asked, "what?" and I said, "this" and I kissed her."

"Graham!" I squeal, though I try to keep my voice down. "That's amazing! Way to go!"

He laughs again and I love it. I love how happy he looks. "She kissed me back. And then said, "I was wondering if you were ever going to do that.""

I laugh and give him an affectionate nudge. "That's awesome. I'm so happy for you!" I can't help but think about the kisses I've shared with Jefferson. For public display or not, you can tell a lot from someone's kiss.

Graham nods and his gaze finds something—or rather, *someone*—over my right shoulder. "Yeah. Me too. Best festival ever."

I tip my head. "So is that all you're going to do with your dream girl while you're here?"

The sooner these two get serious, the sooner my best friend is back in Sapphire Falls to stay. Of course I'm going to rush this.

Graham's focus comes back to me. "Should I be telling you about this?"

"You tell me everything."

"Yeah, but this is Margot. Should I talk to you about her like this?"

"Margot will talk to me about you like this if that's any consolation," I tell him.

I'm ninety-nine percent sure that's true. I've never actually been in a situation where one of my friends is serious about and sleeping with another of my friends now that I think about it.

Graham looks a little concerned. "She'll tell you about her sex life?"

"No," I say, shaking my head. "Never mind. I won't let her. Maybe just that you have one? But I don't wanna know the details."

He quickly nods. "By the way, same goes for you and Jefferson. I definitely don't need to know."

I open my mouth to tell him there is nothing to tell, but for some reason, the words won't come out.

There *isn't* anything to tell. But there's one little word that floats through my mind right after that phrase.

Yet.

I think it is much more accurate to say that there is nothing to tell about Jefferson and me sexually *yet*.

"Deal," I finally say. "I will say that I am really happy about you and Margot," I tell him with a huge smile. "You're both really lucky. I hope this turns out to be amazing."

There's no way this won't turn out to be amazing. Two of my best friends getting together? I couldn't be happier.

Then I look over my left shoulder. To where Jefferson has now moved to sit on the end of his truck tailgate. It's a little further away from the fire, but still part of the group. Others are doing the same. Either sitting up on the tailgates or on the logs and chairs people have positioned closer to the fire. Music is playing, drinks are flowing, conversation and laughter rises and falls on the evening breeze. And I suddenly want to go over and join Jefferson.

"I'll let you go hang out with Margot," I say.

"Okay," Graham says with a nod. "Haven't seen as much of you this trip." His gaze also goes to his brother. "But you seem to be having a good time."

I give a little laugh. "I am as surprised by that as you are."

Graham snorts. "You might actually be the only one who is surprised by that."

"You really don't think this is weird?"

"I really don't. Why don't you just give it a chance?" he asks.

"Because I've spent all this time thinking of Jefferson as my nemesis," I say honestly. "He makes me crazy."

Graham looks at me thoughtfully for a long moment, then he says, "I think that's why he's perfect for you."

I frown but laugh. "What? You *want* me to be crazy?"

"I want you with someone who will challenge you," he says. His expression and tone hold affection but it's also clear he's serious. "I want you with someone who will respect and appreciate your strength and will actually want to build that up. I want you with someone who is worthy of you, Harlow."

My smile dies as my chest tightens. Oh. That's really nice. "Graham..."

"You are my best friend. You've *always* been there for me. You've defended me. You've accepted me. You've made me feel like I can do anything."

I swallow. I did not expect this conversation to get sentimental.

"But you've also very seldom let me do anything for you."

"That's not true. You're my best friend too!" I protest.

"I know. But you don't really *need* me. Not for the building up and pushing you stuff," he says. "Because you always know what you believe and what you want and how to get it."

I shake my head, but he gives me a look that says *you know I know what I'm talking about*. Graham does know me. And, okay, so I've given him more advice and pep talks than he's given me. He's definitely listened to me rant. He's definitely listened to my dreams and plans. But no, I guess he's never had to really build me up. And he's never really argued with me.

Unlike his big brother.

"I'm easy for you," Graham says. He gives me a grin. "And I've always liked that. We have such an effortless relationship. We're so comfortable. I can just be myself. You can be you. Neither of us has ever tried to change the other."

"That's a *good* thing," I say.

"There's a time for that," he agrees. "But sometimes we need people who will make us really think. Who will make us question what we believe. Who will be the sandpaper that will smooth off our rough edges."

I study his face. The face I know as well as my own in the mirror. "Do you think Margot can be that for you?"

"Maybe," he says, a soft smile on his lips. "She knows me, but she doesn't know me like you do. There's room to learn and that's good, I think. But we'll have to see. You and Jefferson on the other hand are already there."

I swallow. "Already where?" I ask. And I'm sure Graham can hear the wariness in my voice.

He smiles. "Already to where the pushing and pulling on each other builds you up instead of breaking anything down. Where you can smooth each other out without ruining the beautiful pattern that's underneath."

I stare at Graham.

"What?" he asks.

"You've always been a genius, but when did you get *poetic?*"

He laughs. "I've been reading some interesting shit lately."

I shake my head. "Well, wow, warn a girl before you pull the philosophy out at a bonfire at the river."

He loops an arm around my neck and steers me back toward the bonfire. "Poor baby, making you *feel* things and be a little mushy."

"I don't mind feeling things and being mushy about *you*," I mutter.

Graham kisses the top of my head. "I know. But now, we both know that you want to feel some things for my big brother. And I'm going to give *you* advice for once."

I look up at him.

"Do it," he says simply.

I just sigh. I'm not going to argue.

Because I'm already doing that.

Graham walks me across the packed dirt area that was long ago cleared of grass and weeds to make a space for big bonfires and chairs.

He stops in front of Jefferson. "Found something of yours," he says.

Jefferson's eyes are on my face. He doesn't argue the *yours* part. He just holds out his hand and takes mine, tugging me up against his side where he slides his arm around me and rests his hand on my hip. "Thanks for returning her," he tells Graham. "Didn't know if I'd get her back. There was a time when separating the two of you was impossible."

Graham nods, then gives me a little smile. "I might steal her once in a while in the future to talk all night, watch movies, and whatever again, but I think this is where she'll want to come back to afterward."

I should protest. I should make it into a joke. I should...do something.

Well, something other than look up at Jefferson, meet his gaze, and smile.

Because that seems like I'm agreeing with Graham.

That makes it seem like there's a future that includes me standing in Jefferson's arms while Graham moves on to hang out with other friends.

A future that includes me choosing Jefferson over those friends.

But...fuck.

What if that could be the future? What if our friends would come and go from my house, or Jefferson's house, or Sapphire Falls and I was left behind with Jefferson?

How would that feel?

I watch Graham walk toward the group that includes Margot, Mia, Ginny, and Sloan, I register the feel of Jefferson against me, and...I smile.

I freaking smile.

Oh, man.

"I hate to break it to you," Jefferson says, his deep voice rumbling against my shoulder and across my chest. "But I think my brother thinks you like me. For real."

Again, I tell myself to make a joke. Mention that we must be good actors. Say something snarky. Anything to keep this from being serious. Or from being true.

But Graham got to me. More than even my parents. Or Jefferson's parents for that matter. Graham knows me. Graham loves me. And if he sees something between Jefferson and me, it's real. And not just a flirtation or attraction or crush. Graham thinks we could be good together.

So, I look up at my now ex-nemesis and say, "Well, he *is* a genius."

At least Jefferson looks surprised for one second. I appreciate that. But then his expression grows...hot.

And I'm definitely in trouble.

Or maybe I'm the opposite of in trouble.

Maybe this is fantastic.

My stomach suddenly does a little swoop-y thing that I kind of like and I think, *yeah, this could be fantastic.*

Either way, things are about to change for Jefferson and me.

"Harlow—"

"Come on," Sasha says, grabbing my wrist and tugging me closer to the fire. "S'more time."

There's a fleeting look of frustration on Jefferson's face and I feel an echo of it in my chest.

We need to talk.

We also need to kiss.

We really need to kiss. More than talk. Kiss, *then* talk.

I really, really want to kiss him some more.

In front of people, in private, whatever. Just very not-faking-it kiss.

I'm caught up for a few minutes, toasting marshmallows, and sliding them between chocolate-bar-covered graham crackers. And I've never not been in a good mood when s'mores were involved.

Especially, when Jefferson joins us, and gets in right next to me. He steals a marshmallow off the end of my stick, and I turn to protest but instead find myself watching him put the gooey morsel in his mouth and then lick his thumb and forefinger.

He looks down to find me watching him suck on his finger.

He drags it out slowly, then reaches for my face, dragging his thumb, that's still wet from his mouth, over the corner of my lip.

He shows me the bit of chocolate he removed, then slides his thumb into my mouth.

Oh, *yes*.

I close my lips around his thumb and suck gently, then swirl my tongue over the pad.

The look in his eyes is scorching.

I feel heat flare in my belly and a tingle between my legs and suddenly, I can't wait to get back to his house.

Things are changing, for sure, and as far as my panties are concerned, it is all for the better.

Someone cranks up the music and my friends, who now have alcohol and sugar coursing through their systems, start to dance.

"Dance with us!" Mia says, coming up next to me.

This is a regular part of the agenda. Dancing with my girlfriends around the bonfire is one of my favorite ways to blow off steam.

The thing is, I haven't had the kind of steam that's building up inside of me right now, in a long time.

The corner of Jefferson's mouth curls up. "Go on," he says. "I always love watching you dance."

Wait, just a second. He *always* loves watching me dance with my friends?

Yes, we're both often at these bonfires. But I've never noticed him watching me before.

But as I let Margot and Mia pull me back away from him, I love the way his eyes travel over me. I remember that he wanted me to wear this dress. I remember the kisses that we've shared so far.

And I fully intend to put a little extra shimmy in my hips tonight.

Jefferson Riley wants to for-real flirt with me? Wants to have a couple of hours of bonfire-party foreplay?

Game. On.

CHAPTER 19

JEFFERSON

I SETTLE BACK against the tailgate of my truck again, my eyes glued to Harlow. Again.

She seemed surprised when I told her that I loved to watch her dance. But this is definitely not the first time I've been unable to take my eyes off of her at a bonfire.

She and the girls often get a little tipsy and then crank up the music.

I'm also not the only guy here who loves this part of the evening. Sapphire Falls grows some beautiful women. And this time of year, the hot weather means there's flirty sundresses and short shorts everywhere we look.

Harlow is swaying, twirling, and wiggling to P!nk with the orange-yellow glow of the fire behind her. She looks like a fucking goddess. And even if I was trying to forget the way Graham brought her over to me and the way she looked up at me when he said that by me was where he thought she wanted to be, my dick has not forgotten the way she sucked on my thumb. Or the look in her eyes when she was watching me lick melted marshmallow off my fingers.

Or hell, the way she looked at me shirtless at my house. Or the way she drank me in at the dunk tank.

Harlow might not like it, but she's attracted to me.

There's heat between us and I know she feels it too.

Something has shifted between us, and if I was a betting man, I'd put money down on the fact that she's wanting to do something about that heat.

Well, I am very happy to accommodate that desire. Fuck, every desire this woman has now or ever will have.

Even on nice sunny days in the middle of sweet summer festivals, sparring with and vexing Harlow Hansen is the most fun I've ever had. In the middle of the night, naked, sweaty, with the lust turned all the way up? Making her crazy, pushing her boundaries, taking all of the sass she can dish out will be the fucking pleasure of my life.

I'm so ready.

Will it complicate things?

Actually, I think it's going to make a lot of things easier.

Harlow and I are on a path to something bigger and lasting.

Sleeping together—okay, fucking each other's brains out—will be unlike anything either of us has experienced before and it will help her understand that we're the real deal sooner versus later.

My eyes narrow as I notice a group of newcomers to the party.

Of course, Zach is here.

I'm not shocked, just disappointed. He has a few guys with him who I get along with fine. I'm annoyed to remember that they are friends of his. When he's not around, Mark, Cade, and Tanner are perfectly good guys. I don't need the reminder that they have shit taste in friends.

But it's a bonfire. There are dozens of people here and it's the great outdoors. Plenty of space for all of us.

Unless of course, Zach decides to talk to Harlow.

I know the second he notices her.

She hasn't seen him yet, but he stands and watches her for far too long.

Of course, even ten seconds is too long in my mind.

I decide there's no reason to turn this into another confrontation like in the town square and I might as well cut this off before it turns into anything.

That's my girlfriend, and if I want to go over and dance with her, I will.

I push off my tailgate, and cross to Harlow. I move in behind her, resting my hands on her swaying hips.

She immediately presses back against me, clearly not upset to have me there. Not seeming surprised either.

I put my mouth to her ear. "I realized that after all those times just watching you, this time I can join in."

"You could've joined in before," she says, snaking her arm up and draping it around my neck as our bodies sway together. That causes her body to arch enticingly, and I cannot keep my hand from running from her hip up her side to the lower curve of her breast and down again.

"Could I?" I ask. "Really? I don't think we were there before tonight."

She turns her head to look up at me. God, I would only have to lean in a few inches to kiss her.

"Are we there tonight?" she asks.

"If 'there' is me getting my hands all over you, pressing up against you, doing this—" I bend and drag my mouth from her ear down the column of her throat to her collarbone where I nip lightly. Under the music and conversation around us, I hear her moan. "Then yes, this is where we are tonight," I finish.

"I like being there with you then," she says tipping her head to the side slightly, a clear invitation to put my mouth on more of her sweet, silky skin. "But you're right, we weren't before."

My hands grip her hips a little tighter as I place a kiss on her neck. "Something's changed."

She straightens and turns in my arms. She links both hands behind my neck, pressing her entire body along mine. My hands move from her hips to her ass.

"Yeah, something's changed."

"I don't think you've had too much to drink. Am I right?" I ask, wanting to be sure this isn't fueled by liquor.

She shakes her head. "I've been careful. One beer."

"Careful?" I ask.

"I didn't want to give you a reason to say no."

Lust licks down my spine and I feel my cock hardening. "Say no to what, Harlow? Be specific."

A playful smile teases her lips. "To making out at a bonfire with me."

"You want to make out with me at a bonfire?"

"I really do."

It's high school stuff, but even the couples our age still find it fun to flirt and tease and make out a little at these bonfire parties. For Harlow and me though, this is all brand new. And it *will* lead to more.

"I've only got one chair. If we were going to go sit down, we'd have to share."

"And I'm just wearing this little sundress. If we were going to go sit down, we'd probably need a blanket. It might get chilly."

"I don't think there's gonna be anything chilly about us sitting together under a blanket on my lawn chair," I tell her.

She grins up at me. "Big talker."

I slide my hand up her back and into her hair. I tug slightly, tipping her head back. "There's lots of big when it comes to me, Harlow."

I cut off her laugh with a kiss.

If someone had told me a month ago I would be kissing Harlow Hansen at a bonfire party in front of all of our friends, I would've assumed they were drunk or giving me a code for *help me, I've been kidnapped.*

But as she lifts on tiptoe to get closer, and I press my hand into her lower back, bringing her more fully against me, it feels like the most natural, right thing in the world.

Fuck. I really need to sit on a lawn chair under a blanket with this girl.

Right now.

"Let's go," I say, lifting my head and turning her toward my truck.

She trips slightly as I hustle us to my truck, but I have an arm securely around her, so she stays on her feet.

"I'm flattered you're in a hurry," she says breathlessly, as I let go of her only long enough to haul the lounge-style lawn chair from the back of my truck.

"To get my hands on you...*really* on you?" I ask. "You have no idea."

She laughs and I turn with the chair to find her hands on her cheeks. I grin and step close. "Are you *blushing*, Lily?"

"I think I am." She looks almost like she can't believe it.

"Is it that? Or are you just really turned on?" I ask, lifting my free hand and tugging one of her hands away from her face. I trace my finger down her cheek. "I think maybe you're flushed because you want my hands on you as much as I want to put them there."

She wets her lips. "I think you might be right." She moves closer to me, pressing her body against me. "Now that I've admitted that I want you, it's like everything in me is just all revved up and I can't stop it or ignore it."

I know the grin I'm giving her is absolutely wicked. "Well, hell, Harlow, I don't think you could have said anything hotter to me."

I hold the chair out and jerk it, causing it to unfold. She laughs.

I bend to arrange it at the end of my truck. I also reach in and grab the blanket I keep out here in my truck bed. Spontaneous bonfires are kind of a regular thing. "You sure you want to stay? I have a whole big house. And bed."

She gives me an equally wicked grin. "Oh, let's have fun. I haven't had a great bonfire make out in a long time."

I don't want to think about her making out with anyone else out here. Ever. "It would be fun at home." My voice is far gruffer than I intended.

Her grin grows. "It *will* be. I'm sure."

This girl. I'm toast. Done. Gone.

"All right. Come here." I sit down, stretch my legs out, and shake out the blanket. I spread my legs, making space for her.

She sits down and starts to scoot up. I reach down and wrap an arm around her waist and haul her up until her ass is pressed against my cock. My very hard-for-her cock.

She sucks in a breath, and I don't have to wonder if she feels what she's doing to me.

I put my mouth against her ear and say, "Whichever of us says 'let's go home' first has to make breakfast in the morning."

"Deal," she says, breathlessly.

I lift one knee, making a tent over us and then, I have my hands on Harlow Hansen.

I rest my hands on her belly first, just drawing small circles, getting her used to my touch. But she has one hand on my extended thigh, the other on the knee of my bent leg, and the way she's already gripping me, I can tell she's into this. I slowly bunch the skirt of her dress up to her waist, exposing her thighs. I smooth my hands up and down both.

"I did a really good job with the lotion," I tell her. "Your skin is like silk."

She gives a soft laugh. "I told you it was important. Apparently," she adds dryly.

My laugh is husky. "You were very insistent." I move a hand up and down her thigh, moving closer to her panties this time. "Are you always so demanding when you want something?"

"You know me pretty well. What do you think?"

I stroke my hand up to her belly under her dress this time. I just skim over her panties, but definitely note they are bikini style. I rest my hand on her warm, bare stomach. "A lot I bet," I tell her. I run my hand back-and-forth. "But in all things, I also think you might appreciate it when someone else pushes back and takes some control."

I slide my hand up, my fingers brushing the bottom of one breast.

No bra. I suspected. This dress has thin straps and I didn't see a bra strap. And yes, I looked.

She catches her breath, and I ask, "You okay?"

She squeezes my thigh. "You can be very assured that if I am not okay, I will let you know."

That's true. Harlow doesn't do things she doesn't want to. And she has absolutely no trouble telling me no. While I always appreciate that, I especially value it in this situation.

I slide my hand up and cup her breast. She gives a moan and arches closer. The hard pebble of her nipple presses into my palm and the heat simmering in my gut flares as my cock pulses.

I squeeze gently, rubbing my thumb over the hard tip. Then

I take her nipple between my thumb and forefinger and give it a slight squeeze.

Her head presses back against my chest and I can see she's breathing more raggedly.

We're facing the fire and the party, but even if I'd had to list all of the people in attendance or face life in prison, I wouldn't have been able to.

My entire world has been reduced to the woman in my arms and the way her breast fits perfectly in my hand.

I lean in and kiss the side of her neck, dragging my beard against the sensitive skin. Her nipple pulls tighter, and I tug gently.

"Jefferson," she says raggedly.

"Fuck, I love hearing my name from your lips with that turned-on-begging tone," I tell her. "So much better than when you're arguing with me."

She shakes her head, her hair rubbing against my shirt. "I'm not begging."

"No?" I pluck at her nipples again and she gives a little moan. "Let's see what we can do about that." I slide my other hand up under her dress, to play with her other breast.

Both of her hands squeeze my legs tighter.

"You like that?"

"Yes," she tells me. "But no."

I rub my jaw against hers. "Tell me."

"You know what I want," she says.

"Yeah, I think I do. But I would really love to hear you say it."

I roll both nipples between my fingers.

She arches and her fingers curl into my legs.

"Tell me you want my hand in your panties. Tell me you want me to finger your pussy."

Her legs move restlessly on the chair, and she squeezes her thighs together.

"I know you're hot and wet for me, Harlow," I say against her jaw. "I know you want me to make you feel good."

"Please, Jefferson," she says.

"Tell me you want my fingers in your pussy." I drag my hand from her breast to rest on her panties, rubbing over the silk that crosses from one hip bone to the other. My hand is huge on her. "I know my fingers are going to stretch you so well. Think of how good that will feel."

She turns her head and tips her chin, looking up at me. "*Please.*"

I can't resist and I lean down to kiss her. Our lips are hungry on each other and our tongues tangle deliciously. I continue to play with one breast and I slip one finger behind the silk of her panties, but I simply drag it back-and-forth over her smooth, hot skin, and don't go any lower.

She pulls her mouth away. "Please put your fingers in my pussy."

I wanted that. Oh, fuck I wanted that. But I actually had no idea the way it would punch me in the gut. Or the way it would make my cock ache.

"Fuck, Harlow."

"Jefferson—"

But I heard her and I am not going to make her say it again. I'm a gentleman.

I slide my hand into her panties, my middle finger gliding over her clit. I pause for a moment, pressing, then circling on that sweet spot.

Her hands grip me as she lifts her hips. "Jefferson!"

"Yeah, I fucking love hearing my name like that." I circle a little faster. "This good?" I ask her. "Do you like this?"

"Oh my God, yes," she says, her voice ragged.

I slip my hand lower, sliding my middle finger into her slick heat. And holy fuck. She's tight, hot, and so wet. The way her pussy grips my finger makes my cock press painfully against my fly. I want to unzip, rip these panties off of her, and shift her up into my lap right here and now. I want to be buried inside her so badly, I almost can't form the words.

"This is going to feel so good around my cock," I tell her, pumping my finger deep, then dragging it out slowly.

She gives a soft whimper and presses up into my hand. I reward her with another finger. That definitely stretches her, and I thrust in and out a few times.

Dammit, I need to spread her out. I want to see her. I need to taste her.

But I really want to make her come like this.

I rub my thumb over her clit, moving my fingers in and out, relishing the tight, sweet fit.

"Oh my God, Jefferson," she says softly in the sweetest, breathy voice.

"Come for me, let me feel it," I urge gruffly.

Suddenly a big fat raindrop hits my cheek.

She gasps and I wonder if it's from also being hit by rain or from my fingers dragging against her inner walls. Perhaps a combination.

I tug on her nipple and thrust faster.

The raindrops pick up speed as well and I hear thunder rumble.

Our friends start gasping and laughing. People move to put out the bonfire and gather up supplies.

Harlow stiffens in my arms, but I say against her ear. "You're not going anywhere till you give me this orgasm."

"Oh God," she gasps, squeezing my leg.

"Better hurry, people are packing up."

The bonfire has been doused and coolers and lawn chairs are being gathered.

And then I feel her pussy clench.

"That's my girl," I coach.

The blanket is getting wet and rain is running down my face, but I keep going.

"Jefferson," she says, and I can tell she's close.

"You're so fucking hot. I should've known that I couldn't even finger you at a bonfire without it being the best I've ever had."

And she breaks apart. Her pussy grips my hand, her hands grip my legs, and I hear "Jefferson!" gasped sharply as someone slams a car door.

I withdraw my fingers, bring them to my mouth and suck them clean. "Delicious. I need more."

She looks up at me and nods. "More."

I smirk at her. Watching as her hair continues to get wet and raindrops trail down her cheeks. "Just say the word. Or words."

Her eyes widen as she realizes what I'm talking about. Then she laughs. "How about we say them together?"

God, I *really* like this girl. I nod. "On three."

"One, two, three," she counts.

"Let's go home," we say together.

CHAPTER 20

HARLOW

WE GATHER our stuff up quickly, throwing the soaked blanket and lawn chair into the back of Jefferson's truck and then climbing inside.

I'm so wet. And not just from the rain.

Damn. Jefferson just gave me an orgasm on a lawn chair at the bonfire.

Easily.

I shouldn't be surprised he's good at that. He's good at *everything* and as turned on as I was, it shouldn't be a shock at all that he was able to make me come so easily and quickly.

But dang, that was hot.

Things have definitely shifted between us and I like it. I like this change and I like that we've talked about it and we seem to be on the same page.

But now that we're in his truck and headed toward his house, I'm chewing on my bottom lip and wondering if we're making some of this up.

Is it just the festival? Is it just wanting to make Zach jealous? I noticed him after we'd gone over to Jefferson's truck to get the lawn chair. I hadn't seen him before, but he was there by the time Jefferson came over to dance with me. Is that a coincidence or did that have something to do with my fake boyfriend joining me and putting his hands on me?

And the make out... it had been so good. So, so good. But it had been dark and we'd been caught up in bonfire stuff and we hadn't been looking at each other. Maybe that all made it easier to get lost in the moment. To kind of forget who we were and what we were doing.

"Hey, can you pull over?" I ask, looking over at Jefferson.

He looks at me quickly. "Are you okay?"

"Yeah. Mostly."

He frowns. "Mostly?"

"Can you pull over?" I scan the road in front of us. "There." I point at a turn in. That road also leads down to the river. There's not a wide bank here so it's not as good for parking a lot of vehicles, building a bonfire, and hanging out, but it will be fine for one truck.

"Are you sick?" Jefferson asks, taking the turn.

"No. I just need to stop for a second."

He grips the wheel a little tighter. "This can't wait until we get to the house?"

Actually, I don't think it can. "No."

He gives me another quick glance, but he keeps driving. "How far?"

"To the river."

He seems frustrated, but he does it.

Two minutes later, he puts the truck in park twenty feet from the river's edge. "Okay, what's going on?"

"Just this." I open my door enough to make the overhead light come on.

He frowns and blinks in the sudden light. "What?"

I lean in, our faces six inches apart, and meet his eyes.

"I just need to see if this is awkward with the lights on, no other people around, just us and our very clear intention to have sex."

He lifts a brow and lets me study his face. "You think it would be awkward with the lights on?"

"Maybe. I just want to be sure we weren't caught up. Or that the dark wasn't making it easier to do all of that."

He leans closer, our noses almost touching. "You think I need something to make it *easier* to touch you? Because I would really love to find something that made it easier *not* to."

I smile at that. "So this wasn't just a caught up in campfire smoke or Zach being there thing?"

"Wanting to get my hand in your panties and feel you come around my fingers?" he asks, his gaze locked on mine.

I feel my cheeks heat, but like before, I don't think I'm blushing. I think it's lust. "Yeah," I say, my voice husky.

"Absolutely not." He reaches up and tucks my hair behind my ear. "I want nothing more than to turn the lights on bright, spread you out where I can get at every inch of you, and make you come around a lot more than my fingers."

Oh, yeah, it's definitely lust coursing through me.

No, this isn't awkward with a light on, and looking directly into his face. Thinking about *Jefferson Riley* having his fingers inside me, feeling me coming apart, only makes me feel hot and very horny.

"Good." I pull my door shut, then slide across the center console and into his lap, straddling his thighs. I sink my fingers into his hair and kiss him.

His hands grip my waist, and I can feel his thick, hard cock pressing against my center.

We kiss, deeply and hungrily for nearly a minute, then he pulls back. "Bed. Spread out. Lights."

"Later. I want you right now."

"Harlow—"

I take his face in my hands. "Jefferson. Fuck me. Right now, in the front seat of your truck, where you will think about it every time you get in this thing."

His hands grip me tighter, and he groans, his head tipping back against the seat.

I smile, running my hands down his neck, then back up to his face. "Please."

His head comes up. "You are *such* a brat."

My grin grows. "And I know your big secret."

"What's that?"

"That you really like brats."

He growls and brings me in for another kiss. Then he says against my mouth, "I really like *you*."

Then he reaches for the side of his seat and hits the switch that sends the seat sliding back away from the steering wheel a few more inches.

I grin, sit back and pull my dress up and over my head. That leaves me naked in his lap except for my panties.

There's enough light from the moon filtering into the truck cab that I can see the way his eyes flare with heat. He drags in a breath through his nose. "Fuck, Harlow."

"Touch me."

His hands come up to cup my breasts, thumbing over my nipples. I put my hands on the backs of his, arching into his touch.

He kneads, plucks, and squeezes. "You are so gorgeous," he tells me. Then a hand goes to my back, between my shoulder blades and he brings me to his mouth, his lips latching onto one nipple, sucking softly, then harder, before biting me gently.

Heat streaks from my breasts to my pussy and I gasp. "Yes!"

I immediately start bunching his shirt up, gathering it under his arms until I can push it up over his head. He lifts his arms and helps me whisk it off. I run my hands over his shoulders and chest, down his ribs to his abs. All that glorious tan skin and muscle that I've been ogling for days.

"You're so gorgeous too," I tell him honestly.

"We really should have been doing this long before now," he says, bringing me forward so he can tease my nipples with his tongue and teeth again.

I nod even though he can't see me. "We really should have."

I continue to stroke his back and knead his bunching biceps as he stokes the fire deep in my belly with his mouth on my breasts.

When I'm wiggling against his cock he finally pulls back. "Lose them." He plucks the elastic waistband of my panties away from my hip and lets it snap back.

"You too," I say, sliding momentarily to my seat so I can wiggle out of my underwear.

He watches me raptly as he unbuttons and unzips his jeans. He pushes the denim and his boxers down past his knees. I drop my panties on the floor and then kneel on the seat.

I take in the sight of him naked—mostly—for the first time.

The gray sweatpants he wore at the house gave me an idea, but it was nothing compared to him naked and aroused.

"Come here," he commands, his voice low and rough.

I reach out and wrap a hand around his shaft. "Just a second."

His breath hisses out between his teeth. "Harlow."

I stroke up and down, measuring his length and girth. "You are—"

He reaches over, grabs me, and hauls me into his lap. "You are a brat. Need you."

"Yes." I sink into his lap, pressing my lips to his. "But we're going to come back to me staring at your huge cock later."

His hand cups me, sliding a finger into my pussy. "I was thinking we're going to come back to you on your knees in front of my huge cock later."

I shiver with lust. His finger, his dirty words, the idea of... all of everything with him is just a big fat *yes*.

"Reach down and grab a condom out of my wallet," he says, his fingers doing magical things between my legs.

I do, somehow. He has an arm around my waist while his other hand torments my clit, so I don't fall out of his lap. I find his wallet in the jeans around his knees, open it, pull out a foil wrapper, and rip it open.

He removes his hand so I can move back far enough to roll the condom down his length. Which is regrettable for about twenty seconds.

Then he brings me forward, positions me over his cock, and then I'm sliding down, taking him in and...Oh. My. God.

Nothing regrettable about this.

This is so good.

He's definitely bigger than any of the men I've been with before. Definitely bigger than my vibrators. And I'm almost immediately ruined for anything else ever again.

"Jefferson," I moan as I still, just adjusting.

"Jesus, Harlow," he says. It sounds like he's talking through gritted teeth. "You're *so* fucking *good*."

I nod. "Yeah. This is...so good."

And we haven't even started moving yet.

"Okay, brat, move this gorgeous body." He squeezes my hips.

"I have to do the work?" I ask, lifting and lowering myself.

He gives a low growl that tightens my nipples and my pussy. God, I love affecting him.

Then he grips my hips tighter and moves me. "I'll help. But I'm already up one orgasm."

"Oh, we're keeping track of who gives who the most orgasms?"

He gives me a grin that makes me as hot as his huge cock or his growly voice. "Of course we are."

I laugh. Of course we are.

So I start moving, and he keeps moving me, and the truck gets very hot, and there are lots of growls and moans and *yes,* and *fuck,* and *Jefferson,* and *Harlow,* and then I come very hard, just before he shouts and presses me down firmly against him and comes just as hard.

Then he holds me against his chest for nearly ten minutes, stroking my hair and my back. I breathe so easy with my cheek pressed over his heart.

And I realize that I hope this "competition" between us never ends.

I hope none of our little competitions and games and arguments ever end.

And once we get back to his house, I manage to even up the score.

Of course, I do.

We wake up the next morning three to three.

CHAPTER 21

JEFFERSON

WAKING up with a naked woman in my arms is never a bad thing. But I am amazed at how much better it is when that naked woman is Harlow Hansen.

I lie wrapped around her, my hand splayed over her stomach, breathing in the scent of her hair, absorbing the feel of her soft, warm body against mine, and replaying last night for several long minutes.

It's about fucking time.

Worth the wait.

Those are the two things that keep going through my mind. Everything about last night felt like we had been building toward that for years. Not just the last few days, but at least since we've been working together with Alex, and I truly think long before that.

I take a deep breath and nuzzle my face against her neck.

I could wake up like this for the rest of my life.

But I need her awake now too. I stroke my hand back and forth over her stomach, I kiss her neck, then run my hand a little lower.

I hear her breathing change, then a soft moan as I drag my hand down one of her legs, and back up.

"Good morning," I start.

But just then I hear a meow from the floor and feel a soft weight suddenly land on my foot.

Oh yeah, we have cats.

"Not the pussy I was hoping for," I mutter against her shoulder.

She laughs softly and rolls to her back. "At least they left us alone all night."

Fuck she's gorgeous in the morning. Okay, she's gorgeous all the time. But her, soft and a little sleepy, and in my bed, takes my breath away.

Another meow and I feel four little paws against my leg. At least two of the cats are in the room.

"True," I say ignoring the animal on the bed for now. "At least I was able to get up four to three."

Her eyes widen. "What? We are three to three."

I shake my head slowly. "Oh, I don't think so, gorgeous. I had my face between your legs around three a.m. and that definitely put me up one."

I see her cheeks flush slightly.

"Oh," she says a moment later. "I thought that was a dream."

I give a surprised laugh. "You thought me making you come on my tongue was a dream?"

She blushes a little darker, but admits, "Well it's not the first time I've had that dream."

That gets her a very long deep kiss. But the cats are not patient. A minute later, we have two on the bed and another on the floor meowing.

"Let me go take care of them, then I'll come back and take care of you."

She sits up as I climb out of bed. "We're supposed to be making breakfast together."

My gaze drops to her naked breasts. "I'm hungry for something else."

She's watching me as I pull on sweatpants.

Yeah, I fucking love this. Us together, still teasing, but able to do it completely naked in the bedroom? Huge improvement.

"Well, someone helped me burn off a lot of calories last night and I'm actually starving," she says, swinging her legs over the edge of the bed. "Can we have breakfast and then do other things?"

"In case I wasn't clear," I tell her. "We're going to be doing those 'other things' in between all of the normal everyday things we both do from now on."

The smile she gives me makes my heart kick against my ribs. She looks pleased and a little surprised, and definitely turned on.

"That sounds amazing," she tells me.

We make our way to the kitchen with three cats weaving between our feet. Obviously, they've already gotten over feeling scared or shy of us.

She feeds them as I get French toast cooking. Yes, I remember her teasing me about that the first morning.

She comes over to the stove and wraps her arms around me from behind. "By the way," she says. "I wasn't joking about the fact that I basically can only make peanut butter toast."

I dish up the French toast and move the pan off the burner. Then I turn and wrap my arms around her. "I'm not kidding when I say I'm not with you for your cooking skills."

She looks up at me through her lashes. "And why are you with me?"

"I am so fucking glad you asked me that."

I scoop my hands under her ass and she wraps her legs

around my waist. I carry her over to the table, sit her on the edge, and then tip her back. She's only pulled on a long t-shirt of mine and panties and I quickly strip both off.

I pull up a seat, putting me right between her legs.

"Jefferson," she laughs softly. But she sure doesn't try to get away.

"What?" I ask, running a hand up her inner thigh.

"I'm a mess."

I stand, leaning over, bracing one hand beside her hip, keeping the other on her thigh. I look her directly in the eye. "I think you are the most gorgeous woman I've ever met. All the time, Harlow. But I want to tell you something."

She looks a little worried, pulling her bottom lip between her teeth. I reach up to free that lip with my thumb and then run my thumb back and forth.

"I've known you for years. I have seen you muddy from head to toe. I've seen you dressed up for prom. And everything in between. You don't have to impress me. I love when you wear sexy blue dresses for me, but I don't need that to want you. The most beautiful you have ever been to me was after you hadn't slept, showered, and had barely eaten for twenty-four hours when we were trying to find Alex. Your emotions were all over your face, you couldn't hold any of your worry or anxiety or love for him inside. You didn't care about anything except that kid. That was the most beautiful you have ever been." I reach up and run my hand through her hair, then down the side of her neck and down her arm to link our fingers together. "Your hair, or your face, or this amazingly gorgeous body are all sprinkles on top. What I love about you is your heart."

She sucks in a deep breath, her eyes welling with tears.

"You just said love."

I nod "I did not intend to tell you that when you were laid

out naked on my kitchen table," I tell her. "But it's true. It's been true for a little while."

She reaches for me and I let her take my face between her hands and pull me in for a long deep kiss. "I love you too," she says against my mouth.

Relief washes over me. Not so much that she feels it, but that she's admitted it. To me and to herself.

I kiss her again and then sit back in my chair and run both hands up her inner thighs. "Now excuse me, I have very bright, full sunlight here, and I want to see every inch."

She covers her face with her hands and laughs. "Oh my God."

"By the way," I say leaning in and kissing her inner thigh. "Five to three."

She looks down at me. "You can't count an orgasm ahead of time."

I grin. "Give me three minutes."

I'M in the best fucking mood I've been in in months. And I'm a generally pretty happy guy. And I finally left my house. I definitely got up five to three and it was halfway to number six before she slid off the table and into my lap and we ended up at six to four. Then we ate French toast, showered, and dressed for the day. We're splitting up for a little while now. She's going to the bakery to help her mom. I'm actually heading over to help with some set up for the wedding tomorrow.

I text her as I remember I've forgotten to tell her about tonight.

Going out with the guys for Carver's mini bachelor party. Basically just at the Come Again. Will probably be late.

She texts back, *Good. I can finally have a movie night with my friends without you bothering me.* Then she sends a kissy face emoji.

Jefferson: *You better plan on being home later and working on evening things up. I've been doing a lot of work.*

I just get another kissy face followed by an eggplant and then a water spray emoji. I'm grinning like a dumbass for the rest of the day.

CHAPTER 22

HARLOW

THIS MOVIE IS GOOD.

It's not a thriller but I still really like it.

The popcorn is even good. Not spicy, but again, I like it.

And I'm surrounded by many of my favorite people.

Including Graham and Margot who are cuddled up together on one of the couches.

And we're at my house.

I'm home.

But I want to be at home with Jefferson. At his house.

Naked. Of course. But I'd even be up for a movie first. Or even just talking to him.

And if you'd told me two weeks ago that I'd want to spend time just me and Jefferson Riley talking about random shit for no other reason than just to be together, I'd have asked for a couple of shots of whatever you were drinking.

But here I am, doing one of my favorite things with my favorite people and wishing I was with Jefferson instead.

Ugh. I'm so pathetic when I'm in love.

My phone starts ringing and I dig it out from between me and the pillow I'm leaning on.

"Sorry!" I tell everyone.

Sloan hits the pause button.

I frown at my screen. "It's my dad."

That makes everyone else frown, too.

You don't want a dad to call during movie night anyway, and you definitely don't want the cop dad calling.

"Dad? What's going on?"

"You need to come get your boyfriend."

He sounds...amused.

I pause. Then ask, "Jefferson?"

"Do you have more than one boyfriend?"

There is something about my father casually referring to Jefferson as my boyfriend that does funny things to my stomach. And my heart.

Yeah, yeah, everyone has been telling us that it's obvious we make a great couple. No one else is surprised. Yada, yada, yada. It's only fully sunk in for me in the past twenty-four hours, so I'm still in the stomach-swooping and heart-skipping stage.

And I kind of like it.

"Okay, no. But why do I need to come get him. Where is he?"

"At the station. In a cell."

I sit up on the couch, my feet hitting the floor. "Jefferson Riley is at the police station *in a cell*?"

Everyone in the room swivels to look at me.

"He is," my father says. "With Zach."

Now I'm standing. "What happened?"

"They got into it at the Come Again. Derek called me. I've talked them both out of pressing charges, so they're just drunk asses who need rides home." He pauses. "I don't suppose you would take Zach home, too? Since he's staying right across the street."

"I don't—"

I start, but my dad raises his voice and calls, "Settle down, Riley, I was joking."

I laugh. "Jefferson heard that?"

"Jefferson's usually a friendly drunk," my dad says. "Seems that Zach brings out a different side of him."

I'm grinning. "Yeah, I've noticed that too."

"You coming?"

"Yeah," I say. "Be there in a minute." I pause, then ask, "How drunk are we talking here?"

"Drunk enough that he's informed me he's madly in love with you and would like to ask for your hand in marriage."

I freeze. "Um..."

"I said yes, of course, but he needs to sober up and ask me again. With your mom there. She'll kill us both if she misses that."

"You're ruining the surprise, Scott!" I hear Jefferson yell in the background.

"Yeah, sorry," my dad says dryly. "We'll have to come up with something big and fun to surprise her with."

"Okay, Peyton will have good ideas," I hear Jefferson say.

I laugh. Loudly. And admit that I think my pounding heart is hammering more out of oh-my-god-I-love-him-and-I-think-I'd-say-yes instead of shock.

Why am I not shocked that Jefferson is thinking about marrying me?

Or that my dad doesn't sound a bit shocked.

"Harlow?" Dad asks. "You coming?"

"I'm on my way." I hang up and look at all my friends. "Zach and Jefferson got into a fight at the bar."

Sasha is already texting someone. I assume it's her mother who will have more details.

Graham just shakes his head. "A hundred bucks says I know exactly what the topic of their 'conversation' was."

I have a feeling I know too.

Especially if Jefferson is talking this freely to my *father* about us getting married. God knows what he said to my ex. Who he hated even without adding me into the mix.

Five minutes later, I stroll through the front doors of the Sapphire Falls police station.

My dad is sitting at his desk, doing a crossword puzzle in an actual puzzle book with a pencil.

"I hope he doesn't have to pay a fine. I didn't bring any money."

He lifts his head and gives me a smile. "I broke it up before they broke anything, including each other. Really brought them down here just to cool off and sober up a little." He tosses me the keys. "You can let them both out. Up to you how they get home."

"Zach is not my concern or responsibility," I say, raising my voice enough that I'm sure the two men down the short hallway in the cell can hear me.

"Damn right," Jefferson calls back.

Dad chuckles. "Would think he'd be more concerned about making a good impression on his future father-in-law."

My stomach does that flippy thing at the way my father refers to the future and Jefferson and me being married so casually.

Then Jefferson calls out, "You already loved me, Scott."

"That means you can only go downhill, Jefferson," my dad calls back.

I laugh. One, because all of that's true. Two, because Jefferson sounds so confident in how my dad feels about him and I kind of love that. Three, because Jefferson's words are slightly slurred. I haven't been one-on-one with a drunk Jefferson ever. This might be interesting.

"Do I have to carry him out to the car or anything?" I ask, keeping my voice a little lower now.

Dad shakes his head. "He should be able to walk just fine. Maybe not straight. But he'll stay upright."

I head down the hallway to the holding cell. Jefferson and Zach are sitting on benches on opposite sides of the small square space. They're both pouting.

"This is not how I expected to end my night," I tell him, inserting the key into the lock.

Jefferson gets to his feet and crosses to the door. "Don't worry. You'll get to end this night just the way you want to."

I swing the door open and Jefferson steps out. I peer in at Zach. "You coming out?"

"I think I'll give your boyfriend a head start. I'm tired of hearing him talk."

I grin up at Jefferson. "Are you being annoying?"

"Zach just happens to find my being madly in love with you annoying. No one else feels that way."

I look at Zach. "We've been telling you this all along. Why are you so annoyed *tonight*?"

Jefferson points at Zach. "He tried to get me drunk, thinking I'd be more honest."

"Honest about what?"

Jefferson slides his hand to the back of my neck and pulls me closer. "You. How much I love you. That we're gonna get married and have babies and live happily ever after."

Of course, all of this comes out a little slurred, but my stomach and heart and my panties react.

I look back at Zach. "So you thought he was lying and that if he was drunk, he would tell you the truth?"

"Worked in high school. But I guess he's still willing to fight for you."

I frown. "What are you talking about?"

Jefferson puts a finger against his lips. "*Shhhhh,*" he says to Zach. "That's between us."

Zach laughs. "She doesn't know? Even after all these years? You're not gonna tell her that you broke your hand in high school over her?"

I look up at Jefferson. "Wait, what? When you broke your hand, that was fighting *Zach?* About me?"

"Dammit," Jefferson says, tipping his head back and looking at the ceiling. "You don't need to know that."

I turn to face him fully. "You missed the championship game because you hurt your hand! And that was because of *me?*"

"Harlow..." Jefferson sighs. "Fuck." He glares at Zach, then looks back at me. "Yes. No regrets."

My mouth drops open. I stare at him. "Why?"

"He wasn't getting away with what he did." He glares at Zach. "He's lucky I didn't put him in the hospital."

I look over at Zach, then back to Jefferson. "Graham told you?"

Jefferson shakes his head. "I knew, Harlow. I was at the party. Graham came and got me when he realized you needed to go home. He couldn't drive. He'd had too much to drink. I took you home and put you to bed that night."

He's drunk. I should just chalk this up to that. But if he's drunk, he's obviously not thinking fast enough to cover any of this up. "*You* took me home that night?" I ask.

"I took you to our house and put you in Graham's room. Then I went and hunted that fucker down." He points at Zach.

I look at Zach. He doesn't dispute any of this.

Jefferson broke his hand, took himself out of the champi-

onship game—the biggest thing in his high school career—
for me.

"You did it because you were drunk, right?" I ask.

Jefferson shakes his head. "No. I wasn't drunk that night. I
knew you both were going to be at that party and I wanted to
make sure nothing happened. But..." He looks so *pained*. "He
still got to you."

"Why would you think something was going to happen?" I
ask.

"Because earlier that week I told Zach that I was in love
with you and that he needed to leave you the fuck alone. That's
why the fucker tried to get you back. That's why all of that
happened." Jefferson cups my face. "It was my fault, Harlow.
So, I *had* to do something."

I take a hold of his shirt with both hands and shake him a
little. "Absolutely not. It wasn't either of our faults. It was all
Zach." I step back from him and look at Zach. "You are *such* an
asshole. Oh my God. I wish he'd had a chance to hit you once
before Derek called my dad."

Zach shakes his head. He just looks...tired. "Wouldn't
change anything."

Yeah, well... He's probably right.

Still I step around Jefferson, stomp into the jail cell, pull
back my hand, and punch Zach as hard as I possibly can.

He howls and covers his nose.

And the next thing I feel is Jefferson pulling me back,
hauling me up, and throwing me over his shoulder. Though I
swear he's laughing as he does it.

In the end, there are charges filed.

Just not against Jefferson.

Totally worth it.

CHAPTER 23

JEFFERSON

I MADE a lot of mistakes last night.

I really wish I could remember them all.

I remember a couple of big ones. The first being starting a conversation with Zach Nelson.

But many of them are more a *sense* that I did something stupid rather than a specific memory.

For instance, there's no way I actually told Scott Hansen that I wanted to marry his daughter, but I definitely thought about it, and I might've said something inappropriate about my feelings for her.

I roll to my back and press my hands to my pounding head.

One of my mistakes was absolutely drinking shots with Zach, determined to prove to him that no matter how drunk I was, my claim that I am madly in love with Harlow was not going to change.

I am absolutely regretting *that* this morning. I feel like shit. In a few hours, I'm going to have to start getting ready for my brother's wedding. As one of the groomsmen, I don't have all of the hair and nail appointments the bridesmaids do, but I need to be available to my family for any last-minute errands or tasks, and this evening I have to stand up in front of the town next to Carver. And not throw up.

At least I get to dance with Harlow. And kiss her. And take her home at the end of the night.

I'm definitely going to have to get over this need to retch.

Harlow won't kiss me if I've been puking all day.

Speaking of... I reach an arm out to the side of my bed where she should be lying, even though I don't feel her curled up against me.

But it's empty.

I also don't hear or feel any cats.

Which means Harlow is up and has fed our furry roommates.

She better still be here though. I want to see her before we go our separate ways for the next several hours.

I frown as I think about her.

Hazy memories of her coming to the police station to pick me up last night filter into my brain.

Oh shit. I'm eighty-five percent sure it's a memory and not a dream that Scott called Harlow to come get me.

Then I sit up quickly—and immediately regret the motion.

Harlow punched Zach last night. In the jail cell.

After he told her the truth about my broken hand.

Those two things aren't a dream.

Dammit.

I've kept the truth about my injury and missing the championship game because of a fight over Harlow from her and most of the town for years.

I'm not embarrassed by it. I've just always known that it would cause additional tension between Harlow and me.

Prior to this week and our fake relationship, the last thing Harlow and I needed was additional messiness between us.

The night I told Zach to stay the fuck away from Harlow and he'd asked why I cared so much was the first time I had admitted to any other human how I really felt about Harlow.

I've always hated that Zach Nelson was the first person to know that I was in love with her.

Honestly, until I had blurted it out to him, I hadn't even admitted it to myself. It had come out of my mouth and I had been as shocked as he was. But the fact that it was true hit me a second later.

And I'd known that he was going to use her against me.

I told her I didn't have any regrets about hitting him and missing the football game, and that's true. But I do regret telling Zach how I felt about her. I have always felt guilty about poking at his jealousy and that it pulled Harlow into the stupid tensions between him and me.

I swing my legs over the side of the mattress. I need to get started on a hangover cure and get my ass in gear.

First, I need to find Harlow.

But as I stand and take my first step toward the bathroom, my gaze snags on a collection of items on my bedside table.

There's water, Gatorade, ibuprofen, and a note.

I'm smiling before I even read it.

You're so lucky you're amazing in bed, because before I knew that I would've really enjoyed torturing you while you were hungover.

It's followed by a little heart and a simple H.

I laugh. Not only because I'm *sure* a couple of weeks ago she would've loved torturing me while I was hung over. But also because I am getting a glimpse at my future. I know I'm going to have dozens of notes with little hearts and Hs collected in my bedside table.

I open that drawer now and drop the note inside.

I partake of all of the items left out for me before padding into the bathroom and cleaning up for the day.

After a shower, plus the electrolytes and ibuprofen hitting my system, I'm halfway back to normal twenty minutes later.

In the kitchen, I find bread and peanut butter sitting next to the toaster and another note that says *Made you breakfast. Some assembly required.*

I laugh and shake my head.

There's no way I can't be in love with this woman.

I find my phone on the counter and type out a text to her.

I assume I rocked your world last night and you can't stop grinning, remembering it. And that you're walking a little funny.

She answers my text within a few seconds. There's a sweating faced emoji and then she says, *that's quite a dream you had. I had similar plans for you, but you passed out on me while I was brushing my teeth.*

Yeah, that's what I was afraid of.

Her: *I take it you don't remember the filthy things you said to me on our way up to the bedroom.*

Me: *Please remind me.*

Her: *Maybe this will keep you from the tequila shots in the future.*

Me: *If you come home right now, I can do my best to re-create it.*

She sends me a blushing emoji and says, *helping my mom with the wedding cake but now I'm thinking about THAT again so thanks for that.*

I chuckle. *You're welcome. Want me to add a few things to it?*

Her: *No, I don't. Not when I can't get you alone for several hours.*

That's fair. We both have a lot to do today and the last

thing I need is going through all the wedding prep with an erection.

Me: *Okay, but all your dances are spoken for tonight.*

Her: *Ditto.*

I grin. I like possessive Harlow.

Her: *Also, the charges were dropped.*

The charges. Now it comes back to me. Not only did Harlow punch Zach, but he threatened to press charges. That fucker. I would've happily gone to talk to him today about that.

Your dad? I ask.

Her: *No. He doesn't like to use his authority that way.*

Her: *My mom.*

I chuckle. Despite his badge and gun, Peyton is much scarier than Scott. And another little bit from last night flickers through my mind.

Did I ask your dad if I can marry you? I ask her. I hesitate before sending, but then push the button.

You did.

Me: *What did he say?*

Her: *That you have to be sober and include my mom next time you ask.*

Yeah, that's what I thought.

Me: *I think you're right about no more tequila.*

Her: *Regretting asking already? I know my breakfasts need some work, but geez.*

I smile. I'm absolutely asking Scott and Peyton that question. And I'm glad Harlow knows that.

Me: *Not that. I just cannot be on your mother's bad side for the rest of my life.*

Her: *Good call.* <winky face emoji> *God knows what she'd teach our kids to get back at us.*

My heart almost stops.

She's just rolling with this planned asking-for-her-hand thing.

And kids.

She just talked about *our kids*. Just casually. Like it's a foregone conclusion.

She's either messing with me—which, honestly, is possible —or she's practicing writing Harlow Riley on her notebook. Figuratively, anyway.

Then I realize a moment later that she will absolutely insist on being Harlow Hansen-Riley.

I grin. I'm suddenly even more in love, even hornier, and very interested in heading to the jewelry store right fucking now.

Maybe I can pull Peyton aside tonight and ask her for over-the-top proposal ideas.

Knowing her, if Scott told her about last night—and I'm one-thousand percent sure he did—she's already got several things in mind for me.

I can handle whatever it is as long as the younger Hansen woman says "yes" when I ask the question.

With that in mind, I send Harlow one more text.

By the way, everything I said last night, I completely meant. Despite the tequila.

Even if I can't remember it all, I'm not too worried. If we were talking about marriage and stuff, I'm good.

Her: *So we really can adopt all three?*

I freeze.

Adopt? Three?

I mean...

I'm not surprised at all that Harlow wants to adopt. That's completely who this woman is and her heart is why I love her so much. So... yeah. Of course.

Three is a lot at once but it's me and Harlow. We're an

amazing team and we've got an amazing family and a whole community around us to support us.

I definitely want a family with Harlow and any child would be so fortunate to have her. Us.

Me: *We'd be kick ass at being adoptive parents. Three. Twelve. Sure. Of course. Whatever you want, I'm in.*

Her: *That was so the right answer. *heart emoji**

I look at that text and grin.

Then take a deep breath. Are these three babies? Maybe at least toddlers? Oh, God, what if they're all teenagers? Actually, it's more likely they're a set of siblings she knows from work so...it could be a baby, a toddler, *and* a teen.

I run a hand over my face.

It's okay. I'm ready. We'll be great at this.

It is absolutely appropriate that Harlow Hansen would bring happy chaos into my life.

I'M FEELING human again by the time the wedding set up really kicks into high gear, thank God. And my family's excitement, and my brother's calm happiness about this big day, seep into me.

Life is good.

My family is amazing, I love that Carver and Kaelyn are so in love, and I just love this fucking town.

I'm also really glad I have finally convinced Harlow of that fact.

Carver and Kaelyn's wedding in the gazebo in the center of town, surrounded by any and every citizen who wants to show up, in the midst of the summer festival, is absolute perfection.

When they first suggested the idea, I agreed that it sounded like fun. But now, standing on the steps of the gazebo, watching my brother say his vows to his longtime love, and looking out over the square in the town where I've spent my life, and looking into the faces of the people—everyone from our Boy Scout leader, to my third grade teacher, to friends who have been by my side since kindergarten, to my parents and all of their friends, to the woman who I have fallen in love with slowly over probably nearly a decade—I can't imagine a more perfect place to have the ceremony.

I catch Harlow's eyes.

She gives me a soft smile.

It's a just-between-us smile.

My heart clenches in my chest, and I feel a sense of right-ness that only occurs when I'm in those rare but perfect moments that are not only just so fucking good, but that I'm tuned in enough to recognize and soak in.

This is how I want our wedding to go.

Right here in this gazebo, at next year's festival.

"Jefferson," I hear my brother's harsh whisper, then Graham elbows me in the side.

I jerk my attention back to the gazebo.

"Do you have the ring?"

Oh crap. I dig in my pocket as the entire audience softly laughs.

I hand the beautiful diamond ring to my brother and he gives me a little wink.

I *so* appreciate Carver's laid-back personality.

"Quit staring at your girlfriend," Graham tells me in a whis-per. "You're being obvious as hell."

I just grin. I really don't care.

CHAPTER 24

HARLOW

"SO I'VE BEEN THINKING about the adoption thing," Jefferson says as we dance. "How will that work? You'll adopt them? And then later, I will?"

I look up at him with a smile. This whole night has been so great. He wasn't lying when he said he was claiming all my dances. Not only have I not danced with anyone else, he and I have barely sat down since the street dance started. We've had a couple of drinks, but mostly have just been soaking up the night and the celebratory feel in the air underneath the twinkle lights that are strung over Main Street. A local band has set up on one end and people ages eight to eighty-eight are dancing on the cobblestones.

"You don't have to officially do anything. Unless you want to. I can adopt them all. Or I can adopt a couple and you can adopt one. Whatever works."

He frowns as if confused. "I would adopt one and you would adopt two?"

I shrug. "We could do it that way."

"I was thinking it would be great to get married in the Square like Carver and Kaelyn did."

I blink at his sudden change of topic. But then I grin. "You of all people were made to get married in the gazebo in the heart of Sapphire Falls."

"Yeah?"

I laugh. "Carver and Kaelyn did it because it was practical. Everyone they wanted at the wedding was already going to be home for the festival. And this way they didn't have to find a venue big enough and didn't have to decorate. Plus they just agreed to pay for the band for the dance that was already going to happen. And that definitely made the festival committee happy. But as far as nostalgia and theme, getting married during the festival is way more a you thing."

He smiles as if that pleases him, then sighs. "I was thinking we would do it next year."

My heart thumps. Is he actually going to propose like this? Here? Now?

"Oh," I say, not really sure if that's the right reaction.

"But that's a year away," he points out, unnecessarily.

"Right."

"But it seems that you're talking about adoption right now."

I frown. "Yes..."

"It seems like it would be a lot easier for everyone if we were married when we did it, right?"

I frown. "Why would we need to be married to adopt the cats?"

He stares at me for three heartbeats. "Cats," he repeats.

"Yeah. The foster cats." Then suddenly everything makes sense. I start to laugh. "You thought I was talking about adopting *kids*?"

His eyes are wide, and I realize we've stopped moving, even

though everyone around us is still dancing, and the music is still playing.

"Of course I thought you were talking about kids."

Oh my God. I said I could adopt two and he could adopt one. I laugh even harder. "Why would you think that?" I ask.

"Because adopting kids is exactly something you would do. Even three at a time."

That makes my heart melt a little. And he's not wrong. I'm still grinning, but I admit, "It is. But I would definitely talk to you about it first. I wouldn't just spring that on you in a text."

He pulls me closer. "You could, you know." His voice is soft and husky. "I want whatever makes you happy."

And I do know I could. My heart melts further. I reach up and put my hands on either side of his face, just looking at him. "Yeah, I guess I do. Wow."

"So, I guess it's safe to say, I am open to adoption."

I smile. "If someone had asked me that, I would've already known the answer."

His return smile is soft. "But it *would* be easier on everyone if we were married right?"

I nod. "Yeah."

"Good to know."

And it's good for me to know that he wants to get married in the town square at next year's festival.

"You know, a week ago, I didn't even like you," I tell him.

He shakes his head. "A week ago, you didn't *admit* you liked me."

"The gazebo might not be big enough for you, me, *and* your ego to stand in."

He just laughs.

"Let's go sit for a minute," I say.

"How much longer do you want to stay?"

"Shouldn't we stay until Kaelyn and Carver leave?" I ask.

"Probably. But they went to ride the Ferris wheel, then I saw them over by the ring toss game. I know Carver will want funnel cakes before they leave, but they could have been gone for thirty minutes by now and no one would have noticed."

I laugh, looking around and *not* spotting the bride or groom. "Another pro for having a wedding during the festival. Makes sneaking off easier."

He grins a mischievous grin that makes my stomach flip. "Exactly."

Those grins of his...I like them too much.

Hand in hand we head for the table where our parents are sitting with some of their friends. All of the couples have been out on the dance floor—can you call the street a dance floor?—but Jefferson's parents have been out there the most.

One thing I really love about knowing my parents' friends so well is knowing lots of stories about them from before all of us kids came along.

I know that Adrianne and Mason first met when Mason bid on dancing with her at a fundraising auction. He'd only been back in town for an hour or so and had no intention of getting involved in what the town had going on, but he'd taken one look at Adrianne and immediately offered an amount that no one else in town could possibly outbid.

I think of the story and smile every time I see them dance at any event.

The group is technically taking up four tables in the beer garden area at the opposite end of the street from the band, but they've more or less arranged their chairs so they're in one big huddle.

We start to take two empty chairs near Jefferson's parents, but a voice says, "Hey, Harlow, come sit by me."

I arch my brows at TJ Bennett, Margot's dad.

He grins and pats the seat of the chair he's just pulled up between him and his wife, Hope.

"Oh boy," I say as I sit down. "What's this about?"

"Just wondering what you all had for breakfast this morning, that's all," TJ says.

I look from TJ to Jefferson, confused. "I had peanut butter toast. Why do you ask?"

"Huh. Margot doesn't usually eat a lot in the morning before a run."

"O-k-a-y."

"She did the 5k race this morning. So did *she* have peanut butter toast?" TJ asks.

I look at him with wide eyes. I'm supposed to know what Margot had for breakfast. I get that. But why?

"Um...I didn't see her this morning," I hedge. Honestly, if she did the 5k that was *way* before I was awake.

"Since she spent the night at your house, I was just curious," TJ says, draping an arm along the back of my chair.

Right. Margot was watching movies at my house last night before I had to leave to pick Jefferson up. Apparently, she told her parents she spent the night with me. Or they're just assuming that because she didn't go home last night.

Yeah, now I want to know about where she spent her night and what she had for breakfast too. Kind of. Except for the part about how she probably spent the night with my best friend who's like a brother to me. I don't really want to know too much about what Margot and Graham do when they're naked together.

I grin at TJ. He is a big guy who has the reputation for being a major grump. Then I smile at Hope, his sunshiny, sweet wife. I love the fact that Margot is not only a perfect mix of the two of them in looks, but also in personality.

"Aren't we a little old for you to be checking up on where

Margot sleeps, TJ? Especially by asking her friends instead of just asking her?" I tease.

TJ shakes his head. "We did ask her."

"Well then my answer is whatever Margot said," I say with a laugh.

"Come on," TJ says. "Tell us what you know about Margot and Graham."

I notice how Adrianne leans in slightly.

"What makes you think I know anything?"

"You're best friends with both of them," Hope says, her eyes bright. "You know we would be thrilled if they're dating. Just tell us a little bit. Is there something going on?"

"I'm not saying a word," I tell them. "Margot will tell you when there's something you need to know."

"That's not a no there's nothing going on," TJ points out.

I laugh and quickly get up and claim a new chair next to Jefferson and closer to my mom.

"But you do know something right?" Adrianne asks.

"I know that this has been a really fun festival week for a lot of us," I say diplomatically.

"Not for Zach Nelson," Mason comments.

His dry sense of humor is so much like Jefferson's, I laugh out loud.

"I didn't say it's been fun for *everyone*," I tell him with a grin.

"If you want someone to spill their guts, buy this guy a few tequila shots," my dad tells TJ, pointing at Jefferson. "Maybe he knows something about his brother and your daughter."

Jefferson groans. "Scott, give me a break."

My dad laughs. "You've been around all of us long enough to know that it's very hard to live things down."

"Shots? That Scott knows about?" Mason asks his son. "What happened?"

I jump in. "He just had some fun down at the Come Again with the guys last night. I had to go pick him up and drive him home."

"Typically seeing the sheriff after too many tequila shots isn't a great thing," TJ says.

"Oh, it was a *great* thing," my dad says. "Tequila is like truth serum with this guy."

Jefferson just groans again, then turns to me. "You ready to go yet?"

I laugh and start to reply, but Mason asks my dad, "What was he so truthful about?"

"That he wants to marry Harlow."

He just says it. Just like that. Out loud to all of his friends. Including Jefferson's parents. Like they're discussing the weather.

And they all take the news with about the same level of surprise as they would if my dad had said it's going to be sunny and ninety tomorrow: they nod and smile as if the information is exactly what they expected to hear.

Jefferson sighs. I sigh.

Then we look at each other and grin.

"I heard Harlow finally punched Zach," Phoebe says.

They all look at me with more surprise at *that* statement.

"Good for you," Hope says.

"Don't encourage her," my dad says, but then adds, "In front of me anyway."

Everyone chuckles. They know very well that my dad is fine with me defending myself, it just helps him have plausible deniability if he's not the one encouraging it out loud with witnesses.

That doesn't mean that he's never given me a private pep talk about not taking shit from anyone, how to throw a punch, and that he always has my back.

"I also heard a rumor that he was going to press charges," Phoebe adds. "The little shit."

"That's all been dropped," my dad says.

Phoebe is looking at my mother with a smile. "Oh, I heard that part too."

"Tell us what happened there, Peyton," Hope says.

Everyone seems as surprised that my mother had some words for Zach as they are to find out that it's going to be ninety degrees in June in Nebraska.

"I'm going to get drink refills," my dad says. He looks at my mom. "Tell the story quick."

Again, he would rather not hear whatever threats my mother made to Zach. Not because he's upset she made them, simply because it's better for the cop to not be included.

He moves toward the bar and my mom looks around the group. "Zach and I have a previous understanding that I simply needed to remind him of."

Hope, Phoebe, and Adrianne share a look, but TJ, Joe, and Mason all look puzzled.

"What am I missing?" I ask.

My mom shakes her head. "Nothing. It's all taken care of."

I lean in. "Mom, how can you and Zach have a *previous* understanding?" I don't mind having personal conversations in front of the rest of these people. I consider them all aunts and uncles. They've known me, and loved me, my entire life. It's almost impossible for me to be embarrassed with any of them.

Studying my mother right now, it hits me she knows more about what happened with me and Zach than I realized.

"Mom," I say, reaching out and touching her arm. "What did you and Zach talk about in the past?"

My mom is one of the most honest and open people I know. She is also fiercely protective of the people she loves.

As our eyes meet, I realize with a jolt that she knows everything that went down with Zach and me.

"I just reminded him that I saved his college career. I am the reason that he is...anything. I could've ruined him, but I didn't, and for that I expect him to leave you the fuck alone for the rest of your life."

I look at Jefferson, but he looks as stunned as I am.

"You know what happened that night? In high school?" I ask.

"You mean the night that he drugged your drink?"

My mom looks around the table and I realize that Adrianne, Hope, and Phoebe also know. This is part of my mom's girl squad. She told them. Hell, they might've been the ones that kept her out of jail after she found out Zach had drugged her daughter.

But it's also clear the men did not know. They all look stunned. And pissed.

I can only guess that my father doesn't know either.

The women clearly had decided how to take care of it and had just done it.

"You went and talked to him?"

She takes a breath, and nods. "I did. I threatened to press charges. The only reason that I even considered not going to your father, or other law enforcement, was because Graham and Jefferson got you away from him." She straightens and looks at me. "It was also too late to really *prove* anything by the time I found out. I was afraid he'd get a slap on the wrist, if even that. It would have killed your father to know what had happened and not be able to really do anything about it through the system. He might have..." She swallows. "He might have actually done something really out of line and ruined his career."

Basically she's saying if she'd told my father, he would have found Zach and beat the hell out of him. Or worse.

Adrianne reaches out and takes my mom's hand. My mom smiles at her and goes on. "Thanks to Graham and Jefferson, you were okay. You had a hell of a hangover, but nothing worse happened. So...I decided to just let Zach know that I knew everything and hope that the threat that I could expose him at any time would keep him in line." Her eyes get a little shiny. "And that it would keep him from doing that to you or *anyone* else again."

I look at Jefferson. He's staring at our mothers. I turn back to her. "But how did you really find out? How did you know I wasn't just hung over from the beer?"

She looks at Adrianne again. "Graham was beside himself after he brought you home."

I frown. "He left after he dropped me off." I had gone upstairs to shower.

My mom shakes her head. "He did. He tried to. But he was so upset, he came back. He felt awful for not calling me the night before. There's only a small window where the drugs are still present in your system and we were past that. You weren't sexually assaulted—"

I hear a rumble, almost a growl, from Jefferson and his arm comes around me and he pulls me closer.

"*Thank God,*" my mom adds. "But the drug would have still shown up in your urine for a few hours. It was too late by the time you got home." She takes a deep breath. "Graham told me what happened and...I went to find Zach, but—" She looks at Jefferson. "Jefferson had already been there. Zach was in really bad shape."

I suck in a breath and look up at Jefferson. His jaw is tense, and he doesn't meet my eyes, but I feel his hand on my shoulder tighten.

"That actually helped me get my shit together," my mom says. "Seeing there had already been some consequences for Zach's behavior, knowing others knew what happened, helped me gather my emotions a little. He was a very stupid, selfish young guy. But Jefferson showed him that he couldn't get away with everything. I realized that I wanted to scare him, hurt him, but..." She sighs. "Not ruin his whole life." She looks at me with a small sad smile. "Trust me, if he had actually hurt you in any other way, I would've ruined him."

"There wouldn't have been anything left of him to ruin," Jefferson says from beside me, his voice low and tight.

My mom looks at him again and nods.

"I told Zach that I was going to watch him. Keep tabs. That if he ever *thought* of making a woman do something she didn't want to do, I would come forward with the story. Even if it was too late to do anything legally to him, I could ruin his reputation, ruin his *family's* reputation here in town, make things very difficult for him."

I nod, my thoughts spinning.

One thing about small towns like Sapphire Falls—people will have your back, but they'll also hold you accountable.

My parents are upstanding parts of this community. People like them, respect them, and trust them. The town would have believed my mom if she'd made public what Zach had done.

Zach would have never been able to come back to Sapphire Falls if this story had gotten out. His dad's heating and air conditioning business would have suffered. His mom's job at the school would have been very difficult. Their friends would have thought of them differently. Their social connections and simply life as they knew it would have changed.

Sure, jail would have been a huge threat, but honestly? Upending his family's happy, content life here in their hometown was a pretty big ultimatum to give him.

"As far as I know, he's still been a jerk, but he didn't mess around with drugs, not himself or with anyone else the entire time he was in college, and he had good relationships with the girls he dated."

I nod, all of these revelations swirling.

"And I didn't worry about you," my mom says with a smile. "I knew you had the Riley boys looking out for you. And all your friends. And all of us." She looks around the table again and all of the women nod.

I take a deep breath. "I...wow. I just...didn't know that you knew."

"I wanted you to tell me when you were ready. If you ever were."

"I'm sorry I never did," I say quietly. My mom is the best. Both of my parents are. I know I could have told them about this.

But I realize...I didn't need to. I was okay. Even immediately following the incident. I was hurt by Zach. I was angry. I'd felt betrayed. But I'd always known I was *okay*. I'd felt supported and taken care of by Graham and my friends.

But I didn't know that Jefferson was a part of it and *that* is what I regret more than anything.

I look at him now. "I had guardian angels I wasn't even aware of, I guess."

My mom smiles at Jefferson. "I was aware of them."

I take a deep breath, feeling a weight lift off my shoulders. Nothing that happened with Zach was my fault. I've always known that. But I'd kept it from my parents because I didn't want them to worry. I never should have doubted how they'd respond.

I give my mom a smile and tease her, so she knows I'm okay. "Yeah, yeah, none of you are surprised that Jefferson and I got together. Whatever."

"Yeah, when he was that in love with you that long ago, I knew it was only a matter of time." My mom sits back in her chair and smiles as my dad rejoins the group.

"Okay, *now* you're being dramatic," I say. I reach over and take Jefferson's hand, squeezing. "We are in love now. For real. But this hasn't been ever since high school or anything."

My mom looks at me as if I just said something ridiculous. "Of course it has been."

"Maybe you thought he had a crush," I tell her. "But he's just a good guy."

"For fuck's sake, Harlow, it wasn't a crush," Jefferson says.

I look up at him and he's looking at me with a mix of affection and heat and a touch of exasperation that I'm pretty sure is just always going to be there.

"I suppose we're going to argue for the rest of our lives about you being smart enough to realize how great we'd be together first?"

He shrugs. "Well, obviously."

"But *you* actually had a crush on *him* first," my mom says.

I look over at her quickly. "What? No, I didn't."

"When you were nine, I distinctly remember you and Margot and Mia and Graham playing wedding. You were the bride and Graham was the groom, but you made Graham go by the name Jefferson."

I'm staring at her. Not because I don't remember that—it's all flooding back to me now as a matter of fact—but because she's talking about this in front of Jefferson.

But of course she is.

"That was only because Graham and I were best friends, and that was weird," I say. "He just needed a different name."

My mom nods. "That makes total sense," she says. "Obviously he couldn't have a name like Tom or Wyatt or any other name at all. Jefferson was really the only option."

"*Now* it's time for us to go," I say to Jefferson, standing.

He chuckles. "I don't know. I'm really enjoying the conversation now."

"It's *really* time to go," I insist, tugging on his hand.

"Also of note, she always wanted to get married in the gazebo in the center of town during the festival," my mom says.

I gasp. "Not *always*."

"Well, as a little girl that's what you would pretend when you played wedding."

"*Very* interesting conversation," Jefferson repeats.

"Jefferson," I say calmly.

"Yes, Harlow?"

"If you ever want to stand in the gazebo with me ever again for *any* reason, you will get up and take me home right now."

He immediately gets to his feet, but he and everyone else laughs the entire time we walk to the car.

CHAPTER 25

JEFFERSON

FOR A SAPPHIRE FALLS STREET DANCE, that had gotten a little intense.

I glance over at Harlow.

She's watching the town pass by her window as we drive toward my house.

She's been quiet ever since we got in the truck. My hand is resting on her thigh and she's got her hand on top of mine, but we're not talking.

I have no idea what to say.

I'm still stunned by what her mom—and *my* mom and their friends—had revealed tonight.

But I don't know why I feel that way.

All of that is completely in character. If one of their kids needs something, they all rally around. It's always been that way. And Peyton is the epitome of a mama bear. She would have absolutely beat the shit out of Zach herself. And the other moms would have covered for her.

If I hadn't gotten there first.

I'm glad I did. Peyton didn't need to confront all of that, deal with all of that.

I definitely needed to.

I suppose my surprise is simply because I didn't know they all knew what had happened with Zach.

Now that I know, everything makes sense. Including the fact that Zach has left Harlow alone.

Until now.

The guy really does have balls coming back here now, for this wedding, and telling Harlow he wanted her back.

"You could have waited until after the championship game."

I look over at Harlow as she finally speaks. "What?"

She keeps her gaze on the street in front of us. "You could have waited to confront Zach until after the game."

I grip the steering wheel tighter. "No, I couldn't have."

"Why not? The game was huge and—"

"Harlow." I cut her off, squeezing her thigh. I look over. She's looking at me with wide eyes. "He *drugged* you. He would have done even worse given the chance. That was *not* going to stand. *That* was huge. That was bigger than any fucking football game."

I hate that I have to concentrate on the road. We're only a couple of blocks from my house though and we need to get there. She doesn't say anything so I just focus on the drive.

We pull into my driveway, and I let out a long, relieved breath. I shut off the truck and turn to her. "Okay, what are you thinking? Wondering about?"

She swallows and then looks over at me. "Let's go inside."

I start to respond, but then close my mouth. Yes, we should go inside. I'll tell her whatever she needs to know, but now, with all the emotions stirred up again, I want to do what I couldn't do back then—hold her, assure her she's safe, tell her that I love her, and *no one* will ever hurt her as long as I'm around.

I nod and get out, coming around to her side of the truck. She's got the door open, but she lets me swing her to the ground and take her hand as we head up the path to the porch. I open the door, letting her past me, then I step in, shut and lock the door behind me.

"Harlow—" I start.

But she turns to me. The only light is the small lamp on the table just inside the door. "You would have gone after him no matter who he'd drugged at a party. You never would have let him get away with that. I want you to know that I know that. And...I love that. You're a really amazing man."

That hits me directly in the chest. I take a breath and blow it out. "Thank you. But, I..." Fuck, does she need to know this? I suppose so. "I would have talked to him, probably punched him once or twice, definitely threatened him if it was anyone else," I say. "But it was you. I hurt him a lot more than I probably needed to. More than I should have." I shake my head. "I'm really not proud of it, but I'm also not sorry."

She's watching me as I confess. "I don't think you need to be sorry."

Good. Because I'm not sure I've got that in me.

"Why didn't you ever tell me?" she asks.

"About beating the hell out of him?" I shrug. "You didn't need to know. It was between me and Zach."

"I did need to know." She moves closer. "You were in love with me. Why didn't you tell me *that*?"

Oh, that. I smile. "Because it wasn't time."

Her brows pull together. "But you felt it. I should have known. It would have changed...so many things."

I shake my head. "I was leaving to go to school. It would have actually been unfair to tell you. Definitely harder on me.

Besides...you weren't ready yet. You weren't in love with me. You needed more time."

She seems very bothered by this. "But maybe if I'd known what you did and how you felt..." She frowns, looking up at me. "Fuck, you're right."

I lift a brow. "I will never get tired of hearing those words from you."

She rolls her eyes, but then gives me a little smile. "If you'd told me you were in love with me and then still left, I would have been hurt and angry. The leaving thing...that would have been hard."

I nod. "Yeah. I know." I lift my hand and cup her face. "And it would have made leaving harder. And if I hadn't..."

"You would have missed out on a lot," she fills in quietly. She reaches up and wraps her hand around my wrist, holding my hand against her cheek. "You would have missed out on things that made you who you are today. The man I really do love now."

I swallow hard, my throat suddenly tight. "Do you really believe that? That me leaving was a good thing?"

She nods slowly. "Yes. There's a big world out there full of people and experiences—good and bad—that make people into who they turn out to be. It happened for you. It's happening for Graham, and Ginny, and Alex. It even happened for Zach. He's not quite the same person he used to be."

I feel relief washing through me. "I'm glad you feel that way."

"Yeah, I guess I have to be glad that you left." The corner of her mouth tips up. "I mean glad for reasons other than the reasons I was glad at the time."

I crowd close. "You thought you were getting rid of me."

"I did." Now her smile is full. "Then you came home to torture me."

I slide my hand back into her hair, the other around to her ass, bringing her up against me. "Yes, yes I did."

Her pupils dilate and she watches me with true love in her eyes. I will never get over that.

"I shouldn't say this, but it's really hot that you beat Zach up for me," she says, her voice husky.

"Yeah? How hot?"

"Really, *really* hot."

I lean in and brush my mouth over hers. "Are you wet for me, Harlow?"

She sucks in a little breath. "Yes," she says against my lips.

"Prove it."

She pulls back, her lips pressed together. She studies me for a moment. Then those lips I intend to be kissing for the next eighty years of my life curl up into a mischievous smile. She reaches behind her, unzips her dress, and lets it fall.

I step back, leaning against the door, and cross my arms over my chest.

She thinks I've tortured her in the past? She hasn't seen anything yet.

"Take off the rest," I tell her.

She unhooks her bra and drops it, then slips her panties over her hips and they hit the floor.

"Now sit on the couch," I tell her.

My beautiful, completely naked girlfriend—I fucking love that term—backs up and sits down on the middle cushion of my sofa.

"Spread your legs." My voice is husky now. "Show me where you need my attention."

Her boldness, in all things, is one of the things I love most about her. She doesn't hesitate to part her knees. Then she lifts one foot up onto the cushion, and lets her leg fall to the side.

Jesus. My cock is aching, and I have to grip my hands and

force myself to stay where I am. But yes, I'm going to torture her a little. Okay, torture us *both* a little.

She cups her breasts with both hands, running her thumbs over her hard nipples, making sweet needy noises. Then she runs her hands from her breasts over her stomach to her inner thighs, then back up.

"Harlow, touch yourself."

"I am touching myself."

She knows what I want and, of course, has already taken some of the control back. "Play with your pussy for me," I say, more firmly.

Her eyes are locked on mine as she slides a hand down her belly and between her legs. She circles over her clit. "I wish you were doing this."

"Imagine it's my hand. How do you want me to touch you? Show me."

She circles a little faster, her breathing increasing, then she slides her fingers down and into that sweet pussy.

I groan silently, imagining the hot, tight feel of her.

"Keep going," I say, low and gruff.

I watch as she teases herself, the flush spreading up her chest to her neck. Her breathing continues to increase, and she says my name again on a soft moan.

I am rock hard and it's taking everything in me to stay where I am.

I watch her speed up, circling over her clit and I can tell she's getting close.

"Stop."

Her eyes fly to mine. Her hand does pause, then she starts moving it again.

"Harlow, stop."

"You're just teasing me."

"Yes. Stop. We're just getting started and you're not going on without me."

"Then come over here and stop me." But her hand has stopped moving.

Oh, we're gonna play. Okay. "You think you don't like being bossed around," I say pushing off the door. "But you need to trust me. Let me tell you what to do. I promise it will be good."

"You stopped me short of an orgasm. How is that good?"

I walk over to the couch and stand, looking down at her. Fuck, she is every dream come true.

"Delayed satisfaction just isn't in your vocabulary?"

She gives me a sexy smile. "Definitely not. Not as long as I have fingers and toys."

I drop to my knees in front of her and pull her hand away. "You don't need those tonight."

Then I lean in and give her a long firm lick.

She cries out and her hand goes to my hair, gripping tightly.

She is my absolute favorite flavor and I could stay here for hours. But she was just on the verge of coming, so she's almost immediately arching closer to my mouth, her stomach and thighs tightening. I continue to lick and suck, bringing her closer and closer to the edge. I slip one finger, then two into her, thrusting slow and steady, as I work her clit with my tongue.

"Oh my God, Jefferson!"

I feel her fingers pull on my hair and her thighs tighten around my head. I lift up and look up at her.

She gasps in outrage. "Jefferson!"

"Trust me." I lick my lips and notice that she watches the movement of my tongue intently.

"You better finish what you started, because you have a detachable showerhead, and I will absolutely lock myself in the bathroom alone."

I chuckle and get to my feet. "Why lock the door? I'd love to watch that."

"Because I'd rather torture you through the door with moans and *oh, yeses*, and calling out some hot movie star's name when I come."

I shake my head. "Wrong thing to say." I reach down and grasp her wrist, tugging her to her feet. I bend and hoist her over my shoulder. With my hand spread over her ass, I start for the stairs.

"The wrong thing to say?" she teases. "Or absolutely the *right* thing?"

I give her ass a swat. "You think you're in charge here, but you're wrong."

"Am I though?" she asks as I toss her onto the bed.

I start stripping and she props up to watch.

She licks her lips. "Because this is going exactly as I planned."

Once I'm naked, I reach into the bedside table, pull out a condom, and roll it on. Then I climb up over her, bracing myself so I can look down at her. "It's going exactly as *I* planned."

She grins. "Well maybe it's a really great thing that we both have the same plans now."

I lean in and kiss her deeply for long, delicious seconds. Then I lift my head, drape one of her legs over my shoulder as she gives a surprised and delighted gasp, and then I slide home in one long, hard thrust.

We both groan.

"For the record," she says breathlessly as I pump deep. "I didn't come with my fingers or with your tongue."

"I'm aware," I tell her, thrusting hard.

She moans. Then says, "Okay just making sure you're keeping an accurate count."

I pick up the pace, working us both closer to an orgasm. "I'm keeping a *very* accurate count."

I see the sly little smile on her face as she arches her neck, and her pussy tightens around me.

"Exactly. As. Planned," she pants.

"Yes, Harlow," I tell her sincerely, as I feel the start of her orgasm and know mine is only seconds away. "It is a *really* great thing that we have the same plans now."

CHAPTER 26

HARLOW

"I DON'T WANT TO GO."

Jefferson runs a hand up and down my back and kisses my shoulder. "I know. But we have to."

It's very unusual for me not to want to go to brunch.

But brunch the day after the wedding is an exception. It's Leaving Day and this brunch is to say goodbye to Graham and Ginny. Both of them are leaving Sapphire Falls this afternoon to go home. Well, not home. They are home while they're in Sapphire Falls, dammit. But they're going back to where they live now.

I fucking hate saying goodbye to them.

There is one way this brunch will be different. I roll to my back and look up into my boyfriend's face. "Can I spend the night here tonight?" I don't want to be alone at my house tonight.

Jefferson looks puzzled but pleased. "You never have to ask permission for that. I'd have you here every night if it was my decision."

I grin. "That was a very good answer." I put my hand

against his cheek. "I have to go back to work tomorrow, but I don't want to go home alone tonight. Or wake up in the morning alone."

I know he understands that the days when I say goodbye to friends make me lonely. I hope he understands that he is already making that better.

He leans over and kisses me. "From now on, you are only alone if you want to be. Got it?"

I nod. "Got it."

We get up, get ready, and head to the Blue Stone.

I think I fall even more in love when Jefferson nudges me toward the chair between Ginny and Graham while he takes a chair a couple of seats down and across the table. I like that he's not clingy and understands that I need to be with my friends.

On Graham's other side, Margot is sitting close and as I take my seat, I notice Graham's hand on her thigh under the table.

He gives me a grin and leans into the side hug I give him.

"I'm going to miss you," I tell him. "But maybe it won't be so long before I see you again." I look pointedly at his hand on Margot's leg.

"I love you," he says. "But when she comes to visit next, you're not invited."

My mock pout is ruined by my laugh. "Wow, it took you zero time to shoot me right out of your number one girl spot."

He chuckles. "Well, my trial kiss with Margot went a lot better than yours and mine did."

I shake my head and lift the mimosa that has magically appeared in front of me. "It's always about sex, isn't it?"

Graham very obviously widens his eyes, looks toward his brother, then back to me. "Hi, black pot, I'm kettle."

I laugh and Jefferson's gaze meets mine across the table. He gives me a look that makes butterflies kick up in my stomach.

And in that moment, it hits me that I truly believe that is going to happen for the rest of our lives. He will be sitting across the table from me in this very restaurant, surrounded by a lot of these same people, thirty years from now, and he'll shoot me that look, and my stomach will swoop.

I take another drink and try to ignore the idea that I wish I was sitting next to him, and he had his hand on my thigh right now.

The best part of my teasing with Graham is that I am thrilled he and Margot are doing well. The more in love they are, the closer I am to having my best friend move back home. Having brunch on a regular basis with Jefferson, Margot, and Graham is my idea of heaven.

Ginny leads over and whispers, "So what's going to happen now?"

I don't know where to start. There's so much to look forward to. "If you wanted to move back, I would rent you my house for really cheap," I tell her.

She blinks at me. "What are you talking about?"

"Just thinking that Jefferson and I will probably be living together soon. His house is bigger, so I'll probably move in there. But I could keep my place and rent it to you if you wanted to move back."

She rolls her eyes. "I wasn't asking you about real estate. But I guess you answered my question about you and my brother anyway."

I sip more orange juice and champagne. They put a splash of peach juice in the mimosas here and it's delightful. "What was your question?"

"If you and Jefferson were going to keep dating."

I look across the table again and find him watching me. This time I wink at him. Then I turn to his little sister. I prop my chin on my hand and give her what I assume is a goofy, stupid-in-love grin. "Harriet Ginger Riley, I am going to *marry* your big brother."

She grabs her mimosa glass, dings it against mine, then tips it back, downing the drink at once. Then she crosses herself.

I laugh. "Are you praying for me or for Jefferson?"

"For Sapphire Falls. They are not ready for the gaggle of little overachievers the two of you are going to unleash on them."

All that does is make me grin even bigger. And my stomach to swoop even harder.

God, Jefferson and I are going to have the best kids.

Brunch continues, with everyone in high spirits. The food and conversation are amazing.

But it's over too soon. Graham and Ginny are leaving from here to go to Omaha to the airport.

We all linger in the parking lot as long as we possibly can.

I hug them both tightly and try my best to hold back my tears. But, as usual, they fall as soon as their car doors shut.

However, *unlike* usual, this time two big strong arms wrap around me from behind and pull me back against a warm, hard body.

Jefferson hugs me as we watch them drive out of the parking lot. In my ear he asks, "What do you need?"

I shake my head. Nothing specific. I know from experience that time is all that actually makes it better.

Instead of pressing, he puts me in his truck and takes me to his house. There he takes me up to the bedroom. He takes my clothes off, but instead of trying to distract me with sex—and for a moment, I thought he would, and I was not opposed—he pulls out a soft, worn t-shirt and a pair of athletic shorts. He dresses me in the comfortable clothes, even knotting the shorts at my waist with a ponytail holder. Then he leads me back downstairs, settles me into the corner of the couch, turns on the television, and pulls up one of my favorite thriller movies. He hands me the remote and disappears into the kitchen.

One of the cats strolls into the room and jumps up next to me on the couch.

Okay, *that's* a very nice additional perk to being here at Jefferson's.

I pause the movie when I smell the popcorn.

I'm crying by the time he carries the bowl of spicy popcorn and two root beers into the living room.

"Shit," he says when he sees my tears. He sets everything down on the coffee table quickly and sinks down next to me, reaching for me. I immediately climb into his lap, and he wraps his arms around me.

"I thought this would help." He kisses the top of my head.

I bury my face in his chest. "It does."

"Are these tears I'm going to have to learn to decipher?"

"Yes."

His warm chuckle and his hand cupping the back of my head soak into me, and I take a deep breath.

I blink and the tears are over. My friends left today. But I had an amazing time with them and there are lots of amazing times ahead. And I've got Jefferson. I'm happy. Content. My life is here. So is his. Theirs aren't. And...that's okay. It's not *perfect*, at least by *my* definition, but mine isn't the only one that matters. And it's all still really good.

"The movie and popcorn and everything are wonderful," I tell him. "For future reference."

His arms tighten around me. "Noted."

The cat moves in closer, curling up next to Jefferson, against my leg. He reaches out a hand and strokes the cat's head and I feel like purring a little too.

I reach for the bowl of popcorn, settling it in my lap, but not moving off of Jefferson. I point the remote at the TV, but don't press play. "Please also note that I will also need to be distracted from my sadness by sex later."

"How do you know that? Do you have sex every time your friends leave and who do I need to kill for helping you through all of that in the past?"

I giggle. I never giggle on Leaving Day. "No, just a theory I'm working on."

He chuckles and settles more deeply into the sofa, snuggling me against his chest. "Oh good. I'm not sure I'm up for murder today. A hot brunette's been wearing me out lately."

I giggle again.

"But I'll see what I can do for you later. I'm really hoping this hunch plays out."

I look up at him. "On second thought, maybe I don't want that theory to be true. You'll probably make me sad on purpose just so you can make me happy again."

He grins and kisses my temple. "Nah. I'll keep you happy because I know I can always make you even *happier*."

"You sure about that?"

"Harlow, I'm very aware that I make you happy just walking in a room."

I roll my eyes and turn back to the TV, pressing the play button on the remote...but only so he doesn't see my big *happy* grin.

I can't let him get *too* cocky.

I have to put up with him for the rest of my life after all.

CHAPTER 27

JEFFERSON

SO, not only am I a sucker for Harlow's tears, but I really, really like being the one that can comfort her.

Holding her while watching her crazy thriller movies might be the best Sunday afternoon I've ever had. And I'm a *huge* sports-on-Sunday-afternoons guy.

My phone rings just as the credits are rolling and she carefully pushes up from my lap, avoiding disturbing the two sleeping cats next to us.

"Be right back," she tells me, hitching up the loose shorts on her hips. She grins. "And I'm feeling better but still sad enough that you need to make me feel better." She wiggles her eyebrows.

"Should we bake cookies?" I ask.

"Cook..."

"Or should we bake cookies naked?" I finish before she can.

"Oooh...Yep. Madly in love with you." She turns down the hall. "And if you don't know the answer to that question already, you're not the man I think you are."

I'm grinning as I pull my phone out.

I immediately frown when I see Margot's name on the screen though. "Hey," I answer, checking to see if there are any missed calls or messages from Graham or Ginny or any other family member or friend.

Nope.

"Hi, I need you to tell me again that it's not completely crazy for me to move to Denver," she says.

Oh. That.

I glance down the hall and lower my voice and immediately feel guilty. "Did you talk to Graham about it?"

Obviously saying goodbye to him today got her thinking about this even more.

"I didn't," she says. "Because I don't want to move *because* of him. He's an extra perk." She pauses. "Even more so now."

So something definitely happened between them. Okay, that matters.

"But I want to do this for me. I want it to be something that's a good idea even if things don't work out with him."

"That makes sense," I say. "I think that's really smart."

"Yeah."

She's quiet. I let her think for a long moment. I know from the last time we talked that she hasn't discussed this with anyone else. I also know she came to me because she knows that I would say she should definitely go. That's what I do.

But...now Harlow and I are together. And that changes things for me. Not that I don't think people should still see the world outside of Sapphire Falls and try new things, but because I can't keep these conversations from her and not feel like I'm going behind her back.

"If you don't go, you'll always wonder," I finally say. "You don't want to stay here and always be wondering if there was another path that would have been better. The thing about home, about Sapphire Falls, is that we're always here. There will never be a time when you can't come back." I pause. "There's not really a risk here. You have a huge safety net. Go. Try it. Come back if it's not what you thought it would be."

"There's a risk to my heart," she says softly.

"So it is about Graham. More than you thought."

"Yeah."

"Well," I say, taking a breath. "Sounds like that risk is there no matter where you live."

She's quiet for a moment. Then she says, "Yeah. It is."

"At least in Denver, you can give that a real shot. And again, you won't be wondering 'what if'."

I hear her deep breath. "You're right."

I let a moment stretch, then I say, "Hey?"

"Yeah?"

"You *have* to tell Harlow. I can't keep this just between us anymore."

"Yeah, I know. I was planning to call her and ask her to have dinner with me tomorrow."

I'm relieved. "Awesome. Great."

"Maybe I'll just stop at her place now though. I don't want to wait."

"Oh...uh..."

She laughs. "She's with you?"

"Yeah."

"Are you...busy?"

I laugh. "We just finished a movie."

"Can I steal her for a little bit?"

She's spending the night here tonight. She's already a little sad and this will definitely make it worse but, she's handling Graham and Ginny leaving. I seem to really be helping her feel better. Maybe this is the best time, actually. She can get all of this sadness over with at once.

"Of course. But call her. Invite her for dinner tonight. This is between the two of you. I shouldn't be around."

"Okay. I'll do that. And...thanks."

"Any time."

"I'm really glad you and Harlow figured your shit out," she says.

"Me too," I say sincerely. "Me too."

We hang up as the bathroom door down the hall opens and Harlow rounds the couch just as her phone starts to ring where it's lying on the coffee table. She looks at the screen. "It's Margot."

I make a noncommittal noise. "I'm going to get drink refills." I stand and head for the kitchen.

I hear her say, "Hey," then, "Um, yeah, I guess. Are you okay?" then, "Absolutely, that sounds nice, see you then."

I return to the sofa with glasses of iced tea, setting them on coasters.

"Margot wants to have dinner tonight. Just the two of us. I think she's extra sad about Graham leaving this time." She snuggles in close to me. "I'll come back over after though, okay?"

I drape my arm around her and sink into the cushions with her. "Of course."

"It will be so nice once they get really serious and Graham just moves back here," she says, starting to scroll through more movie titles on the screen. "We can all have dinner together all the time. That will be so fun."

That would be fun.

It *will be* fun.

When they come back to Sapphire Falls to visit.

Fuck. I should just tell her what I know.

But she and Margot are going to talk in a couple hours. It can wait that long.

And it will be okay. Fine. She'll come back here, and we'll talk about it, and she'll realize how great this is for Margot. And for Graham. And that *she*, Harlow, is great right here with me. In Sapphire Falls.

I look at the cats stretched out on the other end of the couch, oblivious to us, even as Harlow tucks her toes underneath one of them.

I sigh.

Yeah, after this news from Margot and the realization that Graham is not moving home, Harlow is not going to be happy.

I might need to get more cats.

CHAPTER 28

HARLOW

I WALK into Dottie's just after six. Margot is already here.

"Hey!" I give her a big smile as I slide into the booth opposite her.

"Hey." Her smile doesn't quite reach her eyes.

"Oh, no. You're really sad this time." I reach across the table for her hand. "You've got it bad, huh? We're going to need cookies and cream milkshakes," I say.

Margot raises her brows. "That's what you get when you're celebrating."

I lean in on both forearms and give her a smile. "Don't hate me. I'm sorry you're sad. But I *am* celebrating that you're in love with Graham."

"You are never in this good mood after Ginny and Graham leave," Margot says, sitting back and crossing her arms.

I sigh. "I know, it's all Jefferson's fault. He actually has the ability to put me in a good mood. Who would've guessed?"

She laughs. "Most of the town?"

"Shut up." But I'm grinning.

"Well, I didn't actually ask you here to talk about Graham," Margot says. "I mean...well, it's adjacent I guess."

I frown and lean in further. "Are you pregnant?" I ask in a whisper.

She frowns and looks around quickly. "No. Harlow!"

"What? I'm trying to figure out what adjacent means."

"If you can be patient for two minutes, I'll tell you," Margot says with an eye roll.

Just then, Lizzie, one of the teenagers who waitresses here part-time, comes to the table. "Hi! What can I get you?"

We both order our usuals and wait until she brings our drinks back. Then I say, "Okay, spill it."

"I'm...getting a new job," Margot says after a deep breath.

I straighten. "Really? I didn't know you were looking for something else."

The thing about small town Nebraska, as much as I love it and find it charming and cozy, is that the jobs are somewhat limited.

"What's the job?"

"You know that new company that's coming to town to partner with IAS?" she asks.

I nod. "I know a little about it."

As much as anyone else in town who has read the city council's meeting notes that are published on the Sapphire Falls website. IAS is Jefferson's dad's company, and they do a lot with agriculture. The new company is a green energy company. They are based in Colorado, but they're partnering with IAS on a project and will have an office here.

"I'm going to be an executive assistant with them," Margot says.

My eyes widen. "That's amazing. Good for you!"

She smiles, clearly proud. "In Denver."

Those two words take a little time to sink in. "Excuse me?"

She takes a deep breath, straightens, then leans in, resting her elbows on the table. She meets my gaze directly. "They actually offered me the job here in Sapphire Falls. But they also have a position open in Denver. And I started thinking, if they like me enough for the job here, maybe they'd give me the job in Denver. And they did."

I stare at her. "If they gave you the job here, why do you want to go to Denver?" As soon as I say it out loud, I realize that's a really dumb question. "Oh, Graham."

But she shakes her head quickly. "Actually, I applied for the job and got it before I knew anything was going to happen with Graham. He's kind of just a perk. The sprinkles on top. I wanted to see if maybe I could do something outside of Sapphire Falls. Just to...try something new."

My stomach knots. This sounds so familiar. "I didn't know you wanted to try something new."

"I love Sapphire Falls," she says. "You know that. But it's a good feeling to know that someone somewhere else wants me too. And I just want to see what it's like. To live somewhere bigger, different. It's like a new pair of shoes. It doesn't mean I don't like my favorite pair and want to wear them again. But a new pair can be fun sometimes too."

I swallow and nod. "And you can't wear two pairs of shoes at the same time."

She reaches across the table and. "I have no idea if I'll like Denver. It might not work out. It might be terrible. The new shoes might pinch my feet or look terrible with all of my outfits. But it's like Jefferson said, if I don't try it, I'll always wonder. And Sapphire Falls is a fabulous place to come home too. It's always here. It's always home."

My throat feels thick. "Jefferson said that?"

She smiles. "Yeah. And he would know right?"

"Yeah." My voice sounds funny. "He would know."

Our food arrives and we eat while she tells me about the job. It's Executive Assistant to the CEO of the company. It sounds incredible. She'll be making a lot of money, even though living in Denver will cost a ton more than Sapphire Falls. They are going to help her find an apartment and get settled.

Apparently, I am only the second person she's told. After Jefferson.

I also find out that she leaves in two weeks.

Actually twelve days.

We walk out to our cars together and she gives me a hug.

"I'm so relieved that you know. I was so nervous to tell you."

I do hate that she felt scared about telling me something she is clearly very excited about. "I'm really proud of you. I know this is a big deal. I'm glad you're excited."

She gives me a small smile. "You're going to miss me. I'm going to miss you too. It makes this easier knowing that you're with Jefferson."

Right. I am with Jefferson. The guy who keeps making people I love leave me.

But I smile back at her. "Now I have two reasons to come visit Denver. And it makes me feel better that you're not going to be there alone. Graham will help you get settled. I'm sure. He's probably thrilled." I frown. "Wait, Graham doesn't know?"

"No," she says. "I want to get there, and get settled, and start the job. I don't want him to think that I moved for him or that I'm stalking him or expect anything. I'll let him know once I'm there. And we can see how it goes."

I do have to laugh at that. "He's crazy about you, Margot. He's going to be thrilled."

She ducks her head a little shyly. "I hope so. But this move is a big deal for me. I don't want to make it just about him."

"I understand." I give her another hug. "I'm going to try not to meddle and I'll try not to spill your news to him before you do."

She pulls back and gives me a serious look. "Graham and I talked about our relationship and you. We don't need to talk about each other with you. You're too close to both of us. That's a little awkward."

I sigh. "I hear you."

"I guess you're just going to have to talk about us with Jefferson."

I don't say anything to that. But yeah...I have a few things to talk to Jefferson about.

Once I'm in my car, I decide I need to take a drive and think things over.

I need to figure out where I stand on a few things before I go home to Jefferson and yell at him about...

I sigh as I start my car. I don't even know what I'd yell about.

This is Jefferson. And me. This is how it's always going to be.

I drive up to Klein's Hill, the tall hill south of town where the entire village can be seen spread out with the warm lights glowing. It's a popular spot and it's a rite of passage for all teenagers in Sapphire Falls to make out up on this hill.

Thankfully, on a Sunday night, I'm the only one here.

I park my car, get out, and climb up on the hood. I look out over the town I love so very much. The town where I've spent my life. Where I intend to spend the rest of it.

But I'm in love with Jefferson.

And I know that if I spend that life with him here, he is going to really piss me off sometimes.

Okay, I spend that life with him *anywhere*, he is going to really piss me off sometimes.

I blow out a breath.

If I think I miss Alex, and that I'm upset and sad after Ginny and Graham leave, at the *thought* of Margot leaving, I can't imagine how I'm going to feel when our children leave Sapphire Falls to go out and see the world. And how I'll feel when they become amazing whatever-they're-going-to-be somewhere else, far from here. How I'll feel every Leaving Day.

Especially knowing that Jefferson encouraged them to go.

How am I going to handle that?

I need to give that serious thought now.

We're getting to the point of no return. We're talking about the future. We've said the word 'marriage'. Our families are involved. Our friends are all in on this.

Am I all in?

I hear tires crunching behind me and look down at my phone. I've been sitting here for forty minutes.

And I've missed a bunch of calls and texts.

I am not surprised when I see Jefferson's truck pull in next to me.

He gets out and stomps over. "What are you doing?" he demands.

I narrow my eyes at him. "I'm thinking about how much I like you. And how much I hate you."

He tucks his hands in the back pockets of his jeans and blows out a breath. "You can't do that at my house?"

I turn more fully to face him. "You had to know that she'd tell me."

"I told her she had to tell you, or I would."

Okay, well, that's something. "So you had to know I'd be pissed."

"Of course I knew that."

I weaken a little just knowing how well he knows me. "You thought I'd just come straight over after that?"

He spreads his arms wide. "No. I thought you'd go to your house. So I gave you thirty minutes to cool off and then went over to talk. Then when you weren't there, I kind of started to worry. Then when Margot said you didn't tell her where you were going and you weren't at your mom and dad's, and Graham hadn't heard from you, I *actually* started to worry."

Dammit. I love how well he knows me. I thought about going home. But my house doesn't feel right anymore. I didn't think I'd actually be comforted being there alone.

And...I hadn't thought about talking to anyone else.

Jefferson is who I need to talk to about this. Once I've figured out what I want to say.

"And then you drove straight up here?"

"This is the first place I thought of after your house and your mom and dad's."

I turn and look back over the town. "I told you I didn't want to be alone tonight, and I was going to spend the night with you."

"That was before you found out that I talked to one of your very good friends and told her I thought her moving to Denver was a good idea."

"Again."

"Yeah." He sighs. "Again." He shoves a hand through his hair and moves closer to the car. "So how mad are you?"

"On a scale from zero to ten?"

"Yeah."

I shrug. "Two. Now."

He rounds the front of the car to stand directly in front of me. He's frowning. "You're sitting up here alone instead of at home with me and you're only at a *two*? What the hell are you going to do when I get you to an eight?"

I frown. "You're going to get me to an eight?"

"You and me? Over seventy years of life together? I'm sure."

I melt a little more. "I guess I'll need to come up here then," I tell him.

"To do what?"

"Think things over."

"Things like what? Like if you're still in love with me? If you can be with me? Because that's crap, Harlow. You do love me. Of course you can be with me. We're amazing together. You don't need to think that over."

I drop my arms from around my knees, straighten my legs, and scoot to the front end of my car. My knees bump his thighs. "No. I don't need to think about any of that, Jefferson. I'm not an idiot. I know we're amazing together. I just needed a minute to figure out how to explain this to you and I knew if I walked into your house and saw you on the couch cuddling a couple of cats and you looked up and smiled at me, I would...just fall in love with you all over again and not actually say what I need to say."

The look on his face is a mix of relief and exasperation and love. I love that look.

"Okay, what do you need to say? But hurry up. I need to kiss you."

I take a breath. "That I know that you are going to do this same damned thing with all of the people in our lives. Including our children. Maybe especially our children." I sigh. "You are going to push them, you are going to give them wings. You're going to tell them about the great big wide world out there that they should experience. You're going to tell them that there are places other than Sapphire Falls where they can be happy, where they can make a difference, where they can meet other people that will love them and appreciate them."

I scoot even closer to him, narrowing my eyes. "But I'm

warning you, at the same time, I am going to love them so hard that it's going to be difficult for them to leave. I'm going to help them make so many memories in this town with these people that they'll *weep* when they drive away. Our children will be spoiled rotten and *I* will be their favorite. I don't believe that you can love someone too much. So our children are going to have a father who is going to encourage them and push them while their mother is going to coddle them and try to keep them at home, and, well, we're probably going to argue about that."

I take a deep breath. "And I just figured I needed to explain that to you right now so that we're both going into this eyes wide open."

He stands there staring at me for several heartbeats. Then he says, "You've been out here thinking about our children."

I swallow hard. "Of course. And we're probably going to need to have a few. We're going to make pretty amazing kids. We probably owe the world more than one or two. But the more we have, the more you and I will probably fight." I'm watching him just watch me with a look in his eyes that's hot and full of love. "Of course, the more we have, the better chances I have of *one* of them staying close," I add with a small eye roll.

"How many?" he asks.

"How many fights? *Hundreds.*"

One corner of his mouth tips up. "Kids. How many kids are we going to have?"

My stomach swoops as my heart thumps hard. "Oh. At least four. Maybe five." I swallow hard again. "Of course, we can adopt some. Or several."

He takes my face in both hands and says, "God, I love you so much."

I feel tears stinging my eyes, but I smile. "I know. You're very smart."

"You're going to make my life very difficult, aren't you?"

My smile grows. "See? Very smart."

He leans in until our noses touch. "Harlow?"

"Yeah?"

"Are you going to marry me?"

I wrap my arms around his neck. "Yes, Jefferson, I'm going to marry you."

"Finally," he mutters. Then he lowers his head to kiss me.

But I pull back.

He lifts a brow.

"And *we're* going to live happily ever after. *In* freaking Sapphire Falls."

He laughs. "Of course we are. Where else would we possibly go?"

I give him a little growl of frustration. He's such a pain in the ass. "I'm serious. I'm dying in this town. And if I go first, you have to put my urn on your mantle and keep me there until you die. Then our kids—or Graham and Ginny if our kids all live on other continents and never come home to visit us because their grand life adventures keep them too busy—can bury us together."

He rolls his eyes. "Jesus, Harlow."

"I know that's dramatic, but—"

"There is no way you're going first," he interrupts, pulling me even closer. "Even being in a fake relationship with you for a week has aged me a year, I swear."

"Very funny," I say as I pull him down for a long, hot kiss overlooking our beloved hometown.

But the thing is, though I would never admit it, Jefferson Riley *is* actually pretty funny. And sweet. And smart. And sexy.

Okay, fine, I probably will admit that from time to time. If he asks very nicely. And is doing that thing he does with his tongue...

I can't wait to spend the rest of my life with him.

Here in freaking Sapphire Falls.

Thank you so much for reading Make Her Mine! I hope you loved Jefferson and Harlow and this trip to Sapphire Falls!

If this is your first trip to Sapphire Falls, I'm so excited that you're here! If you'd like to read about Jefferson and Harlow's parents (and all their friends) keep scrolling for the list of the entire original series!

If this is a return trip for you, welcome back! 🩶 I'm so happy to be back in this little town and I'm thrilled to have you all with me!

Would you like the RECIPE for Harlow's Spicy Popcorn?? Grab it right here!

subscribepage.com/popcornrecipe-mhm

Find ALL of my books at **ErinNicholas. com**

And the best place to find out all the news about that (including upcoming books and more!) is right here!

bit.ly/Keep-In-Touch-Erin

And this is your personal invitation to my Facebook group, Erin

Nicholas's Super Fans where you can get first looks, behind the scenes peeks, and daily fun with fellow romance lovers (including me!)!

THE SAPPHIRE FALLS SERIES

These are interconnected stand-alones and can be read in any order. Each book contains a full story and an HEA for the couple featured.

ABOUT THE AUTHOR

Erin Nicholas is the New York Times and USA Today bestselling author of over thirty sexy contemporary romances. Her stories have been described as toe-curling, enchanting, steamy and fun. She loves to write about reluctant heroes, imperfect heroines and happily ever afters. She lives in the Midwest with her husband who only wants to read the sex scenes in her books, her kids who will never read the sex scenes in her books, and family and friends who say they're shocked by the sex scenes in her books (yeah, right!).

You can sign up for *all* the Erin news right HERE!

You can also find her here:

f facebook.com/ErinNicholasBooks

instagram.com/authorerinnicolle

BB bookbub.com/authors/erin-nicholas

Editor: Fedora Chen

Cover design: Qamber Designs

Photography: Wander Aguiar

Digital ISBN: 979-8-9908220-7-8

Paperback ISBN: 979-8-9908220-8-5

www.ingramcontent.com/pod-product-compliance
Ingram Content Group UK Ltd.
Pitfield, Milton Keynes, MK11 3LW, UK
UKHW041413270125
4309UKWH00038B/836

9 798990 822085